LAND OF WOLVES

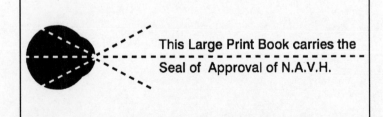

This Large Print Book carries the
Seal of Approval of N.A.V.H.

A LONGMIRE MYSTERY

LAND OF WOLVES

CRAIG JOHNSON

THORNDIKE PRESS
A part of Gale, a Cengage Company

Farmington Hills, Mich • San Francisco • New York • Waterville, Maine
Meriden, Conn • Mason, Ohio • Chicago

Copyright © 2019 by Craig Johnson.
A Longmire Mystery.
Netflix is a registered trademark of Netflix, Inc. All rights reserved. The series *Longmire*™ is copyrighted by Warner Bros. Entertainment Inc.
Thorndike Press, a part of Gale, a Cengage Company.

Thorndike Press® Large Print Mystery.
The text of this Large Print edition is unabridged.
Other aspects of the book may vary from the original edition.
Set in 16 pt. Plantin.

**LIBRARY OF CONGRESS CIP DATA ON FILE.
CATALOGUING IN PUBLICATION FOR THIS BOOK
IS AVAILABLE FROM THE LIBRARY OF CONGRESS**

ISBN-13: 978-1-4328-6806-2 (hardcover alk. paper)

Published in 2019 by arrangement with Viking, an imprint of Penguin Publishing Group, a division of Penguin Random House LLC

Printed in Mexico
1 2 3 4 5 6 7 23 22 21 20 19

For Frank Carlton, gentleman and sportsman —
not necessarily in that order.

Ezezaganen lurraldea otso lurraldea da.
A land of strangers is a land of wolves.

BASQUE PROVERB

The flocks fear the wolf, the crops the storm, and the trees the wind.

VIRGIL

ACKNOWLEDGMENTS

Once, as a young man running fence for a rancher up near Dillon, Montana, I found myself stretching barbed wire over a rocky ridge, having ground-tied my horse below because his shod hooves weren't too fond of the outcropping. It was April and still cool, but I was working hard in an attempt to get back to the line shack where I was staying. I was wiping the sweat out of my eyes with a coat sleeve when I noticed something sitting in the tree line about a hundred yards away.

As my eyes focused, a full-grown, light-gray dog came into view and it was only after a moment I realized I was looking at a wolf. Not having had much interaction with these animals, I immediately thought about the .30-30 in the leather scabbard attached to my saddle too far away.

I straightened, swept my hat from my head, and wiped the sweat away again just

9

to make sure I was seeing what I thought I was seeing, and to make sure my neighbor didn't confuse me with a mule deer. I stayed like that, and the wolf just sat there looking at me for about ten minutes.

Figuring the horse and I weren't in any immediate danger, I went ahead and finished the work under the animal's watchful eye. I gathered up my tools and supplies and looked to where the creature had been, but it was gone.

The next day I came back and didn't see her, having decided she was female, and was a little disappointed. The following day, though, she appeared in the tree line again in the late afternoon to watch me, just as she had before.

Climbing over the fence I had been working on, I stood there for a moment and then took a few steps toward her, but she rose and turned as if to go away. I stopped, and she sat back down, and I'm pretty sure we established a truce.

I never saw her anywhere but on that ridge, and after I'd moved on with my work through the summer I didn't see her at all.

The fall came, and I had finished my tasks on the ranch and was being cut, not because I was a bad hand but because I was young and there were a number of other, older men who needed the limited amount of jobs that there were over winter.

After having a celebratory whiskey in the boss's library, I spent the night and got up early for one last ride before heading east to graduate school. It was early September, but the aspens and cottonwoods had already been touched by a frozen hand and were sporting patches of gold. I rode to that same ridge, left my horse below as I climbed to the knife-edge, and walked along the fence on the jumbled rocks to look for the wolf that had been there.

She never showed in that tree line, but I like to think she was watching me.

I've developed a scenario in my mind where she had had her pups somewhere in a den nearby and was just keeping an eye on me until I'd done what I needed to do and then moved on. I would've liked to have said goodbye, but sometimes that's not the way with magical things. You just have to take them for what they are.

My knowledge of wolves was invariably increased by time spent with Jim Seeman, Wyoming game warden, and Dan J. Thompson of the Wyoming Game & Fish Large Carnivore Section Supervisor and Predator Attack Team, who kept me from chasing my tail.

My gratitude to Bertrand Tavernier for pointing out that to see truly one of the worst Westerns ever made I should watch *Thunder in the Sun* — an hour and a half of my life I'll never get back.

Thanks to Judge Scott Snowden for all the legal counsel that otherwise would've had me howling at the moon, and to Dr. David Nickerson for the medical advice that kept me from being thrown to the wolves.

No acknowledgments would be complete without saying thanks to my pack, starting with Gail "Wolf in Sheep's Clothing" Hochman, and Marianne "Lone Wolf" Merola. Kathryn "Who's Afraid of Virginia Woolf?" Court would howl in attendance, as would Margaux "Wolf by the Ears" Weisman, and Victoria "Wolf at the Door" Savanh. Brian "Wolfman Jack" Tart would be there with Ben "Wolf Whistle" Petrone, and Mary "Cry Wolf" Stone.

Most of all, though, thanks to my own den mate and the true nature of my beast, Judy "Leader of the Pack" Johnson.

1

It's hard to think of a place in Wyoming where the wind doesn't reign supreme; where the sovereignty of sound doesn't break through the parks of the Bighorns with a hoarse-throated howl. I sometimes wonder if the trees miss the wind in the infrequent moments when it dies down, when the air is still and the skies are a threadbare blue, thin and stretching above the mountains. Needled courtesans — the lodgepole pines, Douglas firs, and Engelmann spruce — stand at the edge of the great park like wallflowers awaiting the beseeching hand of the wind to invite them to the dance floor. And I can't help but wonder that when the sway passes and the trees are still, do they pine for that wind; do they grieve?

"It's a dead sheep."

"What?"

"It's a dead sheep, in case you were wondering."

"Yep, it is."

She stopped eating her breakfast Power-Bar and looked straight at me. "Then why have you been staring at it for the last five minutes?"

I swallowed and formed a few words, but they wouldn't come out. It was like that lately, almost as if some inhibitor was kicking in every time I tried to say something.

She studied me for a moment more, and then her eyes returned to the carcass. "Is it me, or does it seem like we've done this before?"

Two men were examining the demised and doing their best to ignore us. "I guess we didn't do a good enough job on the other sheep-o-cides."

She continued chewing. "Why is that?"

"Because there's another dead sheep."

"There's always another dead sheep. It's what sheep do — they die." Victoria Moretti glanced around at the snow-spotted park and the breathtaking beauty of the Bighorn Mountain Range, bold faces of the granite high country rising like magnificent stockades. "Boy, we're in the middle of fucking nowhere."

I sighed and girded up some more words. "Nice, isn't it." I passed her the cup from my battered thermos that was covered in stickers, one of which read DRINKING FUEL. She handed me the remains of her bar, and I watched as she took a sip of the coffee.

"Remind me again why we're here?"

I took a bite. "Public relations."

"Since when does the Absaroka County Sheriff's Department have to worry about public relations?"

"When has the Absaroka County sheriff or any other sheriff not had to worry about public relationships? Or, more important, dealings within the law enforcement community." I took another bite and pointed at the two men. "Aka: the Absaroka County Brand Inspector and the National Forest Service."

"You just don't want to be babysat at the office."

I watched a random breeze push the treetops, dusting the frosted grass with a little fresh snow from the pine needles. "There's that." I undid the top of the thermos again and took my chrome cup back to refill it. "You mind telling me what that's all about?"

"What?"

"Why everyone is treating me like a Fabergé egg?"

"After Mexico, all parties have decided

that you need a little more adult supervision."

I nodded and handed her the last bite. "Sancho follows me to the bathroom."

At the mention of our Basque deputy, Santiago Saizarbitoria, Vic smiled. "He's taking his orders very seriously."

I started to lift the cup to my lips, then stopped. "Whose orders?"

"I am not at liberty to say at this time."

"My daughter."

"Pretty much."

I sipped my coffee, a slight huff building. "If she's so worried about me, why doesn't she come up here and see about me for herself?"

"Um, because she has a life and a career in Cheyenne." She studied the side of my face. "She's been through a lot, Walt."

I nodded. "Yep."

"What, you're lonely? I can get Sancho to go *in* the bathroom with you."

"Thanks, but no thanks." I took a deep breath, feeling the stitch in my side. "I know she's been through a lot, and I just think we need to talk about it."

"So call her."

"I hate phones."

"Go to Cheyenne."

"I'm not particularly fond of Cheyenne

either . . . Besides, after the amount of time I've been gone from the county, I think I need to be around here." I turned to look at her just as the two men approached. "Well?"

Don Butler, who had been the county brand inspector for years, gave me an unsettled look. "Difficult to say on a three-day-old kill."

"Could be a wolf." We all turned to look at Chuck Coon. "Well, it could be."

Vic made a face. "I thought you Rabbit Rangers say there aren't any wolves in the Bighorns."

Butler pushed his stained hat back and scrubbed a hand over the lines on his face. "Of course there aren't, which is why we're collecting DNA."

Coon sighed. "Anyway, there aren't supposed to be."

"Are you saying the wolves aren't co-operating?"

"Like any other adolescent, they have a tendency to wander . . ."

Butler glanced back at the remains. "If it is a wolf, it's a young one, I'd imagine."

"I'm betting a two-year-old." Chuck leaned against the tailgate of my truck, the official mantra spilling from his lips like a teletype machine. "It will be dealt with swiftly."

17

"You're gonna kill it?" Vic shook her head. "Doesn't the Fed just pay for the sheep?"

"Yeah, but once they get a taste for mutton, they usually keep hitting the herd and it becomes a problem — besides, it's a predator zone, so they're not supposed to be here."

She glanced at me. "What's a predator zone?"

"Neither protected nor trophy, they are considered to be in an agricultural area and a nuisance or predator, and you're allowed to shoot them at any time, like coyotes."

She looked back at the ranger. "They were here before we were."

I changed the subject. "More important: whose herd?"

Don cocked his head with a grim look. "Extepare. Abarrane Extepare."

Vic looked confused.

"Son of Beltran Extepare, the man who blew Lucian's leg off." The sheep rancher's father had been the Basque bootlegger back in the late forties who had relieved my predecessor of an appendage.

Her tarnished gold eyes sparkled the way they always did at the mention of mayhem. "Ooh, shit. This is getting interesting."

I looked past the two men at the hundred or so sheep grazing a good fifty yards away.

"So, I don't suppose the old man is up here?"

"Not that we've seen."

"How 'bout the herder?"

"Haven't seen him either."

"Well, who called in the sheep?"

Coon thumbed his chest. "I did."

"Then first you need to find the herder and talk with him. Then we can go have a little chat with Abarrane and hope we don't get shot." I watched as Coon, in search of a needle, looked behind him at the expanse of haystack mountains. I turned and looked at Butler. "Any idea what Extepare's permits for grazing are?"

Disgruntled, Don started off toward his truck. "Got 'em on my computer."

I threw out the rest of my coffee and, slowly sliding off the tailgate, limped after him with Vic and Chuck in tow. Coon pulled up beside me.

"How are you doing, Walt?"

"Good — a little stiff, but I'm fine."

"That sounded like some pretty hairy stuff down there in Mexico."

I nodded.

"Sure you're okay?"

"Yep."

He continued talking as I opened the passenger side door. "You lost a lot of weight

19

— I guess you can count that as a positive."

The brand inspector had a nice truck with carpet, a leather interior, and all the electronic gizmos, including a swinging table that held a laptop computer. "Jeez, Don, the Cattleman's Association is making way too much money."

He grumbled as he climbed onto the seat. "I practically live in the thing." After tapping a few keys, he stared at the screen. "Extepare all right. One section — looks like it's mostly west of here." He peered through his windshield. "Odd, those sheep scattered this far east and nobody checking on 'em."

Studying the large meadow, my eyes followed his. "Maybe the wolf spooked them?"

Don pulled the brim of his hat back down, low over his eyes, still seemingly puzzled. "Maybe, but hell, we've been here for an hour and you'd think somebody would have shown up . . ."

I turned, looking at the expanse. "How big would you say this park is?"

"At least a couple square miles."

Vic studied the large, open space. "Why do they call them parks?"

"Bastardization of the French term that the trappers used when they first came to this part of the country." I sighed, seeing the lunch I'd planned at the Busy Bee Café going up in grilled smoke. "All right. We can split it up — you take the right, Don. Chuck, you take the middle, and Vic, we'll work the tree line to the left. I don't think there's much of a chance that he'd set up camp out in the middle, but you never know." I glanced back at Butler. "Does the herder have a name?"

"Miguel Hernandez."

"Chilean?"

"Yeah."

Walking back to the Bullet, I called over my shoulder. "Our standard frequency." Climbing in, I was met with a copious fog of Dog breath as he hung his bucket head over the seat and whined. "I know you want to get out, but you can't — like the butler, they might think you did it."

Vic pulled the passenger door closed behind her. "Chile?"

Glancing around at all the remaining April snow, I slipped the truck into four-wheel drive.

"H-2A — temporary-agricultural-work program that allows companies to hire foreigners if no Americans want the jobs."

She leaned forward, scanning the area ahead of us. "The scenery's pretty great, but I can't imagine the amenities are plentiful."

21

"If we find Miguel's campito, you'll see."

"They stay up here?"

Following the slope of the meadow, I drove slowly, keeping my eyes on the tree line. "You've seen the sheep wagons at the Basque parade; they generally live in those."

"So, this guy, Extepare, he's Basque, and he hires some guy from Chile?"

"Yep."

"Why not another Basque?"

"The economy is good there, and nobody wants the jobs. Most of the herders you're going to see out here these days are South American — *borregueros* they call themselves."

"What do they get paid?"

"About six hundred fifty dollars a month."

"Jesus. I'd run off too."

Hoping to spot something, I kept peering into the dense forest as we drove. "Tough to eat scenery. It's lonely work."

"You mean they just leave them here?"

"There's usually a camp tender who comes up with supplies and might spell them out for a day or two, but it's rough with no other human interaction — some never learn English."

"Do they have dogs?"

"Usually, why?"

She pointed. "Because there's one."

I turned to see a border collie at the precipice of a ridge ahead. Slowing to a stop, we waited a moment, but then the dog disappeared. "Damn." Gunning the engine, I turned the wheel and drove to the spot on the ridge where the dog had been. "Do you see anything?"

Vic sat up in her seat and turned around to the right and back toward me, finally looking past me to a spot on my left. "There."

I turned and could see the dog hightailing it into the forest, so I spun the wheel again and then drove to the edge of it and parked.

Vic held her hand on the rear door. "You want Dog out?"

"No." He looked at me, deeply hurt. "Sorry, but if you run off chasing some strange dog, I'll never find you." I met my undersheriff at the front of the truck and peered into the mist, where the sun was attempting to melt the snow. The meadow behind us resembled an impressionist painting, evaporating before our eyes. "See him?"

"No."

Leaning against the grille guard and staring at the snow patch in front of us, I shook my head, raised a hand, and motioned to the right. "Looks like he's headed that way."

Letting Vic break ground, I followed,

dodging between the trees and wishing the pain in my side would let up. After getting back from Mexico, Docs Bloomfield and Nickerson had given me the once-over and explained that the doctors in Juárez had actually done a pretty good job of patching up my stomach, spleen, liver, and part of a lung, but I still felt like hell.

They'd warned me that I needed more bed rest, but I'd finished rereading all four volumes of *A Dance to the Music of Time* and I was going stir-crazy. They'd informed me that with deep-tissue, solid-organ damage, the repair was really up to the organ itself, and that if I wasn't careful, I was courting disaster — or at least asking it out on a first date.

"You all right?"

I looked at Vic, who was standing on the trail still ahead of me. I placed a hand on a nearby lodgepole pine. "Yep, just a little winded."

She approached. "Go back to the truck."

"No."

"Let me rephrase: go back to the truck or I'll shoot you."

I shook my head. "No, you won't."

Slipping the semiauto from her holster, she aimed the 9mm at my foot. "If you don't do what I say, I'm going to blow the big toe off your left foot — now go back to the truck."

"Is that a new sidearm?"

She held it up for inspection, displaying it like a hand model would. "Glock 19 Gen 4 in Midnight Bronze." She re-aimed it at my foot. "There is a pool at the office on who is going to be responsible for letting you do something stupid that causes you to hurt yourself, and that is not going to be on my watch — got it?"

I smiled at her in an attempt to save my toe. "Who's leading the pool?"

"Lucian, but Sancho coming up fast on the inside."

"That's why he follows me to the bathroom?"

"Uh huh. Now quit stalling and go to the truck."

"Yes, ma'am." I pushed off the tree and started back at a slow pace, wondering if I'd ever pick up the step I'd lost in Mexico. Maybe that was the way of things; sometimes you paid a price and never get to make another deposit into your account and eventually you are overdrawn. Lately, I'd been feeling like I was standing at the counter, the cashier always closing the window in my face.

I wasn't paying much attention as I walked

back toward the truck, but after a while I became aware of some movement to my right and turned my head in time to catch a glimpse of what I thought was the same border collie — but then thought again.

When you see a wolf, you can't help feeling impressed. Maybe it's because we're so used to being around their more domesticated cousins, but this animal is something else. Aside from all the crap that you see on TV and in the movies or even in badly written books, they're not the slathering beasts just outside the glow of the campfire; there's only one word that comes to mind when I've ever seen one in the wild: empathic.

It's like they're reading your mind, because they have to know what you're thinking to simply survive.

Back in the day, after that first nomadic hunter tossed a greasy leg of caribou to a curious pair of eyes, it set off a chain reaction of genetic mutation of over eight hundred thousand years that bred a partner for mankind, and an entirely different branch of the canine tree was born. For the sacrifice of their freedom came security and their role as guard and companion.

That was not the animal I was looking at now.

He studied me, not moving, and if not for

a slight difference in color gradation against the darkness of the trees and the faded snow, I would've never seen him.

What would he have done then?

Eons ago there was a period when we would have been competing with each other as apex predators, but intellect and opposable thumbs gave us an evolutionary advantage and now he lived in our world.

Unconsciously, my hand landed on the holster of my stag-handled .45 — maybe I wasn't feeling so apex after all.

His mouth was closed and his ears were down, but his eyes were wide and studied me. He was massive even if he hadn't eaten a quarter of a sheep. There was no blood on his mouth or ruff, so if he had killed the sheep, who knew when he had?

Coon said he was probably an adolescent, but that didn't jibe with what I was looking at right now — this fella must've weighed at least 175 pounds, and his muzzle was covered in gray, which contrasted with his broad, dark body.

I thought about what I knew of wolf societies and figured he wasn't long for the world. A mating pair dominates most packs, and interlopers are usually killed outright. This poor old guy was on the prowl for a new life, likely pushed out of his old one in

Yellowstone. Little did he know that the majority of other packs in the Lower 48 were in the far reaches of northern Wisconsin and Minnesota, and I doubted he would make it that far — with Coon and Butler on his tail, it was unlikely he'd make it to South Fork.

I watched as he shied away, giving the impression that he might bolt. I just stood there looking at him — hell, it wasn't very often that you got such an opportunity. I didn't pull my sidearm — that wasn't my job.

"Hey."

His ears perked, and I noticed he wore a transmitting collar.

"You need to get out of here."

He held his post and watched me, but every time I began to make a movement toward him, he'd duck his head and act as if he were going to take off, so I just stood still. "You haven't seen a shepherd around here, have you?"

I took another step, and this time he loped away, but I followed quickly enough so that he kept turning back to look at me now and again to see if I was still there.

I'd only gone about fifty yards when the radio on my belt sounded.

Static. "Walt, where the hell are you?"

Pulling the two-way up, I whispered honestly, "Um, in the trees."

Static. "What is that supposed to mean?"

I keyed the mic again. "You wouldn't believe me if I told you . . . You find the shepherd?"

Static. "No, but you need to get back to the truck. Now."

"We need to find the herder."

Static. "Yes, *we* do, but *you* need to get your ass back to the truck right now."

"What? I can't hear you — you're breaking up . . ."

Static. "Walt, do not try that shit with me. I invented it."

I turned off the radio and welcomed the high-altitude silence as the wind scoured the treetops like a powerful hand. The big wolf was still watching me expectantly, but I was left with little choice if I was serious about finding Miguel Hernandez.

"You know, if you lure me out here and there are a bunch of your buddies waiting for us, I'm not going to be happy." I pushed off again, but the pain in my side was really getting to me, so I stopped and leaned against a sizable trunk, resting with my hat in my hand and an ear pressed against the bark.

I listened to the blood rushing in my head,

29

regulated my breath, and waited for the pain to go away, but it didn't. Focusing on the ground, I became aware of something lying there, something out of place. Using the tree as support, I knelt and reached out to pick up a small piece of white cardboard with some blue printing on it. I held it a little closer and breathed a laugh.

"Are you okay?"

Raising my head, I glanced around, but could see nothing, not even the wolf.

"Over here."

I leaned a little forward, looked around the tree that I was crouched behind, and could see a woman standing a little ways off. She had wide cheekbones, dark hair, and startling blue eyes, and wore snow boots, leggings, and a hunter-green down jacket. She adjusted what looked to be some kind of Tibetan *dharma-chakra* hat complete with tassels.

Slowly standing, I stuffed the card into my shirt pocket. "Howdy."

She took a step closer, and I noticed that the border collie we'd been chasing was standing at her feet, looking at me and whining. "Are you okay?"

"Um, yep."

"You don't look so good."

I swung a finger toward the dog. "You

need to keep a sharp eye on her: there's a wolf right around here, a very big one."

"I know — 777M." She gestured toward the dog. "Gansu's been around wolves a lot and knows to stay clear." The dog came closer than the woman had and sat at my boots. "She likes you."

"Who is 777M?"

"That wolf you're following, his designation is 777M from the pack he got kicked off of in Yellowstone."

I straightened. "He's a long way from home."

She shrugged. "Old and gray . . . I'm guessing a newer, younger version has taken his place in the pack. It happens, no matter what the species." She smiled, but I watched as the smile faded when she saw the semi-automatic at my hip. "You Predator Control?"

"Depends on the predator." I pulled my Carhartt back, revealing the solitary, partial constellation on my chest. "Sheriff, Absaroka County."

She relaxed a bit. "Where's that?"

"You're in it."

"I thought I was in Big Horn County."

"You would be, about a quarter of a mile that way." I pointed west, then held out my hand. "Walt Longmire."

"Keasik Cheechoo." She shook my hand with a surprising grip and then shrugging the canvas rucksack off her shoulder pulled a Nalgene water bottle from it. "You still don't look so good, Sheriff."

I sighed a wheezing laugh. "I've had a rough couple of months."

Handing me the plastic bottle, she glanced around. "Drink up."

Unscrewing the attached top, I took a few swallows and then wiped off my mouth with the back of a glove. "You mind telling me about your relationship with 777M?"

"Relationship?" She smiled and took the water back, taking a slug for herself. "Is that cop talk?"

"Pretty much." I tossed a thumb over my back. "We've got a dead sheep."

Her eyes stayed on me, their sky blue offset in her deeply tanned face. "Oh, no."

"Oh, yes. Anyway, your buddy 777M is number one on the suspect list."

She stiffened again. "What makes you think he did it?"

"Um, the fact that he may be the only wolf in the Bighorn Mountains at this time?"

"How do you know a wolf did it?"

"I don't, but the brand inspector and the forest ranger back up in the park seem to be pretty certain of it and are collecting

32

DNA as we speak."

"If it was the wolf, he was desperate and starving."

"I don't think the Stockman's Association is going to care . . . Anyway, you haven't answered my question, Ms. Cheechoo. What are you doing up here running with the wolves?"

She smiled again; it was a quick smile, but a toothsome one nonetheless. "Jungian analysis? Are you sure you're a Wyoming sheriff?"

"So the citizens tell me every four years, and you do what for a living?"

She handed me the bottle again. "The wolf conservancy out of Missoula, Montana."

I smiled at her. "I know where Missoula is — kind of a big town."

"I'm a nurse at St. Patrick's hospital and volunteer for the WC."

"And 777M is one of your projects?"

"He is, and you're looking to kill him?"

"Not really, I'm actually looking for a shepherd."

She stepped in closer. "Miguel?"

"You know him too?"

"I do."

"You know where his camp is?"

"He was moving it two days ago."

33

"And you saw him?"

"I had dinner with him. He was lonely, and I'm female and can listen — kind of a rarity here in the mountains."

"Well, his sheep, or more specifically Abarrane Extepare's sheep, are scattered all over the meadow up there, and there's nobody in sight."

She thought about it. "I can show you where his camp was."

"That'd be a start." I lumbered up and stood there looking at her, taking in her features. "Assiniboine or Blackfeet?"

She smiled again, easier this time. "I'm always amazed when white people feel free to do that. I mean, what would you say if I walked up to you and said, 'Scots-Irish; English, with a little bit of Nordic; possibly Swedish or Norwegian'?"

"I'd say those were nationalities, and nowhere near as important as tribe."

"In case you haven't noticed, Sheriff, it's all tribes." Pulling the pack onto her shoulder, she turned to go, with the collie following at her heels. "Cree-Assiniboine/Young Dogs, Piapot First Nation by the way."

"Idaho is where I grew up, but I lived in Colville Reservation for a while."

"Washington." I noticed she was slowing

her pace to accommodate me. "You might know my friend, Henry Standing Bear?"

"Standing Bear?"

"Northern Cheyenne."

"I've heard of him, I think." She stopped. "Did he break a guy's arm in Spokane one time, arm-wrestling back in the eighties?"

"Not that I'm personally aware of, but it sounds like his MO."

She studied me. "Big guy, almost as big as you. Handsome."

"That's Henry, especially the handsome part."

"It was my uncle's arm he broke."

"Oh. Sorry."

She shifted her shoulders in an easy shrug. "He was a jerk."

"Well, the Bear can be an acquired taste . . ."

She started off again. "No, my uncle."

Keeping up, I noticed we were moving farther and farther from the park. "Any idea why Miguel might've moved his camp so far into the tree line?"

"He didn't. There's a spur opening up here, and he had the sheep gathered. It's boxed on two sides, and it was easy to watch the stock from an outcropping or from the wagon."

"You sound like you know him pretty well."

"I do on-site inspections for the Wage and Hour Division of the Colorado Labor Department." She stopped, turned, and looked at me. "Because of the itinerant nature of the job, there's no way to enforce any kind of code for the working conditions, so I am on salary for the department part time." She gripped the shoulder strap of her pack. "Miguel was working in Colorado and was going so hungry he ate part of a rotting elk carcass, and the rancher he was working for had the nerve to charge him with poaching and dropped him off at the immigration office for deportation. He almost died of food poisoning, but an agent took him to a local emergency room and saved his life."

"And he came back?"

"Miguel has a wife and two children in Rancagua, south of Santiago — he sends them all of his money." She glanced around. "He was deathly afraid of wolves. I tried to explain to him that they really weren't all that ferocious, but he heard of a child being dragged off by one when he was young and never forgot it."

Kicking off again, we broke into the spur she'd mentioned, a clearing about half the size of a football field, a red and white sheep wagon with a set of mules tied to the rear at the far end. I was always seeing the wagons as a metaphor, like tiny ships on the rocky seas of the Bighorn Mountains, tidy little resources with everything in its place, prepared for the long journey of solitary months to come.

"That's funny."

"What?"

"That's where his camp was two days ago, but he was in the process of moving it."

"Maybe he changed his mind."

"And let the sheep wander off? He'd never do that."

Walking across the clearing, I could see a narrow aperture where the trees got thin and joined the larger park. "Nice little spot."

She paid me no attention and continued toward the wagon with the collie loping alongside. "Miguel! *¿dónde estás?*"

It looked like many of the other sheep camps I'd seen before but remarkably neat and orderly with the wagon buttoned up. There were two mules that twitched their ears at us when we arrived, and I noticed they'd eaten all the grass their leads would allow them to reach. I filled a nearby bucket from a water container attached to the wagon and then moved the mule and the jenny to the other side where they could reach it and fresh grass.

The young woman appeared alongside the wagon. "Animal lover."

"Rancher's son." I turned to look at her after watering the mules. "Find him?"

"No, and the wagon is closed up as if he was getting ready to move."

"Do you want to look inside?"

She hugged herself. "I'm not comfortable doing that."

"I am." I headed toward the front. "I'm not going to spend hours out here looking for him if he's asleep in there."

I checked the latch on the front of the wagon. It was unlocked, so I opened the top part of the miniature Dutch door and peered inside. The canvas gave the interior an amber tone, and inside it was warm. I was tempted to climb in and take a nap.

The woman joined me in the opening. "This is so strange."

Reaching over, I picked up a few books from the bench beside the tiny cook stove. "He keeps an immaculate camp." Turning the books over, I was surprised to find a number of political pamphlets along with George Santayana's *The Last Puritan* and *Philosophy and Poetry* by Mariá Zambrano.

There was a handwritten piece of paper in one book, and I pulled it out and read it:

I would I might Forget that I am I. Sonnet VII. George Santayana

Closing the poem back inside, I gestured with the book. "Hmm . . . Not the usual reading material you find at sheep camp."

Looking past my shoulder, she nodded. "He is incredibly intelligent and writes a great deal of poetry himself. I think he was something of a dissident and might've not been welcome back in Chile."

I noticed there were some theme notebooks stacked neatly on a bench, and I was tempted to sample Miguel Hernadez's poetry but decided I was being intrusive.

Closing the door, I turned to glance around and suddenly froze. "Where's your dog?"

Keasick patted her leg, and the collie came from under the wagon. She sat at her feet, wagging. "She's right here, why?"

I pointed to a spot in the tree line where, in the drifting cloud of evaporating snow, stood 777M.

Carefully slipping the pack from her shoulder, I watched as she opened the top and took out a large digital camera, but just as she got it up to her face, the dark wolf vanished into the mist. "Damn, I can't see him. Are you sure he's there?"

"Until a moment ago."

39

Sighing, she slipped the camera back into the sack. "The O-Seven lineage goes back to the midnineties, but this guy is something different. Maybe from another pack."

"Do you think he knows you?"

"I don't know, I guess I never thought about it."

"In my experience with wolves, they get away from human beings as fast as they can, but this guy seems to be loitering around — and that's not good." Half turning, I gestured toward her dog. "The two of you stay here."

I'd taken a few steps when she called after me. "Is that an order?"

"Do what you want, but if that was my dog I wouldn't want her anywhere near ol' 777M."

Crossing the small meadow, I approached the forest and was suddenly glad I wasn't wearing a red hood or out visiting grandma.

I stopped for a moment, noticing some carvings on one of the trees. They were fresh, and I could make out the general design but not their meaning. Pulling out a small field notepad, I copied the designs and then returned it to the inside pocket of my jacket.

The roof of the cloud ceiling had lowered to the point where I could only see about seven feet above the ground. Trailing my eyes in and out of the visible world, I thought something moved off to my right, but as my eyes adjusted, I could tell it was only a branch, swaying in the mist where the treetops shimmied like the seed heads of alpine grass and dropping curtains of powdery snow through the fog.

Even though the last known case of wolf rabies in America had been back in the forties, I still wasn't willing to take any chances, so I unsnapped the safety strap on my holster and took a few investigative steps forward. Glancing in all directions, I moved slightly toward an open area to my left where I thought I saw something move again. Thinking that the wolf might've found some way to get above me, I slipped the Colt from my holster, flipped off the safety, and aimed upward, but there was nothing there.

There were tracks in the snow, a lot of them, and bloodstains, and I was getting more than a little concerned about Miguel Hernandez — still, lone wolf attacks were rare. With roughly a dozen wolf fatalities in the last century, almost all, if not captive animals or the few with rabies, were the result of attacking packs. Wolves worked in numbers, making them such impressive predators — but this was a lone wolf, and why, of all things, would he attempt to take on a human being?

I knelt down and ran my hand over the surface of the snow where the blood seemed coagulated, but there wasn't nearly enough of it to indicate an attack on something as large as a person. Maybe there was an initial assault that had disabled Hernandez enough for him to be carried off, no mean feat for a single wolf — or damaged him enough that he limped away to be attacked again in another location.

Something struck the brim of my hat, splattering off the edge and falling onto the leather surface of my glove. Slowly raising my face, I looked up just as a brief window in the mist revealed the grisly remains of Miguel Hernandez's naked feet, stripped of all flesh and hanging high above the ground.

2

"I think it's safe to assume the wolf didn't
hang him."

"Probably not, but I don't think we should
jump to any conclusions."

"Yep." Sitting on the stool in room 26 of
the Durant Memorial Hospital along with
Saizarbitoria, my custodian-of-the-moment,
we watched as Isaac Bloomfield and David
Nickerson carefully went through the findings of their autopsy with us. "Were there
any other signs of predation?"

"No, just the feet, which I imagine were
the only portions the animal or animals
could reach — excluding birds, of course."

Isaac adjusted his glasses. "How high
would you say he was hung?"

"His feet were at least five feet off the
ground, probably closer to six."

Nickerson looked at me, pausing in his
work. "Wow."

"I've jumped that high for a beer."

43

Isaac interrupted. "You are six and a half feet tall."

"Well, this wolf is almost that tall." I made a face at Santiago and gestured toward the body. "So, what's the verdict?"

"Well . . ."

The silence hung in the room like a caul. "Now, why do I not like the sound of that?"

"Second most common method of suicide." The senior doc pulled at his lower lip. "The neck was not broken, which is not that unusual in suicides; rarely does the individual do the job correctly, and most asphyxiate." He pointed to the neck of the herder. "But the knot was correct in this case, and the drop should've been substantial enough to break the neck . . . but it didn't."

"The knot?"

"Textbook knot, and it should've broken the spinal cord along with the dislocated vertebrae, but it didn't. Not that unusual, I suppose. Hanging is a very technical form of execution and difficult to perform properly; much crueler, painful, and primitive compared with other methods."

Sancho got off his stool and approached the body. "So, it's a suicide."

"Most don't attempt it from eight feet above the ground, and you found no stool, ladder, or anything he could've climbed onto?"

"No."

The Basquo glanced at me, but I'd played this game many times before with Isaac and was happy to just let him think out loud. "So, it's a homicide."

Nickerson shrugged. "He could've climbed the tree and swung out into the air, which would've done the trick."

"So, suicide?" Sancho looked at me, but I still said nothing.

"All the wounds on his arms, those are curious." The younger doctor posited. "Difficult to judge the alcohol level of the deceased, because the bacteria of the body produces its own alcohol as it decays, but the vitreous humor sample verifies that he was intoxicated."

"How drunk?"

"Three times over the legal limit." Isaac glanced at me. "Was a bottle discovered in the vicinity?"

"No." I joined him in studying the body, even going so far as to lumber off my stool. "Hard to climb a tree when you're drunk."

Saizarbitoria made up his mind. "Homicide."

"And there is the damage to his face."

45

I moved forward. "What damage to his face?"

Isaac pointed. "Numerous bruises and a split lip — I'd say he was in a fight, Walt."

Stooping down, I studied the damage I'd missed because of the general swelling and discoloration. "Would you say that was part of the hanging?"

"No, I'd say that he was in a fight two to three days before his demise. Then there's the feet. The decedent was not wearing shoes, which might've assisted in climbing the tree."

The Basquo, having now figured out the drill, said nothing.

"Or the wolf might've carried them away."

I lifted my head a little as a thought struck. "Have you done any fiber testing on his clothes yet?"

"No, we simply bagged them to be sent down to Cheyenne."

"You mind doing a preliminary?"

"And what, exactly, would I be looking for?"

"Horse hair, or mule to be exact."

Isaac nodded. "Interesting . . . that would be about the only way you could get him up that high."

"Folks have been hanging people from their mounts for years around these parts."

I nodded and began for the door. "Let me know what you find."

As I turned the corner in the hallway, the Basquo caught up. "You really think somebody hung him?"

"Hard to say, that line of work has a high suicide rate — they used to call it *sage-brushed.* I know of two who've committed suicide in my lifetime; that much time alone just isn't good for anybody."

"So, which ear do they put the knot behind in a hanging?"

As we turned the corner, Keasik Cheechoo, the woman from the mountain, stood with her hat in one hand, running the other through her impossibly thick hair. She stepped out to block us. "Well?"

I pulled up and stopped. "Hello, Ms. Cheechoo."

"He was killed."

I glanced around the mauve waiting room, where a few heads lifted from last year's magazines and last week's *Durant Courant.* Turning a little sideways, I blocked her from the majority of the room and lowered my voice. "I'd like to speak with you about the situation, but I'd just as soon do that at my office, if you don't mind?"

She shot a look around, her eyes ricocheting off the citizenry. "Um . . . Okay. When?"

47

I patted my shirtfront pocket. "Well, I've got your card here with your cell phone number on it, and I can give you a call when we're ready to speak with you."

"Why not now?"

"Because we have other responsibilities, Ms. Cheechoo."

"Like what? What's more important than Miguel Hernandez's life?" She stepped toward me, lowering her own voice. "You've got important parking tickets to write?"

I stood there for a moment looking at her — I like doing that to convince people that I'm angry, although all I really am is tired. "Ms. Cheechoo, when I spoke with you earlier, I asked if you could let us know if you were considering leaving town and that if you were, would you please contact us, and you said you weren't leaving anytime in the near future. Now, have your plans changed?"

She crossed her arms. "No."

"Then I will be contacting you shortly." With that, I turned and walked past her and outside, toward my truck. Saizarbitoria was staying to my right with a slight smile on his face. "What?"

"Nothing."

We climbed into my truck and were buckling our seat belts when she appeared on

48

the other side of my hood. Santiago's smile had faded, and he began to remove his belt when I stopped him. "No."

Climbing out, I closed the door behind me and placed a hand on my fender. "Ms. Cheechoo . . ."

"Keasik."

"If you're concerned about the speed of the Hernandez investigation, I'd advise you to stop impeding it by hampering me in my duties."

Her head kicked sideways. "I'm not so sure there's going to be any Hernandez investigation."

"Well, you're entitled to your opinion, Ms. Cheechoo."

As I climbed into my vehicle, she shouted after me. "I'm not moving."

I started the truck, stared at her for a moment, and then pulled the selector into reverse, throwing an arm over the seat and swinging wide before pulling down into drive and then quickly accelerating before she could run in front of us.

When I glanced at Sancho, he was smiling again. "What?"

"Why didn't you just talk to her?"

"Because I want to think about what I'm going to ask her, and I'm tired."

He nodded.

"Left." He stared at me. "They put the knot behind the left ear in a formal hanging."

"Walt."

There was nothing, nothing I could see, nothing I could hear, nothing I could taste, nothing I could smell, but worst of all nothing I could touch.

"Walt?"

Nothing, and no matter how hard I tried, it seemed like consciousness was leaving me out in the cold — almost like I'd come loose from the earth and was spinning out into space and total desolation.

"Walt!"

I started, almost flipping my chair backward. Something pulled in my side, and I was pretty sure I was going to die. Sitting there without moving, I waited till the spasm faded and then raised my eyes to meet the two sets standing in the doorway of my office.

"You okay?" Victoria Moretti studied me.

"Yep, I'm fine." Swallowing, I patted my leg and the other set of eyes came over, resting his broad head on my knee.

She glanced back into the dark, main office. "You fell asleep, and nobody wanted to wake you up — at least we thought you were asleep."

"I was."

"Your eyes were open."

"I'd just woken up."

"No." She glanced at her tactical Timex. "You've been sitting there staring and not moving for seven minutes and thirty-two seconds."

I smiled a crooked grin. "That long, you're sure?" I glanced up at the old Seth Thomas on the wall — it was after nine o'clock at night. "I guess I wore myself out up on the mountain."

She came in and sat in one of my guest chairs, lodging her boots on the edge of my desk, studying me from over her kneecaps. "Walt, something is wrong."

"I'm just tired."

"It's more than that. You've done it about a dozen times that I've witnessed, and other people have noticed it too."

I smiled again, this time putting a little more effort into it. "Maybe I'm cracking up."

"Not funny, asshole." She studied me. "Is it Bidarte?"

"I don't think so."

"He's dead."

"So they say."

51

"You watched him die."

"Yep."

"You killed him yourself."

"Please, don't remind me."

She shook her head and then dropped her tactical boots to the floor. "In case you haven't noticed, the world as a whole is a much better place since his passing."

"I know."

"So, let it go."

I nodded and continued petting Dog's head.

"Wow."

"Wow, what?"

"This isn't so much about him as it is about you, huh?"

"Meaning?"

"This is the moment when you find out you're not ten feet tall and bulletproof." She leaned in and smiled. "You've been shot, stabbed, punched, kicked, run over, and generally abused in just about every way possible, and it's only now that it's gotten to you?"

I stopped petting Dog for a moment, so he gave my hand a lick. "Maybe so."

"I mean, I can see your point — the fucker did more damage to me than anybody ever has or ever will, and I wanted to wring the life out of him with my bare hands, but I'll settle for having you skewer him like a campfire marshmallow."

"Thank you."

"You're welcome." She settled back in the chair. "Let's go have dinner."

"I'm not really hungry."

She stared at me. "You've lost what, thirty, maybe forty pounds since your adventure in the desert?"

I continued petting Dog's head. "I don't know."

"Not that you don't look good, I mean better."

"Thank you, I think."

She continued to study me. "Not that I don't enjoy your company, but I think you need to go see a guy."

"Any particular guy?"

"Yeah, the guy you usually see when having these internal philosophical debates. I don't mind doing it for a while, but then my head hurts and I want to shoot something."

"Okay."

"So, unless you want a beer, or the horizontal bop or both?"

"I'm not sure if I have the energy for either."

She shrugged. "So, you need me to give you a ride home?"

"No, I think I can make it on my own." I carefully stood, still feeling the tremors of pain from my side echoing through my nervous system like distant thunder. "I think I'm just going to go home and go to bed."

"Without company?"

"I'm afraid so." I held out a hand, and she took it. "I wonder . . ."

"Don't. Don't wonder about you and me right now. Okay?" She curled my arm around her, slipping herself gently into my damaged side as if making it whole. "You've got enough to think about."

Draping my arm over her shoulder, she helped me with my jacket and then walked me out of my office and around Ruby's dispatcher's counter toward the steps.

"Who's leading the office pool?"

"Think our adventures in the mountains."

"Sorry." After saluting the painting of Andrew Carnegie, I held the door for her and Dog as we passed through and into the night. She leaned against the adjacent glass as I locked up and thought about who had the pager that one of us always carried home at night. "Whose got the Rock?"

"Sancho. He said he'd meet you here early and go with you out to the Extepare place — he figures speaking Basque will give you an advantage." She leaned back and looked up at me. "You ever need an expert in sarcasm, you'll let me know, right?"

"Undoubtedly." We'd just started down the remainder of the stairs when I noticed a white Toyota pickup with Montana plates and a slide-in truck camper sitting in the parking lot.

Vic noticed my gaze. "Somebody moving in?"

"I believe that's Keasik Cheechoo's vehicle."

"*Choochoo* the wolf woman?"

"For lack of a better name."

As the three of us approached, I could see a large lump of blankets in the cab and the border collie snugged into the pile with her owner.

"She's sleeping in our lot?"

"I guess so." I gestured toward Vic's vehicle parked next to mine. "Throw Dog in my unit and then get out of here and I'll talk to her."

"Fuck that, you and Dog get out of here and I'll talk to her."

"That will end with you putting her in a cell."

"*Qué será, será.*"

"That means someone has to stay here tonight with her."

My undersheriff slumped, some of the

55

wind having effectively escaped her incarceration sails. "I don't like her."

"Enough to spend the night with her?"

"Point taken. Just don't be long and then go home." I watched as the new and improved Glock 19 Gen 4 in Midnight Bronze bounced off her hip as she unhappily retreated before opening the passenger door of my truck for Dog, then she climbed into her own unit, started it, and circled around, rolling down the manual window. "I'm back here in forty minutes, and if the two of you are still here I'm arresting you both, and she can listen to the two of us having sex in the next cell."

Vic drove off, and I reapproached the Toyota with Dog watching from the passenger seat of my truck. I rapped my knuckles on the window of the white pickup.

The border collie, Gansu, unleashed a series of yipping barks as she stood on the seat. Keasik Cheechoo pulled the Tibetan hat from her face.

I raised my hand again. "Howdy."

She rolled her window down and massaged her eyes. "What time is it?"

"A little after nine."

"What were you doing in there?"

"Working." I lied.

"Yeah, well, I'm waiting for our meet."

56

"I'm sorry, did we schedule something?"

"Not since you drove off and left me standing in the hospital parking lot." She pulled the blanket aside and then reached over and took her cell phone from the dash, the condensation of her warm breath filling the open window. "My plans have changed, and I'm leaving in the morning."

I rested an arm on the roof of her vehicle. "Something come up?"

"Work related, so if you want to talk to me you need to do it now."

"I'm sure we can just do it on the phone."

"Now you tell me?"

"Well, you could've come in the office."

"I don't like police stations."

"Okay." I tapped the top of her truck. "You're off the hook and can head back to Missoula."

"Colorado."

"Wherever, so long as I've got your cell phone number."

She lodged the blanket between her and the dog. "I thought I should let you know, I've already contacted the Chilean government and lodged a formal protest on Miguel Hernandez's behalf, stating that his ultimate death was a result of unsafe working conditions."

"Good to know."

When I said nothing more, she looked up at me. "You're not worried?"

"I didn't employ the man, Ms. Cheechoo."

"It was your job to protect him."

I stared at her for a moment. "Yep, it was." I tapped the roof once more and then turned and walked toward my truck. "Travel safe."

The door opened and slammed shut behind me, and I could hear her rushing to catch up as I got to my own unit. She caught me off-balance just as I was turning, and I tripped over my own feet, falling against my truck and sliding down into a sitting position, my hat landing in my lap.

Dog thudded against the window above me and growled before breaking into a series of barks that only stopped when I beat on the door with my knuckles. "Knock it off, I'm all right."

She'd backed away but now was reaching down to try to help me. "I am so sorry, I didn't mean to —"

Brushing her hand away, I told her, "I'm fine," and started to stand but just couldn't summon up the energy. "Actually, I'm not . . . would you mind helping me up?"

Between the two of us, we grappled myself to a standing position, and I placed an open hand on the window to stop Dog's intermittent motorboat impersonation.

She backed to arm's length as if the beast might come through the window. "What kind of dog is that?"

"I don't really know."

"He's yours?"

"It's more like I'm his."

"I can see that." Allowing me to catch my breath, she held onto my arm. "Would you like me to call someone?" She was distracted for a moment but then raised her head to look at me. "My God, you're bleeding."

Glancing down, I could see a dark stain seeping through my flannel shirt. "Well, hell . . . I must've pulled some stiches in the drainage hole."

"Drainage hole?"

"I was stabbed a while ago."

She stared at me in disbelief. "We've got to get you to the hospital."

"I'd rather go home and bleed, really."

"You can't just go home." She glanced back at the defunct library that served as our office and jail. "You must have emergency equipment in there?"

"Yep, but I can take care of it myself."

"No, you can't. I'm a medical technician for God's sake — if you're not going to let me take you to the hospital, then you have to at least let me patch you up here."

Realizing I was fighting a losing battle, I acquiesced and turned to look at Dog. "Stay here, and don't eat the steering wheel."

I unlocked the door and, with the help of the banister, climbed the steps up to the desk where Ruby kept a large first aid kit. Sitting on the lower section of the counter, I shrugged off my coat and, grimacing a little, began carefully pulling out my shirt-tail and unbuttoning my shirt.

She stood at the top of the steps and looked around. "How did you get stabbed?"

"It's a long story." Getting the shirt out of the way, I could now see that the bleeding was coming from the bottom of the Ace bandage that Bloomfield and Nickerson had wrapped around me at the last dressing change. Giving up on discretion, I shouldered off my jacket, unbuttoned the rest of my shirt, and then slowly unwrapped the flexible bandage to reveal the gauze patch and medical tape that had come loose when I'd fallen.

"Let me see." Pushing my hands aside, she knelt and peeled the gauze back. "It's not so bad — one of the stitches must've pulled, but it's already stopped bleeding." Pulling some antiseptic cream from the kit, she applied it onto a sterile pad and replaced

60

the bloody one with deft hands. "So, who stabbed you?"

"A drug kingpin, down in Mexico."

She continued to work. "Kind of out of your jurisdiction as a Wyoming sheriff, isn't it?"

"A little . . . he had my daughter."

There was a pause. "She in the drug business?"

"No, worse — she works for the attorney general's office in Wyoming." Keasik glanced up at my face again. "It was personal — between him and me."

"Yeah, looks personal all right." Finishing the work, she began rewrapping the flexible bandage around my midriff, her arms surrounding me. "How old is this wound?"

"A month or so, why?"

"It shouldn't be draining like this after that much time."

I reached over, put on my bloody shirt, and changed the subject. "So, why the emergency in Colorado?"

She stared at me for a moment and then reached out and flipped my collar down smoothing it. "Don't you have a clean shirt?"

"No."

Shaking her head, she began buttoning the dirty one for me. "I'm assuming you're not married."

"And why is that?"

"Married men always have a clean shirt — it's one of the perks."

Unmoved by the distraction, I asked again. "Colorado?"

She finished buttoning and stepped away to admire her handiwork. "I made that up. I'm not really leaving, but I thought it might motivate you. Instead, all it did was induce me into aggravated assault on a police officer." She folded her arms. "You gonna book me?"

"It would be a hard sell on a jury, considering you're the one who scraped me off the parking lot and brought me in here to patch me up."

She nodded. "Also, I'm sorry about the parking ticket remark back at the hospital."

"I've heard worse."

She smiled, and there was warmth in it for the first time. "What are you going to do about Miguel?"

"Ms. Cheechoo . . ."

"Keasik, please."

It seemed stupid to try to remain professional after she'd seen my insides. "Keasik, the first thing I'm going to do is find out if there's anything to investigate. I mean, if the man committed suicide there really isn't

62

anything . . ."

"People can be driven to suicide, you know?"

"I do, and if there's anything like the treatment you've mentioned, we'll act on it."

"Honest?"

"Honest." I crossed my heart and did the Cub Scout salute. "You seem sure that wasn't a suicide, and if it was that there were mitigating circumstances." I stretched my neck and looked at her. "How well did you know Mr. Hernandez?"

She studied me, stiffening and saying nothing at first. "What are you insinuating?"

"Just what I asked — how well did you know Miguel Hernandez?"

Still folding her arms around herself, she took a few steps toward the marble fireplace, a remnant from when librarians used to check out books using a card-catalog Dewey decimal classification system. "We slept together. I guess that's pretty well, huh?"

Standing, I tucked my shirttail in, careful to avoid the wound. "Keasik, I'm honestly not trying to pry — it's just that in the course of an investigation I'm going to need to get the lay of the land and I'm going to have to ask some questions that might not be pleasant."

"You knew."

"I suspected." I chose my next words carefully. "You seem to have an emotional investment in all this."

"He was my friend." I stared at her, waiting. "And maybe a little more."

"How long had you known him?"

"A couple of years; since the incident in Colorado."

"And that was with the Department of Labor job there?"

"Yes."

"Do you know of anyone who would wish him harm?"

She crossed back toward me. "Tons of people; he was a political dissident and was on the forefront of decent treatment of nomadic tradesmen."

"In Chile?"

She gestured with her arms wide. "And here."

"I guess what I'm looking for are individuals who had both a method and motive — if he was murdered. First off, someone who could've been placed in the Bighorn National Forest within the last forty-eight hours, which limits the suspects."

"Some of the people who hired him could want him dead."

I took a breath and shook my head. "Now, don't get me wrong, I know the Extepare family and they've got a few rough edges, but I don't see them hanging their own shepherd."

"Someone else, then."

"Who else does he know up here?"

"He worked for some other ranches in Wyoming."

"Can you get me the names from the Colorado Department of Labor?"

"Absolutely."

"Well, that's a start." Standing, I shrugged on my jacket. "I will talk to Abarrane first thing in the morning. Is there anyone else he may have had contact with, other than yourself?"

"I really wouldn't know." She studied on the subject, finally pulling her fingers through her hair. "I know he'd come into town every couple of months, but I wasn't with him, so I don't know who he could've met."

"I'll check into it."

She grinned. "Well, there's a Basque bar in town."

"Yep."

She became even more excited. "And a Basque bakery."

"I know that too. I live here."

"Right." Her enthusiasm dampened, she dropped her head and the smile. "I guess

65

you get that a lot. Junior G-men who want to help?"

Ignoring the question, I thought of something else. "But he wasn't Basque."

"No."

"Then why would you mention the Basque establishments in town and not, say, the Mexican restaurant?"

Her eyes stayed steady on me. "You don't miss much, do you?"

"I try to be thorough, but you still haven't answered my question."

"He had more in common with the Basques than the Mexicans, I suppose. He was always kind of old world, if you know what I mean, at least that's what his reading tastes were."

Remembering that I had taken the books from the herder's wagon, I brought them back into the room and pulled the handwritten poem from the book of poetry. "Any idea whose handwriting this is?"

She studied it. "No."

"Not his?"

"No."

I took the piece of paper back and studied it. "I'm no expert, but I'd say it was a feminine hand, wouldn't you?"

"Yes."

I nodded and placed the sheet back into

66

the book, lodging it under my arm.

She cocked her head and reached out to tap the binding. "What do you think it means?"

"I don't know, but to be honest it's more important to ask all the questions than to have answers at this stage of an investigation." I looked directly at her in anticipation of her next question. "Because at this point some of the answers would inevitably be wrong, and all that does is slow the pursuit."

"Pursuit?"

I nodded, moving toward the door in hopes that she'd get the idea. "If Miguel Hernandez was murdered, then I am hunting for a killer, and the sooner I find him or her the better."

Following me, she paused at the top of the steps. "Before he or she kills again?"

I took a breath and tried not to sound too pedantic. "And for the sake of justice and Miguel Hernandez."

"All this for a three-year working-visa Chilean?" I watched as she went down the steps, turning at the landing to look at me and smile. "They're growing an odd crop of sheriffs here in Wyoming these days."

I stood high above her, attempting to cover my stained shirt with an arm — if you're going to appear epic, it's best to do it without looking like you're bleeding to death. "Yes, ma'am."

"I'm not a bad person, you know?"

I didn't say anything.

"I knew he was married and had kids and everything, but he was so lonely."

I dropped my head to examine my boots. After a moment there was a noise, and when I looked up she was gone. Having carefully avoided the minefield of personal interaction, I turned off the lights and eased down the steps, saluting the painting of Andrew Carnegie, along with all the 8 × 10s of the entire previous sheriffs of Absaroka County who had and had not avoided their own personal perils along the way.

When I got to the door, the Toyota was pulling out onto the main street, the yellow traffic lights strung through town blinking long after all good sheriffs should be home in bed.

I locked up and walked to my truck and was just about to open the door to an expectant Dog when I thought I heard a lone and plaintive sound from the west, high in the mountains.

I paused and listened, but there was nothing more. Figuring it was just in my head, I turned back and opened the driver's side door, but then I heard it again. Still unsure

68

if it was just my imagination, I glanced in at my 145 pounds of canine mix as his eyes glowed and he lifted his massive head, answering with the bellowing call of the hound of the Baskervilles.

Boy howdy.

3

"Did you get any sleep last night?"

We were bumping along the gravel road and over the moguls of ice that remained in the shadows of the Bighorn Mountains south of town, and I was actively failing in an attempt to keep my hat over my face. "Not much." Finally giving up, I slouched against the passenger door and watched the sun slowly burning the late-morning mist from the Powder River Country like it was a doomed ghost.

"Double Tough texted me and says he's happy to come up and meet us at the Extepare place, if you want."

A lazy smile played on my face before my head bounced against the inside of the window again. "He's bored down there in Powder Junction?"

Saizarbitoria laughed, the black Vandyke splitting to reveal his white teeth. "Probably, but he thought that since the family

70

has a propensity to relieve law enforcement of appendages . . ."

Glancing out the window, I watched as we approached the gate of the fifteen-thousand-acre ranch. "Tell him I've got my Basque secret weapon with me and we'll be fine." Pulling the notepad from my pocket, I thumbed it open and held it in front of the Basquo's face as he drove. "What do you make of that?"

"Your drawing?"

"Yep."

"That you made the right choice with a career in law enforcement." He glanced at it again as we bounced along. "Where did you see that?"

"On a tree, near where Hernandez was hung."

"Arborglyphs — carvings. The old Basque shepherds used to do them on the aspens all over the West, but like other traditions, there are less and less of them."

"These were fresh."

"Really?" He studied them again. "The first one at the top is a flower symbol that is supposed to ward off evil. And the two figures below represent a father and son, I think."

Folding up the notepad, I dropped it back into my pocket.

Sancho fought with the steering wheel again. "So, to get it straight, the old man Abarrane blew Lucian's leg off?"

"No, not Abe, his father, Beltran."

"I don't think I know him."

"Well, you missed your chance — he's been dead for quite some time now."

"When did that happen exactly?"

"You mean when did he die?"

"No, when did he blow Lucian's leg off?"

"Late forties, after the war." I glanced over at the Basquo, who still showed interest in the story. "Lucian was over on Jim Creek Hill in Sheridan County, out of his jurisdiction, which explains why it is that he got the drop on Beltran and his brother . . . Jakes, I think his name was."

"Why was Lucian after them?"

"I think it had to do with a woman that Lucian was married to for a couple of hours."

"A couple of hours? Who was she?"

I sat up, a little annoyed, and loosed my seat belt with a thumb. "Which story do you want to hear, because I'm only telling one."

He continued to smile, entertained by my morning grumpiness. "The leg."

"Not that much to tell, really. Lucian slips up on them but then isn't watching, and Beltran grabs a shotgun and blows Lucian's leg off and then walks over and stands there advising Lucian that he should take up another line of work before Beltran leaves him to bleed to death. Instead, Lucian uses the sling from his rifle to tie off the leg and drags himself to that old Nash of his and drives into Durant, and the doctor there took the leg." I sighed. "Shortly thereafter, said doctor left town."

"What happened to Beltran and Jakes?"

"Three weeks later, Lucian sticks the barrel of his .38 in Beltran's ear and sends him down to Rawlins for a five spot. When he got back, he'd calmed down a bit. Heck, I think I even saw the two of them drinking together at the Euskadi Bar on Main Street."

"What about the brother, Jakes?"

I thought about it. "Damned if I know."

We got to the Extepare ranch and drove past the outbuildings and sheds giving the impression that this was most assuredly an honest-to-goodness working ranch. Abandoned, out-of-date equipment was parked alongside the barns with deeply trenched causeways and weather-beaten grayed posts and poles that leaned southeast in the pervasive wind.

I pointed to where some more modern vehicles and a bulbous '65 International

Travelall were parked in front of what must've been the main house, where a man sat on the front steps.

Armed.

Santiago slowed. "Is he holding a sawed-off shotgun?"

"Looks like it."

Sancho pulled up and parked, and I got out, looking at Abarrane. "Mr. Extepare."

He squinted his eyes at me as he stood with what looked to be an old, foreshortened Remington automatic half aimed toward the yard beside me. "Sheriff."

"Are you going bird hunting?"

A short, stocky man with a prodigious nose and earlobes that seemed to comprise the entirety of his body fat, he held the tough-guy look as long as he could and then chuckled. "I did not know if you recognize an Extepare without a shotgun!" He broke out laughing at his joke as I came around the front. "How you doin', Walter?"

He tossed me the old sawed-off Model 11 that probably hadn't been fired since before Sputnik. I looked at the crusty, rusted mechanism of the twenty gauge. "What's this?"

"Dat's the one dat done it."

I stared down at the weapon, the realization dawning on me like the slow morning I'd already endured. "This is it, huh?"

"Dat, or Ma Barker hid it under dat lambing shed over at the summer place."

"Well, I'll be."

"No other reason my old man woulda taken a valuable piece of iron like dat and hid it unless he had a reason — you give dat to that grouchy boss of yours the next time you see him, you know?"

"He's not my boss anymore."

He knocked some knuckles against his lowered head. "I keep forgettin'. G'ttin' old I guess."

"We all are, Abe."

"How 'bout you fellas come in and have a cup o' coffee?" He nodded and stepped off the porch to ground level, looked up at me, and then glanced over at the Basquo. *"Kaixo."*

Sancho extended a hand. *"Ondoeskerrik asko."*

"I knew you was one of us people, you handsome devil you." The old Basquo began laughing. *"Zein da zure izena?"*

"Nire ib zena Santiago Saizarbitoria da."

"Pozten naiz zu ezagutzeaz."

I took a step forward, breaking up the Basquefest. "Abe, I've got some bad news."

He turned and looked at me for a moment and then dropped his eyes to the mud

75

between us. "Yeah, dat Don Butler, he call." He glanced back at Sancho and then me, turned, and thumped up the steps with tears in his eyes. "How 'bout you fellas come in and have dat cup o' coffee."

Abe sat ceramic buffalo mugs on the table with the red and white–checked plastic cover, and I glanced at the frilly curtains that gave the tiny kitchen a European feel. "Where's Wilhelmina?"

He gestured toward another portion of the house. "Oh, she don't feel so good in the mornings, so I try and let her get the sleep, you know?"

As Sancho and Abe sat, I studied the black and white photo hanging on the kitchen wall. "I know that's your father, Beltran, but is the other man his brother, Jakes?" Both men looked as tough as wrought iron.

"Ya, dat ol' dark-looking Basquo was my uncle — the real black sheep of the family — had the bluest blue eyes you ever saw."

"Was?"

"Oh yeah, we figure he be dead."

"Your father was the one who shot Lucian, wasn't he?"

He sipped the coffee, his eyes sparking over the rim of the mug like daybreak.

"There's some argument in de family 'bout dat."

My translator decided to join the conversation. "In what way?"

He shot a quick look to Saizarbitoria. "Hard to believe there would be some differences in a Basquo family story, you know?" He leaned back in his chair and studied me. "There's talk dat Jakes was the one dat actually shot Lucian and that since my dad was the older of the two, he takes the blame."

Rolling the sawed-off from my shoulder, I looked at it again. "Lucian says it was Beltran that shot him."

Abe shook his head and laughed some more. "Yep, dat's what Lucian says all these years all right."

I leaned the dangerous-looking weapon against the wall and came over and sat with them. "Are you saying Lucian was in on it?"

"I ain't sayin' nothin', but you give him dat shotgun and see if the statuary limits is up on dat, then you come back here and tell me, you know?"

I sipped the coffee — it was really good. "Whatever happened to Jakes?"

Abe took a deep breath and slowly let it out, twisting at the hairs in his ear. "Don't know to tell da truth. When my father got out of dat prison in Rawlins, him and Jakes got into it over how Jakes was running the place, and Jakes took off to Idaho and married some Indian woman and started his own spread, a big one — but then he got into money trouble and disappeared back in the eighties. I heard he got hit by a train or somethin'." Reaching behind him, he picked up the old percolator from the stove and freshened our mugs. "It would have taken a train to kill one of those ol' Basquos. We ain't heard nothin' from dat side of the family since."

I glanced at Saizarbitoria and sipped my coffee, letting the silence settle in the cozy kitchen, wishing I didn't have to bring up the next subject. "Miguel Hernandez . . . ."

Abe returned the percolator to the stove and then wrapped his stubby fingers around his coffee mug. "Dat poor young man." He looked up at me. "I never can figure how you get to dat in life — I guess I fought so long for mine dat I can't think of givin' it up without a fight, you know?"

"I know." I waited a moment. "Abe, who saw him on a regular basis?"

"Oh, the camp tender, Jimenez, and my son-in-law, Donnie."

"And when was the last time they would've seen him?"

78

He thought about it. "Jimenez would've seen him last week when he brought him supplies."

"And Donnie?"

He tried to smile, but it faded. "Oh, dat Donnie would've seen him when they move the sheep, but dat's about all. Him and dat daughter of mine, they don't want to work the sheep full time — live down in Colorado."

"And where would I find Jimenez?"

"Up the mountain. I can get you a map or you can check with those Forest Circus guys, they know more about dat stuff than I do."

I ignored the dig at the Rangers. "Did you know Hernandez very well yourself?"

"Oh, I'm the one dat hired him the better part of a year ago."

"How?"

"They have dat thing with the federal government dat allows us to hire folks for jobs the Americans won't do, dat H2O program. Them labor people in Colorado, they sent me his information, and I met him down there in Greeley where he had some family he was staying with. He was a funny guy, smart . . . book-learning smart, you know? Too smart to be herdin' the sheep, but he wanted the job and I gave it to him.

He done real well, 'cept for that one time."

"And what was that?"

"Oh, about a month and a half after we hired him, Jimenez went up to drop off supplies and the place look like hell, and Miguel was layin' there drunk with his arms which was all cut up."

Santiago lowered his mug. "What had happened to him?"

The old Basquo imitated dragging a blade across his forearms. "He done it himself; cut his arms with dat knife he had."

Sancho looked at me. "He was cutting himself?"

"Like I said, he was high strung with all dem books and such. I don't think he ever got used to the mountain and mountain ways; some never do, you know?"

I glanced around the kitchen, a little sorry that I hadn't known the herder better. "Is there anyone else who might've made contact with him?"

Abe twisted the hair in his ear, almost as if he were winding up his brain to answer. "Dat bartender at the Euskadi, he overserved him a couple of times. I come in there, and dat herder, he done drank a good hundred dollars of the money I give him. So, I load him up and get him out of there." He took another sip of his coffee. "Some-

80

time you don't do well on your own and then you turn around and don't do well with people." His eyes came back to mine. "Then what you gonna do?"

"Anybody else?"

"Nope, not dat I know of."

"You say he had family down in Greeley?"

"I don't know 'em, but yep, dat's what he said." He nodded and then rested his eyes on me, and for the first time I could see a glimpse of those hard men captured in the black and white, now residing in the son. "You tink someone did this to him?"

"We don't know, but we're trying to find out." I drained my mug and sat it back down. "Abe, have you ever heard of a woman by the name of Keasik Cheechoo?"

He paused for a long moment and then slapped the table, causing Santiago to start. "The wolf woman!"

"So, you've met?"

"Dat woman, she crazy!"

Sancho laughed. "In what way?"

"Oh, she got all kind of ideas about how those wolves are people and dat we gotta take care of 'em."

"Well, they are an endangered species."

Abe shook his head and pointed a stubby finger in Sancho's face. "You wanna know who the endangered species is, dat'd be us,

81

dat's who. I been losin' my ass in the sheep business my whole life, but nothin' gets me quite like pullin' a squirmin' life out of a half-dead sheep an' nurturin' that thing along till it has half a chance of life, and then some damn wolf or coyote eats the poor thing's legs off and it's layin' there in the mornin' for you to find . . . Market value is what they give me, market value, ya know?, and sometimes dat ain't worth a tinker's damn!"

He broke off his diatribe midsentence, and I turned to see that a very sleepy five-year-old boy in a one-piece set of pajamas, rubbing an eye open, was standing in the doorway.

"Oh, hey. Did Poppy wake you up with dat loud voice?"

The boy nodded and crossed the room to be swallowed up by the old man's arms that pulled him in close and then shifted him onto one knee. "Did you know dese guys are the sheriff and his deputy? They got badges and everything!" He poked a finger my way. "If you ask him nice, that big fella there is the sheriff and he might show you dat badge of his."

Smiling at the boy, I pulled my coat open to reveal the hardware, and he woke up a bit, leaning forward.

Abe smiled at us. "He don't talk all that much, but you should see him fish." He turned the boy in his lap and hugged him close. "Can't you fish, tell 'em."

The boy remained silent and seemed to have a hard time meeting our eyes. But that was nothing new in our line of work — you got used to people not looking at you.

Sancho lowered his head and pushed back his ball cap. With a little one at home, he was quick to break the ice. "Hi, what's your name?"

Abe answered for him. "Liam."

"You want to be a deputy, Liam?"

The little guy didn't respond, but then Saizarbitoria pulled something from his pocket and handed it to the youngster.

Liam opened a hand and took the gift, and I could see it was a gold-painted, metal badge that read SHERIFF with crossed six-shooters at the top.

"That badge is better than ours, because it can make noise. Hold it up to your mouth and blow into it." He demonstrated. "Just blow like a whistle."

Liam slowly raised the badge to his face and blew, and to my surprise, it made a whizzing, siren noise.

"That's it!"

For the first time, the boy smiled.

Abe stood him on his feet and patted his back, sending him off. "You go with Nanna while I say bye to dese nice men, okay?"

The smile faded, and he shot past us like a small fish, darting through the doorway like it was dark water.

"He don't talk much, but he listens, and I guess dat's more important, you know?"

I nodded and stood up, reaching back for the shotgun. "Are you sure you want to part with this, Abe? Like you said, the *statuary* limits on the crime have passed . . ."

He smiled and stood along with me, hitching his thumbs behind his wide elastic suspenders. "Oh, you makin' fun of me now?"

"No, I'm not." I stuck out a hand. "If you hear anything, I'd appreciate it if you'd give us a call."

"Will do." He turned to Saizarbitoria, transferring the hand his way. *"Egun on."*

The Basquo nodded. *"Egun ona izan dezazula."*

"Bai, bai."

Bumping back down the roadway, Sancho sawed the wheel, drifting to the right and then straightening his unit so that we barely missed one of the leaning poles. "Lays it on a little thick, doesn't he?"

84

"I suppose."

"H2O program . . . C'mon, he's what, second, third generation?"

"First."

"Still. He's been here forever . . . why does he sound like he just got off the boat?"

"Because he wants to." I glanced at the Basquo. "Did you know that other than Lucian or Omar Rhoades, that old fellow back there is probably the richest man in the county?"

"You're kidding."

"Nope." I glanced around at the canyons and arroyos trailing from the foothills like chopped waves, the remaining snow looking like froth in the troughs. "This place is about fifteen thousand acres, but he's got two others and that's just in this county. Rumor has it that Beltran got the majority of this one in an epic poker game back in Durant, but Abe's pretty shrewd himself and has done nothing but add onto the empire since he took over."

I watched the country take shape as other thoughts crowded in.

"Something wrong?"

"When I was down in Cheyenne, I had a run-in with Libby Troon about Abe . . ."

"Who's Libby Troon?"

"She owns Liberty Bail Bonds down in

85

Cheyenne."

"The biggest one in the state?"

I nodded. "She said that Abarrane had been taking 'the boy,' whom I assume is Liam, on some unscheduled fishing trips."

"Do you know what I would pay to pass my kid off on weekends?" He shook his head. "And who would complain about a grandfather taking his grandson fishing?"

"I don't know. I never let Libby get that far, but maybe I need to call her up and get the entire story." Watching the sun loosen itself from the low-flying cloud cover like a yoke from a pan, I pursued an investigation of my own. "Where did you get that toy badge?"

Santiago pulled out another and handed it to me. "Ruby was complaining that one of the drawers in her counter wasn't shutting right, so I pulled it and found a crumpled up paper bag full of these."

"Dobie County?" I read the fine print. "Tom Mix."

"Yeah, I looked 'em up. They're from the forties — giveaways from a cereal company. Some of them have the whistle and some have a spinning six-shooter decoder." He jiggled his shirt pocket. "I give 'em to kids when I'm out on patrol." He chuckled. "That cheap ol' bastard Lucian must've done the same thing back in the day."

I raised the tin toy to my lips and blew into it. "Well, he didn't get to be one of the richest men in the county by being a spendthrift."

I stared at the suspicious lack of communiqué on the door of my office. "Why are there no Post-its here?"

Ruby turned on her stool to regard me. "People have been doing your work for you, but you do have an appointment with Nate Laski."

"And who, pray tell, is Nate Laski?"

"The nice young man who is now working for the *Durant Courant.*"

"What young man who's working for the *Durant Courant?*" I walked back over to her desk, sat on the edge, and reached a boot over to pet Dog with the Vibram sole. "What's going on with Ernie 'Man About Town' Brown?"

She pushed back and looked up at me. "He's approaching a hundred years old, so he's hired this nice young man to do his legwork."

"More likely so that he can play with his train set." Ernie Brown had an extravagantly marvelous train set cohabitating in the work area of the small weekly newspaper. "So,

87

what does the cub reporter want?"

"A statement about the wolves."

"Wolf." I shook my head. "What about it? There's a wolf in the Bighorn Mountains. I'm not the Game and Fish, Predator Control, or Barnum and/or Bailey."

Her phone rang, which was nothing remotely new, and she reached back to pick up the receiver and then listened for a moment. "Yes, yes . . . As a matter of fact, he's right here." She hit the Hold button. "Nate Laski, line one. I'm assuming you'd like to take this in your office?"

Attempting to give off an air of nobility, I limped back with Dog following. Evidently, he could feel my mood, or else he was in on the office pool too.

Slumping into my seat, I stared at the flashing red light on my phone, my arch nemesis and all-around annoyance, as Dog sat and rested his head on my knee. Sufficiently anchored, I pulled the thing off the hook, held it up to my ear, and punched the button like a lotto ticket. "Yep."

"Sheriff?"

The voice was very young. I repeated myself. "Yep."

"This is Nate Laski of the *Durant Courant,* and I was hoping to get some comments from you about the wolf situation?"

"Wolf *situation*."

There was a pause. "Yes, sir."

"What wolf *situation* is that?"

"Well, we have wolves in the Bighorns now."

"We have a wolf in the Bighorns — wolf, singular; a lone wolf."

He interrupted. "But there was a man killed."

"There is a man dead, which is not the same thing." I leaned back in my chair, class now in session. "There is a man who most likely committed suicide."

"But he was partially eaten by the wolf singular?"

I had to smile, maybe the kid was smarter than I thought — at least his ass was. "The wolf took part in some scavenging predation, which is what wolves, singular or plural, are sometimes wont to do."

"Yes, but isn't it true that once wolves taste human flesh they acquire a taste for it?"

I sighed. "Not to my knowledge, but I'm no wolf expert. Perhaps you need to talk to the wardens over at Game and Fish or to somebody who deals with these animals and get some professional answers before writing your story."

There was a pause. "So, you say the death

was a suicide?"

"I said, most likely a suicide."

"Can you tell me his name?"

"Not until we've made arrangements in contacting the next of kin."

"Was the man local?"

"No."

"We've heard rumors that he was a shepherd. Could that have led to the circumstances surrounding his death?"

I sighed again. "Circumstances surrounding his death . . . How old are you?"

"Excuse me?"

At the risk of sounding like Lucian, I still had to ask, "How old are you, young man?"

Another pause. "I don't see how that has . . ."

"I've been answering your questions, now you answer mine."

"Twenty-four."

"Where are you from? I'm just curious."

"Casper."

"Brand-new degree in journalism?"

"Yes, sir."

When I was around that age, I got an invitation from the United States Marine Corp requesting my assistance in a conflict on the other side of the world in Vietnam. "Nate, can I call you Nate?"

"Yes, sir."

"Call me Walt, okay?"

"Right, Walt."

"What we have here is a man working up the mountain who may or may not have committed suicide and a registered, radio-tagged wolf most likely from the packs that have been reinstated in the greater Yellowstone region. Now this wolf couldn't resist the opportunity of feeding on a portion of the dead man's body, even after most likely killing a ewe. Now, if that is the case — and from my understanding this wolf will be dealt with 'swiftly,' in the parlance of the Game and Fish Department — then it should be noted that the wolf is alone and that it had nothing to do with the death of the man in question."

"Got it."

"Good. Is there anything else?"

"Excuse my ignorance, but having just moved here, I'm not aware. Have there been wolves in the Bighorns before?"

"I think there have been, but Chuck Coon of the Forest Service or Ferris Kaplan over at Game and Fish would be able to answer that and any other questions you have more capably than I." I reached down and stroked Dog's head. "I am no wolf expert."

"One more thing?"

"Yep."

91

"Do you have a stock photo you could email over to us here at the *Courant* just in case we decide to use it?"

"I don't have a computer or email, and no I don't have a photo of myself. Besides, why in the world would you want a photo of me?"

"Just in case we decide to use it?" There was some rustling. "I'm trying to get some things up to date here in the office, but it's, uh . . . difficult."

"Is the train set getting in the way?"

"It's pretty sizable, Walt."

"Best of luck with that, Nate." I hung the phone up and turned around in my chair to find the majority of my staff standing in the doorway. I addressed the only one that spoke Spanish. "Sancho, you mind getting the number and contacting his wife in Chile?"

"Can do."

"Has anybody run Miguel Hernandez through the National Crime Data Base?"

Vic glanced at Saizarbitoria and then back to me. "He's the victim — we generally don't do that."

"Let's."

She turned to Sancho and dropped her voice. "Sic 'em."

He disappeared, and she hung there in

92

the doorway. "I heard you were met with armament this morning?"

I pointed to the article in question, which was leaning against the wall beside the coatrack. "There it is, the preferred method of amputation for decades here in Absaroka County."

She picked it up and examined it as Dog, bored with the conversation, went out to his usual spot under Ruby's desk. "I thought it was supposed to be a twelve gauge?"

"Evidently, even calibers get bigger in the telling."

She sat down, still holding the shotgun. "What's he like?"

"Who?"

Her eyes came up. "Honest Abe."

"Tough, but kindhearted; colorful. Why?"

"I'm assembling my suspect list."

"Why in the world would he do it?"

She shrugged. "It's a short list."

"Well, you may be getting yourself all worked up for nothing. Abarrane says Miguel had a history of self-mutilation, of cutting himself."

"Oh, boy."

"Yep, kind of textbook. He also mentioned that he had family down in Greeley, Colorado, so we might want to go through the personal effects and see if we can find some information on them as quickly as possible. You say he had a cell phone?"

"Yes, I'm charging it back to life now. It's one of those cheap, prepay deals, but we can get information like a call listing off of it."

"Good."

"So, how goes the great wolf hunt?"

Turning in my chair, I looked at the spring sky, partially cloudy, close, and indifferent. "Like I say, not my problem."

"Who were you talking to on the phone?"

"Some kid from the newspaper, hustling an angle."

She lodged her tactical boots onto the edge of my desk, the only one I let do that. "You give him one?"

"Not really."

"Have him fucking talk to me next time."

"Oh, that's just what we want." I reached out and pulled my Rolodex from between Bancroft's *Works, Volume XXV* and Larson's *History of Wyoming*. Scrolling through the paper cards, I became aware of my under-sheriff smirking. "What?"

"Internet for old people — you know we're going to eBay that thing someday."

Finding the file I wanted, I dialed the number from the business card taped onto it, holding the receiver under my chin.

"Don't you have things to do? You know, *undersheriffy* things?"

She rolled her eyes and retrieved her boots, then curtseyed before flipping her imaginary skirt up to moon me and then made an exit, stage left.

On the third ring, a voice rasping from having smoked too many Virginia Slims, answered. "Liberty Bail Bonds; liberty means freedom."

"Actually, it's more of an ability to choose or a basic right."

The rasp sharpened. "Who is this?"

"I'm hurt."

There was a cackling laugh followed by an uneven string of lung-rending coughs. "Walt Longmire, I've been emailing you."

"That would be a trick in that I don't have a computer."

"Well . . ." I listened as she mumbled, sticking what I assumed was another filter-tipped cigarette in her mouth, which she lit with a quick inhale. "That would explain why you haven't answered."

"Why have you been trying to get in touch with me, Libby?"

"Wait." She took another puff. "Who called who here?"

"Consider it a response to your emails."

She hawed and hemmed and then hawed

95

again. "This is kind of a touchy subject, but a party has contacted me about a man-hunting opportunity, and it's up there in your neck of the nape, so I thought I'd see if that delicious friend of yours, Henry Standing Bear, was available."

"In what way?"

"Oh, I can think of a bunch, but this is simply a snatch and family grab."

"Meaning?"

"This individual wants someone to go and get their kid back from a relative."

"Are they the legal guardian?"

"Yes."

"Then why don't they just file a petition with the court and let one of my deputies take care of it?"

She hemmed and smoked some more. "I think they'd just as soon keep this on an unofficial basis."

"And hire a kidnapper?"

She hawed. "Are you going to help me here?"

"Who are we talking about, Libby?"

"I'm not telling you, if you're not going to help me."

"There in Cheyenne, you mentioned Abarrane Extepare, and I'm assuming this is his grandson, Liam, we're discussing."

There was a pause including both hem

96

and haw. "I was hoping you'd forgotten that part of the conversation."

"Nope. Now who's the potential felon?"

"The son-in-law, Donnie Lott."

4

The Cheyenne Nation lifted the beer from the cooler behind the bar and rested the can on the surface of the coaster that bore the logo of the Red Pony Bar & Grill. No bottles in the Powder River Country — hard to throw a can and hurt somebody and nobody ever threw a full one.

"He has a cousin in Greeley."

Henry Standing Bear pulled the tab on the can, leaving it vertical. I studied it. "Why do you do that?"

He folded his powerful arms and leaned on the bar back as Art Blakey's "A Night in Tunisia" played from the jukebox. "It allows the client to know that the can is a fresh one."

"They can't figure that out on their own?"

"In my line of work there are levels of awareness, and most of my clientele are VIPs."

"VIPs?"

"Very Intoxicated Persons."

As if on cue an agricultural cowboy sidled up to the bar and, adjusting his signature John Deere ball cap, slurred the words, "Hey, um, can we get another round? I'm celebratin' with my brother-in-law about just gettin' divorced from his sister."

"Nothing runs like a deer, or smells like a john." The Bear continued looking at me but spoke toward the man. "Does your group have a DD?"

The younger man looked at him, his face as blank as a shore-leave sailor's bank account. "A what?"

"Is there a sober member of your party who can drive all of you home?"

"Um, yeah . . . JJ's wife don't drink."

The dark eyes shifted to the man, and then to the two other men sitting at the far side of the pool table, one a regular looking fellow and the other a blond-haired guy in a rumpled suit and loosened tie. "I do not see a female accompanying you."

The drunk kid looked — evidently, he wasn't sure himself. "Oh, she's on her way."

Henry nodded. "When she gets here, I will be happy to provide you with a fresh round of beverages."

He stood there for a moment more and then moved to go. After a few steps, he turned back. "He's my lawyer, and like I said, we're celebrating my getting a divorce from his sister. Why don't you just give us those beers now, 'cause JJ's gonna be real pissed if I head back over there empty handed."

"I am truly sorry for the inconvenience."

The kid nodded again and then cocked his head, listening to the jazz. "And could we get something else on the jukebox?"

"No."

If anything, the blankness was enhanced. "Um . . . Okay."

The Bear turned back to me. "Did you call the cousin?"

"Vic did."

"Anything?"

"They were very sad and had no idea why he might've done it."

He studied me. "You hate this part."

"Yep, so much so that I palmed off calling Hernandez's widow in Chile on Sancho." I turned the beer on the coaster. "I do hate it. Telling people that their loved one has gone on to the great beyond? I do, indeed, hate it."

"Lonely work."

I turned the can some more. "Kind of like bartending."

"I wish."

Once again on cue, the young man re-approached, and Henry turned to look at him once more. "No."

He stood there for a moment, almost frozen to the wooden floor, but then turned and retreated without another word.

"Tell me about the wolf."

I brought my eyes back to him and shifted gears. "What do you want to know?"

"What did it look like?"

"Like a wolf."

His head dropped a bit in disappointment in me. "Can you be a little more specific?"

"What do you care?"

"I want to know if I know it."

"What, you're on a first-name basis with all the wolves in Wyoming and Montana?"

"A few."

He waited, and I summoned up the image of the wolf, which was surprisingly easy. "Big." I glanced down at the snoring monster wrapped around the base of my bar-stool. "Bigger than him."

"Amazing, few things in this epoch are."

"Dark, but with a mask sort of over the eyes, along the nose, and to the sides of the muzzle that had a lot of gray. Dark-colored overall with really light eyes almost a cara-mel color." I shrugged. "He also had a four-thousand-dollar transmitting collar on him,

101

and his official title is 777M."

He looked slightly surprised. "Chuck Coon told you that?"

"No, a woman by the name of Keasik Cheechoo who works for the wolf conservancy did. She's, let me see if I can get this right . . . Cree-Assiniboine/Young Dogs, Piapot First Nation."

"Keasik — Cree for 'sky blue.' So, she's Canadian."

"I guess, but she says you broke her uncle's arm one time arm wrestling over in Spokane."

He shook his head. "Doesn't ring any bells."

"Well, if I had as many cases of aggravated assault as you . . ."

He ignored me. "So, male."

"Keasik Cheechoo is female."

"The wolf, 777M. The M stands for male."

"Oh."

"How old?"

"I have no idea, but I'd say old. Probably kicked off from his pack by some young buck." He smiled. "What?"

"You are feeling some empathy for this aged wolf?"

"I hadn't thought about it; maybe so."

"I would not want to meet the younger

102

wolf that could run off something bigger than Dog." He studied the surface of the bar between us, reached behind, and took a sip of the tonic water and lemon juice he sometimes kept on the bar back. "It might be someone I know, or perhaps someone you know."

"What the hell are you talking about?"

"Sometimes people's spirits come back, and some of their favorites are bears, buffalo, and wolves."

"Werebears and werebuffaloes?"

"Not exactly."

Folding the tab down, I finally took a sip of my Rainier. "Uh, huh . . ."

"In my culture, animals are celebrated as beautiful, mysterious, powerful, dangerous, and benevolent. There was a period, before we lost the ability to listen, when the animals took pity on us, protected and taught us to the point where they became human in times of great need."

"Henry . . ."

He held out a hand. "Hear me out. Back in the day, my people wore the skins and furs of these animals, choosing the animals that appealed to them. Say a person were to choose a wolf, or more important, the wolf were to choose this person and the person becomes the wolf without changing their physical form. He or she dreamed of wolves, developed wolf skills and power, acted like a wolf, immersed themselves in wolf lore, talked with wolves, hunted with wolves, was taught by wolves, protected by wolves, painted himself or herself as a wolf, and wore wolf *omotome* in his or her medicine bundle." He reached into his shirt and pulled out the small, beaded pouch he always wore around his neck. "This is where the border between two species is broken, and spiritually the wolf and the human become one."

"Well, I hope it isn't anybody we know, because when the DNA testing gets back from the lab in Laramie, this wolf is as good as gone."

He nodded, dropped his head, and, as the dark hair closed around his face, took another sip of his faux drink. "You said the wolf is older."

"Well, he looked older, but I didn't get a chance to see his ID."

He returned the glass to the flat surface behind him and crossed his arms again. "How long ago was it you met Virgil White Buffalo on the mountain?"

I sat there just looking at him.

His face rose, and he studied me. "What?"

Pulling my horsehide jacket aside, I

reached into my shirt pocket and tossed the card I'd found on the ground on the mountain onto the battered and gouged surface of the bar. I watched as it slid across and stopped just short of slipping off the other side.

The Bear leaned forward and examined the blue printing on the white card that announced CASH PRIZES, MALLO CUP PLAY MONEY 5 POINTS — aware that I had found these selfsame cards left to me by a dead or possibly not dead seven-foot Crow shaman. Henry's eyes focused so deeply, I was afraid the thing might burst into flames. "This was with the dead man?"

"No, it was where I saw the wolf for the first time."

He picked it up and examined it more closely. "You found these before, during your interactions with Virgil?"

"Yep."

"He could have scattered these things all over the mountain."

"Yep."

"There is only one problem." He handed it back to me.

"This one is like new." I placed the card down by my beer.

"I do not suppose Keasik Cheechoo or Chuck Coon are fond of Mallo Cups."

105

"I really wouldn't know." I stared at the card. "If, and this is a big if . . . If Virgil came back in this manner, what would he be trying to say to me?"

"Difficult to know — perhaps nothing."

I raised my eyes to look at him.

"It is possible he is simply checking up on you. Just seeing how you are progressing in the most inconspicuous way he knows."

"A hundred-and-seventy-five-pound wolf?"

"We all have our ideas of unassuming. You have to admit it is more subtle than a seven-foot Crow shaman."

"A little." I spun my can on the coaster. "So, why is he checking on me?"

"Concerned for your welfare."

I curled the corners of my mouth enough to give the impression of a smile. "I could've used his help down in Mexico."

"Maybe you had it." He placed his palms on the back edge of the bar, his forearms turned forward, the blued veins visible. "It is difficult to confront madness, because insanity is a stranger to reason and any reasonable response would be insane."

I stared at him. "I think I got that."

"The only thing more difficult is to return from madness, because we are never again sure that we are truly sane." He fingered the card. "Like a disease, the madness lingers in the system, dormant but never truly gone from the mind, and we must learn to suppress it so that we can once again trust ourselves to be in civilized society."

"So, I have to learn to trust myself again, huh?"

"Possibly." He looked straight at me. "How is this aberration manifesting itself?"

I took a deep breath. "It's like I'm freezing up, my mind and body — like a short circuit."

"How long?"

"Five to ten minutes, or so I've been told."

"Are you aware of yourself in these periods?"

"Some, but removed — like I can't reach myself."

"Perhaps you are being prepared for a vision."

"Well, then why don't I just have the vision?"

"You are not ready for it."

"You have to work up to a vision?"

"Sometimes."

"As opposed to horseshit, which is readily available at all times?"

He didn't have an answer for that, and it was another moment before he surprised me by changing the subject. "We should go fishing."

"What?"

"Fishing — precision guesswork based on unreliable data provided by those of questionable knowledge."

"I know what fishing is." I took a sip of my beer. "If you want to go fishing, we'll go fishing."

"No, I mean really fishing."

"Like a trip?"

"I was thinking Alaska."

I thought back. "A bear almost ate us the last time we were in Alaska."

"That was a polar bear — does not count."

"Where in Alaska?"

"Hyder."

"Why Hyder?"

"I have never been there."

"I'm not sure if I have." I thought back to my period in Seward's Folly. "Where in Alaska is Hyder?"

"Southeast, furthest point east in Alaska, south of Juneau. Ground transport through Stewart, Canada, is the only way there."

"Is the fishing good?"

"Chum salmon."

"Dog food."

Dog looked up, *dog* and *food* being in his twenty-word vocabulary, following his number one word, *ham*. "Forty-pound-ers . . . But we're not going there for the fishing, we are going there for the adventure."

"Okay."

"In the meantime, I may need your help with a project of mine that is closer to home." He smiled. "Have you ever heard of Jaya Long, aka LongShot?"

"Nope."

"Highest scoring girls basketball power forward in Lame Deer history, but there is a situation developing, and I may need your help."

"Any relationship to Lolo Long, Cheyenne Reservation chief of police?"

He nodded, an unidentifiable expression passing across his face. "Her cousin."

I was aware of some movement to my right and noticed that JJ was standing at the bar.

"Hey, Chief, how 'bout that round?"

Henry didn't move, but the mahogany pupils shifted in his head and you could almost hear them clicking like a set of bolt actions as they registered full right. He waited a moment before speaking to the man with the rock and roll hair. "Your companion informed me that your wife is coming by to give all of you a ride home,

109

and I told him that when she did, I would be pleased to provide you with another round."

He snorted. "Well, she's not coming, so you can just hit us with another."

The Bear looked at him.

"Did you hear me?"

"Yes, I did."

The drunk straightened a bit. "Do you know who the fuck I am?"

I started to turn and pull back my jacket to reveal my star, but Henry extended two fingers like an absolution, so I sat there and watched the show.

He stepped toward the man, an easy step like the ones the mountain lions make before sinking their teeth into the back of a neck. "Excuse me?"

The idiot actually leaned in. "I said, do you know who the fuck I am?"

Henry peered at him and actually looked concerned. "Do you not know who you are?"

There is a specific form of confusion that plays across a drunk's face — I'd seen it many times, and I was seeing it again now. "What?" For some reason, the drunk looked at me, then at his friends, finally turning back to glare at Henry. "Look, asshole . . ."

You had to really be paying attention to

see what happened next, but I had witnessed Henry in these situations before, so I knew what was going to happen, maybe not exactly, but certainly a form thereof. Like a timber rattler, the Bear's hand leapt out, snatching the drunk's tie and yanking downward, which caused the man's chin to collide with the edge of the bar with a clack like a Willie Mosconi clean break.

The Cheyenne Nation had let go of the tie and placed his hand to his face feigning concern. He glanced at the man's fellow drunks, who sat there transfixed. "Your friend appears to have passed out, perhaps you should come and assist him?"

Slowly they stood and approached, possibly even more put off by Dog, who had risen from his nap to go over and sniff the man on the floor. When they got close enough, they stooped down and picked JJ up, holding him vertical with his arms draped over their shoulders.

They stood there for a moment before the young one, obviously the mouthpiece of the group, decided to speak. "Um, we'll be going now . . ."

I turned and opened my jacket revealing my star. "No." They seemed indecisive, or maybe they were in a state of mild shock, so I tipped my hat back and draped my jacket to reveal the Colt M1911A1 .45 semi-automatic at my side. "You're going to go back over to your table and sit on your hands until JJ's wife gets here." Dog curled around my stool again, and I picked up my Rainier, taking a sip as they struggled to get the man back to their table. "I don't know, maybe it's a coincidence. I mean, it's just a candy wrapper." When I raised my face to look at him, the Cheyenne Nation was covering his mouth with a broad hand and looked as if he were trying to hold back a laugh. Finally removing the hand, he lip-pointed over my shoulder at the two men and the unconscious body.

I turned around to look at them.

"I was just kidding about the sitting-on-the-hands thing."

"So, you were in a bar fight."

"No." I sipped my coffee and glanced around at the thin crowd at the Busy Bee Café. "Who told you that?"

"Marco." She dumped five sugars in hers, stirring it in with a spoon. "Polo."

"The pool . . . Henry's in on it?"

"Everybody on the North American continent is in on it." Looking out at the fast-moving water of Clear Creek that was wearing away the ice, she sipped her coffee and leaned back in her chair. "How are you feeling?"

"Tired."

"You sleep?"

"Not so much. I stared at the ceiling and pretended."

"It'll fade."

"I hope."

Dorothy, the owner and proprietor, sidled over to our table and studied me. "Nice scar."

Self-consciously, I raised a hand, feeling the different texture of the healed wound that began above and then ended below my left eye. "I don't look like a cocaine dealer in the eighties?"

"No." She reached out and turned my face for a better view. "More of a Basil Rathbone–dueling scar kind of look." She released my chin. "Personally, I didn't think it was possible for you to be even more roguishly handsome than you were."

Feeling the heat of embarrassment rising from my collar, I made eye contact with her. "Thank you."

"But you're too skinny — what do you want to eat?"

Handing her the menu, I smiled. "The usual."

She smiled back at me. "Nice to hear you

113

say that." She turned to Vic. "I've got a Philly omelet with shredded beef and provolone."

"Is that the *special*?"

"Yes."

"Is it also the *usual*?"

"Yes."

My undersheriff handed in her menu. "Sold."

As Dorothy disappeared into the kitchen, I noticed that Vic was studying the side of my face now. "What?"

"She's right. Like I always say, scars make better stories than tattoos."

"I don't think I'll be telling this story to anybody soon."

"She's also right about you putting on some weight."

I studied the ice tracing the edges of Clear Creek, mentally willing them to melt in an attempt to hurry the spring along. "For years, you've all been on to me about taking weight off, and now you're all trying to fatten me like a hog."

She leaned in, sipping the sugar drink she called coffee. "Just more of you to love." Sitting back, she pulled an unfamiliar phone from her pocket. "I charged the departed's cell and came up with a log of callers both sent and received, all of them either the Extepare ranch, a number in Greeley, and a few long distance calls to Chile — nothing out of the ordinary."

I continued to cast my eyes into the frigid water.

"Walt, did you hear me?"

"Does it seem like this winter has been long?"

She snorted. "It's the high plains, Walt, every winter is an ice age."

"Maybe my blood thinned down there in Mexico."

"Well, you lost enough of it." She sat the mug down and looked at me. "Are you sure you're okay?"

Stifling a sigh, I looked down Main Street at the town where I was born, where I'd married and raised a child, where I'd lost my wife, and where now everything felt strange. "I'm . . . I'm having trouble getting back."

She reached a finger out and brushed it against the back of my hand. "What did Henry have to say?"

"He says that I may be preparing for a vision."

"You know, that's just the kind of shit he says that I have no idea what he's talking about." She shook her head. "What else?"

"He wants to go to Alaska."

"Interesting. I wouldn't have come up with that either." She nodded. "Well, it takes time. I mean that wasn't a police action down there, it was a war."

I turned the mug on the table by the handle. "Yep."

"So, you have to treat it like a war and stop judging yourself as if it was part of your job because it wasn't — it isn't like you had any choice."

"Right."

There was a noise from her phone, the Philadelphia Eagles fight song to be exact, and she paused as she read a text. "You're not hearing a word I'm saying, are you?"

"No."

"DNA is in."

"On the sheep?"

"None other." She pocketed the phone, the incredulity writ large on her face. "We have a murder in this state, and it takes us six months to get results, but if it's a sheep we get it overnight?"

"Wildlife lab in Laramie, not the overworked Division of Criminal Investigation."

"Oh."

"Well, don't hold me in suspense . . ."

"Inconclusive. They said the carcass was too old and that they couldn't get a proper DNA analysis."

116

"Well, at least you didn't hold me in suspense." I took a sip of my coffee. "If there's enough of a stir, they're going to want to kill the wolf, never mind the inconclusive."

"Why?"

"The evidence doesn't matter — people are going to hear *wolf*, and it's going to explode into a full-blown monster hunt with torches and pitchforks. Like Chuck said, we're not a trophy zone but rather a predator one, so wolves can be shot on sight. People are going to want that wolf dead, and I doubt Chuck Coon is going to want the job, so that means they'll be bringing somebody in from Predator Control. Usually counties here in Wyoming depend on Game and Fish to provide a professional hunter, but in Absaroka it's under the auspices of the county predator board, and they have a group of hunters they keep on a list."

"So, who will it be?"

"The next person on the list. I think there are about three or four, some with dogs and some with helicopters."

"Omar?"

"Oh, I think he's too big of a deal to bother with this. Besides, he's probably in Borneo or someplace."

117

The tarnished gold eyes looked over my shoulder toward the mountains. "So, we're going to have a wolf hunt."

"Evidently."

"You don't look excited about the prospect."

Turning, I looked at the Bighorns with her. "Maybe I'm feeling empathetic toward the old wolf."

"Maybe they won't get him."

I turned, aware that I was looking at her with the pupil that was bisected by a gash, ghostly and shining like a strike of lightning. "They always get them."

Walking up the steps, I made the landing and glanced past the dispatcher's area at my office door, where numerous Post-its were stuck on the molding like tiny, cautionary flags. "Looks like business is picking up."

Ruby leaned back in her chair and handed me more. "Since news of the great wolf hunt has hit the airwaves, we've had numerous applicants apply for the job of Predator Control."

"The position is open?"

"Evidently."

"They don't apply here, they apply to the Department of Agriculture's Technical Services Division or with the county preda-

118

tor board."

"Chuck Coon gave them your number."

"I am going to shoot Chuck Coon." She handed me the Post-its along with the current edition of the *Durant Courant* with a photo of me on the front page. "What's this?"

"The news that evidently packs of wolves are now clamoring out of the Bighorns and lying in wait behind every mailbox in hopes of seizing our children and devouring them whole."

"Oh, hell."

"Can I quote you on that?"

I took the bundle and trundled off to my office as Vic trailed after me, waiting at the door as I sat.

"Welcome home."

"Yep."

She hung on the jamb. "You'll give me warning if you decide to run off to Hatch, New Mexico?"

Sitting in my chair, I threw the papers on my desk. "I promise."

"You want me to inform Miguel Hernandez's family members in Chile that he's wolf chow?" I looked up at her, and she shrugged. "I'll phrase it differently."

"Sancho didn't do it?"

"Me or him, we're all here to serve, oh

Great One."

Ruby appeared. "Call, line one."

"I'm out."

"It's Chuck Coon."

"I'm in." Stabbing the red button with a forefinger, I flipped the receiver up and clutched it like a cudgel. "I am going to have an open season on forest rangers."

"Walt, before you start, I don't know these people and you do."

Ruby disappeared, but never one to miss an ass-chewing, my undersheriff sat in my guest chair. I shook my head. "Call Ferris Kaplan over at Game and Fish — this is not my job, Chuck."

"Well, as of Thursday, it's not going to be my job either."

"What's that supposed to mean?"

"I'm retiring."

"What?"

He laughed. "Retiring, it's a thing some people do when they feel like they've put up with enough crap for one lifetime."

"Like a rat from a sinking ship." I sighed and hung the phone up without further comment as Vic leaned in. "So, what'd the turkey trooper have to say?"

"He's retiring, so it's our problem, unless I want to hand it over to Ferris Kaplan."

"So, hand it over to Game and Fish."

"He's overworked."

"And we're not?"

I glanced down at the Post-its attached to the *Durant Courant* and covered my face with my hand. "Well, we are now."

Vic leaned across and spun the news-paper, then peeled back a Post-it in order to look at my picture. "It's an old one, before the scar." She glanced at me, the gold flash-ing. "Maybe you should go for a soft focus like those romance authors do."

The red button on my phone began blink-ing as Ruby called out from the main room. "Walt, line one!"

Slumping in my chair, I punched the but-ton again and picked up the receiver. "Long-mire."

"It wasn't me."

I pulled the receiver from my face and looked at it for comic effect, lost on the world as a whole but infinitely humorous to my undersheriff. Placing the thing in the crook of my neck, I pulled the paper back so I could read the article. "Excuse me, but who is this?"

"Jerry."

"Jerry who?"

"Jerry, down here at the Euskadi."

Recognizing the name of the bartender at the only Basque bar in Durant, I nodded.

"Aranzadi. Right, what did you not do?"

"Beat that kid up."

"What kid, Jerry?"

"The one in the paper; that shepherd that hung himself."

I glanced at Vic, whose eyebrows crouched together in question. "Abarrane Extepare mentioned something about fetching him out of your bar."

"Um, yeah, well, I don't want any trouble with that ol' Basquo either."

"How about I come down there, and you can tell me the story?"

There was a pause. "Um, sure. That'd be okay, I guess."

"Bad time?"

"Um, no, no . . . It's just never good to have the Law in the place when people are drinking."

I thought about how Lucian frequented the place on an irregular basis but figured retired Law wasn't as much of a deterrent to the drinking public. "How 'bout we meet you in the alley behind the bar. Have you got somebody who can cover for you for a bit?"

"Um, yeah."

"See you in five minutes." I hung up the phone and glanced at Vic. "How 'bout a drink?"

"Now you're talking." Following me out of my office, Vic ran into my back as Ruby intercepted us and tried to hand me more Post-its. "I don't want those."

Fist on hip, she looked at me, her cat's eyeglasses pushed back on her nose. "What do you want me to do with them?"

I patted the doorjamb. "Put them here on the Wailing Wall."

Vic read the paper she'd purloined from my desk, her boots wedged on the dash of my truck again. "Wow, we've got a real wolf emergency on our hands, huh."

"I told that kid the straight story, but evidently he had something in mind before he called me."

"They do that sometimes." She lowered the paper. "I'm assuming that since it's only ten o'clock in the morning, we're not really going for a drink, so what's the skinny?"

"Miguel Hernandez had multiple bruises, contusions, and lacerations about the head and shoulders, and Isaac said they'd been made a few days before his death. I was going to poke around and try to see who the fight might've been with, but the bartender down at the Euskadi called and said it wasn't him that did it, which leads me to believe that he knows who did."

"Sound detective work." She folded the paper and tossed it on the seat between us. "So, why are we driving down one of our two alleys?"

"We're meeting him behind the bar — besides, I thought it might remind you of your home turf."

She glanced up at the two-story buildings. "Philly? Not hardly. Manayunk, maybe."

Jerry Aranzadi was easy to spot, wearing a white apron and wiping his hands on a dish-towel behind a dumpster at the back door of the bar. "Jeez, Jerry. This looks like a drug deal."

The balding man nodded and leaned in my window and rested his arms on the sill. "Thanks for meeting me like this, Walt. I wanted to tell you, but it's not good for business for me to be talking about customers." He threw a thumb toward the door. "People come in with their problems, and I just don't want to get a reputation as a guy who talks."

"I understand." I waited for him to begin, but evidently he was having trouble, so I primed the pump. "You want to tell me about Miguel Hernandez?"

He looked confused. "Who?"

"The shepherd."

"Oh, right. He was in here, less than a

124

week ago."

"Uh huh."

"He sat where he usually did, at the booth by the window — was reading a book. I mean the kid wasn't any trouble, you know? Anyway, he's sittin' there minding his own business when this other guy comes in, a kind of cowboy."

"You know him?"

"Nope. I mean he looked kind of familiar, but I couldn't place him. Well, he sits in the booth, opposite the Hernandez guy, and they start talking, but low and pretty intense — not like they were friends or anything."

"Right."

"Well, after a while the cowboy leans over and smacks the living shit out of this kid. I mean really lets him have it. So, I walk over and ask them if there's a problem, and they say no and they'll keep it down. So, I go behind the bar, and I'm keeping an eye on them, when I have to go to the back. But I hear a crashing noise and come running out, and now the kid is on the floor with this cowboy standing over him. Well, I grab that ball bat I keep behind the bar and go to push the cowboy off the kid, and he turns around and has some words for me, so I tell him the next argument he's going to have is with you, Walt, 'cause I'm calling 911."

I nodded. "Then what?"

"Oh, he talks some more shit before I go toward the phone, and that's when he says a few more things to the kid and walks out."

"That was the end of it?"

"No. I help patch the kid up and buy him a drink to help make up for it, and when I bring the *izarra* and gin over the kid looks up at me and says that cowboy is gonna kill him."

I glanced at Vic, whose eyes sharpened. "Do tell."

"So, the kid drinks his drink and it's getting close to closing, and I tell him I need to lock up, and he asks me to let him sleep in the bar and I tell him no, that I can't do that, but that I'll be happy to give him a ride home. He tells me that he works on the mountain, and I tell him I can't run him all the way up there, but doesn't he know anybody in town that he can stay with? He says yeah, and so I load him up and run him over to this place on the north end of town out near the airport."

"Okay."

"But here's the thing: when I was driving him out there, there was this car that I swear was following us."

"And you think it was this cowboy?"

"I do."

"What kind of car?"

"New, maybe a truck but I think it was a car."

"Make, model, color, plates?"

Jerry made a face, covering it with his long fingers. "It was dark, Walt, and I was tired. I'm not sure which county or number, and I guess it was a car — an SUV maybe?"

"What happened when you dropped Hernandez off?"

"He got out and went to the front porch, and there was a woman who opened the door, and they talked for a bit and then he went in."

"Did you know the woman?"

"No, not much. She looked kind of familiar, but she was backlit in the doorway, so it isn't like I got a good look at her either." He fumbled in the apron and pulled out a napkin with a number and street written on it. "I remembered the address and wrote it down for you, because I figured you'd want to go talk to her."

"Thanks, Jerry." I took the napkin and handed it to Vic. "I'm sure we will."

5

"So, do we pretend we're Mormons or are we selling Tupperware?"

I walked around the car and met Vic in front of the small house. "I think the uniforms are going to give us away."

Pausing at the mailbox, Vic opened it and then followed after me. "No name, no mail."

Stepping onto the porch, I knocked and waited. After a moment, I knocked again and leaned to one side to look in a window, but all I could see was a room with a couple of cardboard boxes piled into each other along the wall. After knocking one last time, I stepped off and walked around the railing to the window. "The place is empty."

Vic looked up and down the street at the houses on either side. "You take the left. I'll take the right?"

"Sounds good." Retreating to the curb, I approached the next house, when the front door opened.

A middle-aged woman, who was tying her bathrobe closed, was holding the door. "Can I help you?"

"Maybe. Walt Longmire, Sheriff." I took off my hat and stopped at the edge of the porch. "I was wondering if you knew who lived in that house next door?"

"Nobody. It's been vacant for the better part of a year now."

"Have you seen anybody around the house in the last few weeks?"

"No." She clutched the robe a little tighter and pulled a lighter and some Camels from her pocket. "Something going on over there I should know about?"

"Not particularly. We're just looking for the last known whereabouts of an individual."

She lit up one of the cigarettes. "Who?"

"A young man by the name of Miguel Hernandez."

"The one that hung himself?"

"Mind if I ask how you know about him?"

"I read the newspapers, Sheriff." She flipped some ash in one of the scraggly bushes that lined the porch and took a step toward me. "And what're you guys going to do about the wolf problem anyway?"

I sighed. "It's only one wolf, so I don't

think there's much to be worried about, Ms.
. . . ?"

"Schlesier. They say that that wolf ate part of that Hernandez kid."

I handed her one of my cards and slipped my hat back on my head. "If you remember anything or you see anything regarding the house next door, I'd appreciate a call."

I turned to go, but she threw out one last tidbit. "You know, once they get a taste for human flesh, it's hard to break them of the habit."

I stood there for a moment wondering what actual research she'd done in the world of lupine studies. "We'll keep that in mind."

Vic met me at my truck. "I got an old guy who says he hasn't seen anything in months, but wants to know what we're going to do about the —" she raised her fingers, imitating quotation marks — "wolf problem."

I climbed in and fired up the truck. "I got the same thing on the other side — the inhabitant says that the place has been empty for the better part of a year."

Vic closed her door and looked at me. "Anything else?"

"She also volunteered that once wolves get a taste for human flesh, it's hard to break them of the habit."

"What habit?"

"Eating people, I guess."

"What, she's some kind of fucking expert?"

Turning a U, I drove back toward the center of town. "Everybody is these days."

There are lots of ways of approaching the ladies at the courthouse, but the one I always rely on is carefully. I pulled into our parking lot behind the venerable building that replaced the North Star Dance Hall and Stables as the newly formed county offices in 1884. It was clear that a former dance hall, stable, and house of ill repute wasn't a particularly safe place to store all of the official Absaroka County records, so a bid of $81,650 was accepted and construction began on the Italianate building with stilted-arch window openings, pronounced keystones, and what they called consoles on cornices.

Bricks for the building were made of clay soil from just south of Durant, and the town's own kilns provided lime for the mortar. Not much has changed except for the sad removal of a bell tower, which used to house a multitude of bats that my old boss and mentor, Lucian Connally, used to say was a perfectly suitable habitat since all the people who worked in the place were batshit crazy.

There is an emblem of the rising sun over the main entrance at the east, but my intention was to enter subtly from the west to avoid the maximum number of county co-employees as possible.

As I started to open the door, I became aware that Vic had followed me. "Where do you think you're going?"

"With you."

"No."

"Why not?"

"Because you and the courthouse ladies don't get along."

"We get along fine."

I stood there, holding the handle but keeping the door closed. "Fine, like when you threw the trash can over the counter at the county treasurer's office?"

"I was provoked."

"You were not provoked, you were just in a bad mood."

She leaned against the homegrown bricks, folding her arms and studying the sidewalk. "They provoked my bad mood."

"By asking you to pay your taxes."

She shrugged. "Taxes in Wyoming are a joke; it was the *way* they asked me to pay my taxes."

"You were six months delinquent and received three warnings in the mail."

"Who reads that shit?"

"I do, and it would be really embarrassing if I was the one who had to throw you out of your house." I stood there, unmoving, as lawyers Dennis and Ben Kervin came down one of the long, curving stairways; the one with the ornamental stringers. The father and son team recognized a Vic Moretti standoff when they saw one and wisely retreated toward the front of the building.

"I'm not going in here with you."

She studied me for a moment more and then flapped her hands in dismissal. "Fine."

Watching her go, I once again marveled at the hypnotic effect of the Glock 19 Gen 4 in Midnight Bronze bouncing off her rounded flank as she headed back toward our offices in full huff.

I opened the glass door and entered unencumbered. The assessor's office was past the hallway and to my immediate right. Jennifer McCormick was the current occupant and was seated at the desk when I came in. "Are you in here hiding from the wolves?"

I sat in the guest chair she gestured toward. "Pretty much."

She ran a hand through her close-cropped

tresses and studied me. "I have a cheese sandwich and some Doritos we can share."

"Then we might make it through till spring. Got anything to drink?"

"It's a courthouse, people drink in here all day. What do you want?"

"Water would be nice."

She reached behind her and pulled out two bottles from a minifridge and handed one to me. "You've lost weight."

"I have."

She unscrewed the top of her water and took a swig. "That's a nifty scar."

"Thanks." I did the same and then asked, "One hundred fourteen Airport Road?"

"What about it?"

"Who owns it?"

She tapped away on her computer and then turned to look at me. "Abarrane Extepare."

"Hell."

She raised an eyebrow. "Wrong answer?"

"Just sends me in a circle."

"Welcome to my world."

I took another sip of my water. "You're a lot of help."

"You continue talking to me that way, and I'm keeping my cheese sandwich for myself and throwing you to the wolves."

"Wolf, singular."

"Cheese sandwich." She tipped her water bottle to mine in a toast. "Singular."

"Abarrane Extepare."

Ruby stared at me over her glasses. "Do you have a phone number?"

"It's on the Post-it, the one I gave you." I was luxuriating in the fact that for once, I'd given *her* a Post-it.

She glanced back at my door, covered entirely with small squares of yellow paper, giving the impression that a sacrificial paper chicken had been massacred there. "I've had a few for you."

"Would-be wolf hunters?"

"Yes."

I reached down and petted the snoozing Dog at her feet. "Would you be so kind as to get me Ferris Kaplan on the line?"

"After I get Abarrane Extepare?" She stared at me. "You could do it yourself."

I stood and studied her, pretty sure that was the first time she'd ever said that to me. "You're too busy?"

She glanced at the papers surrounding her. "I'm always too busy, Walter. Anyway, there's a gift for you in your office."

I glanced at the door with a feeling of dread. "What kind of gift?"

"Why don't you go and see?"

With one last look, I moved toward my office, still keeping a little distance just in case somebody had gotten the wolf and left him in there. Leaning a little to one side, I could see a large box sitting on my desk. "What the heck is it?"

"A computer."

I turned to look at her. "I don't want a computer."

"You signed the requisition yourself. It's been ten years, and we all got new computers, including you."

"I never had one." Glancing into my office, I ceded ground and went back to her counter. "I sign everything you put in front of me, but that doesn't mean I want a computer."

"Well, you've got one — the county IT guy is coming by later to hook it up."

"What does IT mean?"

"Information technology."

"You're my information technology."

"Not anymore." She sat her pen down and looked at me. "You know how I print out all your emails and leave them on your desk so you can answer them in longhand, just so I can come back in here and type out your responses?"

I dropped my eyes, a little ashamed. "I don't get that many emails."

"You didn't used to." She turned in her chair. "But there are enough now that I don't have the time to do it anymore."

"How about we just stop doing emails?"

"We can't do that in a modern department, Walter."

I glanced at the terminal in front of her. "I don't know how those things work."

"We'll teach you."

"I don't want to know."

"Walt, I don't have time for this."

"Where's Vic?"

"In her office. She's hooking up her new computer."

Walking away without further comment, I went down the hall where my undersheriff sat reading an instruction manual; Saizarbitoria's legs stuck out from under her desk at an odd angle. She looked at me. "Back from the courthouse?"

"This is a conspiracy. You are all working against me." I glanced down at the legs. "What is he doing under there?"

Santiago's voice sounded from below the desk. "Hooking up the modem."

"What's a modem do?"

"Nobody knows what a modem does — they're just magic and then the computer works." She stopped reading and stared up at me.

I started to turn to go. "I don't want a computer."

"You can send emails back and forth with your daughter, and she can send you photos of your granddaughter."

I stopped. "What?"

"Photos, you can send them over the internet."

The voice from below the desk rose up again. "You can look stuff up too."

"Like what?"

Vic raised the proverbial eyebrow. "How to operate a computer, for one."

"This is just the slippery slope toward a cell phone."

"We can only hope."

"I'm not opening the box."

"Fine, see if we care."

I stood there for a few moments more, but when it became obvious that they weren't going to entertain my anxieties, I turned and went back toward my own office. Once there, I stared at the large box for a moment and then picked it up and sat it on the floor by the wall. Sitting in my chair, I propped my feet on it, crossing my boots and thinking maybe the thing wasn't such a bad idea after all. I could get it a small tablecloth and maybe a lamp.

"I see you've found a use for your computer?"

I looked up to find Ruby in my doorway. "I'm not opening that Pandora's box."

"Okay." She walked over and handed me another Post-it. "Unsurprisingly, Abarrane is not answering his phone, but his wife tells me they've owned that house for years and that they usually rent it out, but it's been empty at least the last six months."

I took the Post-it. "Okay."

"You can call her or go visit her yourself. You know she gets things mixed up."

She started to go, but I caught her with my words. "Are you mad at me?"

"Yes, I am." She leaned on the jamb and refused to make eye contact. "I'm too old for this foolishness. Name me another sheriff in this state that doesn't have a computer?"

I sat there, silent.

"Human life is a story of evolution and change, and you are not adapting to the tune of technology. We're not asking you to split the atom here, Walter." With this, she turned and walked out, her voice trailing after her. "It's selfish, and I'm tired of it."

"Dog's not mad at me." I kneaded his ear as he rested his head on my knee and

139

listened to the whine of telecommunication between here and Cheyenne. "He doesn't seem to care if I have a computer or not."

"He's not the one who has to print out your emails and type up all your answers."

I nodded at the air as the monster stretched and then curled up beside my desk, probably wondering why we weren't going home. "You think I'm being selfish?"

"The results are selfish, and since Ruby's the one who is dealing with it, I'd watch my step if I were you."

"Meaning?"

"How old is Ruby, Dad?"

I adjusted the receiver against my ear. "I honestly don't know. I find it best to not ask women those kinds of questions."

"Past retirement age, and the only thing that keeps her there is you."

"You really think she'd quit on me?"

Cady sighed, and I could feel the waves of annoyance drifting north. "It's a possibility, and I don't think what she's asking is all that outrageous."

"I don't want to lose her."

"I can see why — you've never been without her, and I can't even imagine what a cluster that place would be if she left."

"So, take the computer?"

"Take the computer for God's sake; answer a few emails and keep her happy . . . try and keep all the women in your life happy . . . life's easier that way in case you haven't noticed."

I sat there for a moment before continuing the line of thought. "Do I keep you happy?"

"Most of the time."

"Most of the time?" I waited a moment, but she didn't add anything more. "You haven't been up for a visit in a while."

". . . I've been kind of busy, Dad, trying to catch up." There was a long pause. "I'm just attempting to get my life back to normal."

"Normal."

"Yeah, normal." Another pause. "That wasn't easy in Mexico, Dad."

"No, it wasn't."

"I mean, maybe you're used to that kind of stuff —"

"You never get used to that kind of stuff, ever."

She sighed, and I listened as she repositioned the phone. "Well, it's just taking me a while, okay?"

I took a breath and continued out on the thin ice of unhappy women in my life. "I guess I just want to be certain that you don't consider me to be a part of that stuff."

"I don't, honest."

"Okay." I sat up in my chair and placed my elbows on my desk. "How's Lola?"

"Sleeping."

"I figured, but how's she doing?"

"She's growing at a phenomenal rate — the clothes that Vic sent don't even fit anymore."

"Well, Vic hasn't seen her in months."

Pause. "Are we going to keep coming back to this?"

"I didn't mean . . ."

"The last time I looked, I-25 went both ways."

"I'm not . . ."

The twinge of aggravation in her voice was growing. "Look, I'm tired, and I'm going to go."

"Hey, Punk. I . . ."

"Good night, Dad."

The phone went silent in my hand, and I sat there listening I'm not sure for what. I finally lowered the receiver onto the cradle and watched the tiny red light go out, extinguished like a heartbeat. "Well, hell."

Dog looked up at me in hopes that I'd pull out my keys, but I didn't have the energy and just sat there thinking about the conversation in its entirety and trying to figure out what I'd said wrong and promising myself that I'd do better the next call.

There was a noise in the outer office that sounded like someone coming in, and I looked up to check the time with Seth Thomas — nine o'clock at night.

Standing, I walked out into the main room, with Dog trailing behind, and waited for someone to top the stairs just as Saizarbitoria's head appeared.

"You here to protect your position in that damned office pool?"

He shook the head and then continued along with a six-pack of Rainier beer. "I talked it over with Maria, and we decided you might still be here and in need of a little spiritual uplifting." He stopped at the top step and smiled an awkward grin. "Besides, I know what a modem is, and I can put your computer together for you."

"Is it doing anything?"

"Describe *anything.*"

"Is it lighting up or making noise?"

"No."

The Basquo's voice echoed from under my desk. "Hmm . . . Maybe I don't know as much as I think I do." He happily tinkered some more as I sat there on the corner of my desk, sipped a beer, and stared at the blank screen of the computer, as if

143

the staring might prompt it. "So, how's Cady?"

"Mad at me."

"Boy, seems like everybody's mad at you these days."

"Are you mad at me too?"

"Nope."

"Well then, that's you and Dog, so almost everybody." I listened as he struggled with something. "Problem?"

"Yeah, the only phone line you've got is a plug-in, and it's so old I'm having trouble hooking it into the modem, but I'll win." He wrestled some more and then asked, "Have you read any of those Post-its that Ruby put on your door yet?"

"All the wolf hunters? No."

"There's more than that."

"Like what?"

"Have you ever heard of the *Rupert Report*?"

"No."

"It's this guy, Jon Rupert, who does this conspiracy show on cable TV about UFOs, cryptozoology, and occult stuff."

I laughed. "So?"

"He's coming to Absaroka County."

"For what?"

"Are you ready for this?"

"Probably not."

144

"A werewolf."

I assembled my thoughts as every ounce of humor left the room. "Did I just hear you right?"

"Did you hear the term *werewolf?*"

"I did."

"Then you heard right." He crawled out from under my desk and sat in my chair, pulling the screen-thing toward him. "You have to turn it on, Boss."

"Where?"

He showed me. "This little button on the back of the monitor."

"Why do they put it there?"

"Well, you don't turn it off every day."

"You mean you just leave it on all the time?"

He blinked. "Well, yeah."

"Seems wasteful."

"They fall asleep."

"Like people?"

"Um, more like, go dormant." He tapped a few keys and then waited. "It's booting up." He turned toward me. "Starting . . . So, this Jon Rupert guy is going to be here tomorrow with an entire video crew to attempt to get footage of the werewolf that they think is responsible for Miguel Hernandez's death."

145

I sipped my beer. "You're not kidding, are you?"

"No, I'm afraid not." He tapped a few more keys. "First, we need to get you a screen saver."

"What's that?"

"A picture on the screen your computer reverts to when dormant. You can change it to some photos of your daughter and granddaughter when you get some." He turned to look at me. "So, what'll it be for now? A lot of people choose fish or tropical scenes."

"Why would I choose that?"

"Then what'll it be? How about the mountains in winter?"

"Not that."

He tapped some more. "Fuzzy animals?"

"Can this wait?"

"Sure. We'll email Cady and get some shots of Lola and her and have them rotate."

"That's the first good thing I've heard in this entire enterprise. Can we send her an email?"

"Sure, what do you want it to say?" I gave him the three words and watched as he continued tapping with a smile. "Okay, so do you want to see an episode of the *Rupert Report*?"

"Not really."

"C'mon, you gotta keep up, Boss." He

146

tapped some more and then turned the screen toward me where a goofy-looking individual in a poorly fitting suit jumped up and down, screaming into a large microphone in front of him, even going so far as to mimic strangling the thing as screens flickered images behind him along with a large sign that read ON AIR glowing red — kind of like his face.

I listened to the screaming and yelling for the better part of a minute and then turned to my deputy. "Can you understand what he's talking about?"

"Not really.

I watched a bit more. "And this is what I have to look forward to on the World Wide Web?"

He shrugged. "That and cat videos."

"Well, it's going to be a barren source of information."

"So, do you want me to take him on?"

I looked at him as if he were the captain of the *Titanic* and had just asked if I minded him going around the iceberg. "Um, yep. That might be best."

"Better than Vic."

"You can say that again."

He tapped, and the ridiculous man went away. "There's more."

"Oh, now why do I not like the sound of that?"

"There's this internet show, *Mickey Southern — Pervert Hunter,* mostly on Facebook and YouTube. I'll tell you about those later."

"He's hunting werewolves too?"

"No, this guy is a Net crusader that goes around baiting pedophiles and then confronts them on video."

"Sounds irresponsible and dangerous."

"He wants to meet with you and is driving up from Denver tomorrow."

"Good grief. What does he want?"

"He says we've got a major predator here in Durant, and he wants to help us take him down."

" 'Take him down?' "

"His words, not mine."

"What is this individual's official standing within the law enforcement community?"

"None, but he's very popular on social media."

I placed my face in a palm and tried to not seem absolutely desperate, even though the fatigue of a full day had now found me like a missile. "Would you like to take this one on too?"

He sipped his beer and looked up at me. "I think I'm going to have my hands full with Alex Rupert and the werewolves, Boss."

"Then tomorrow is going to be a long day." I stood gesturing toward the crouching technology that now occupied the majority of my desk. "Thanks for all of this, and the beer — but most important, the beer."

He smiled at me, the Basque eyes twinkling. "Get out of here and get some sleep. I'll clean up and get things straightened away."

I patted my leg and Dog stretched and joined me at the door. "How old is your son now?"

He sipped the last of his beer and then sat it on top of the file cabinet. "Two and a half years old."

"They're fun at that age."

He laughed. "You haven't been around kids for a while, have you?"

I nodded in agreement. "You'll lock up?"

"Got it."

I left him standing in my office as Dog and I made our way across the darkened main room and down the stairs. I pulled on my jacket and saluted Andy.

It was cool and overcast, and I couldn't help but stop about halfway across the parking lot to just stare at the sky, the three-quarter moon slipping in and out of the clouds like a pale chrome pinball.

149

You could see the valleys and mountain ranges on the luminescent little rock that orbited the earth, the word *moon* being traced back to the Old English, derived from the Proto-Germanic *menon,* which in turn derived from the Proto-Indian-European *menses* that meant month, forever associating the moon with the passage of time.

Current hypothesis is that the planetary body was formed when debris collided with the earth 4.5 billion years ago, late in our planet's growth process. It has been surmised that a fraction of that debris went into orbit around the earth and aggregated into our current moon.

One of the main indications that the moon did not derive from the earth is the fact that our planet has an iron core and the moon does not; and our planet, in fact, is one of the very few that has a moon an appreciable fraction of its own size.

So here we are, like two entwined lovers in a constantly twirling dance in the vast ballroom of endless space.

I looked down and saw that Dog, who was sitting on my foot, was also regarding the moon. "Always good to have a pal, huh?"

He wagged, and I patted his head, pulled out my keys, and unlocked my truck door as we made the rest of the trek across the parking lot. I opened said door and allowed him to jump into the front passenger seat. He turned and looked at me as I climbed in from the driver's side. I placed the key in the ignition and fired the three-quarter up before spying something sitting on the dash just beyond the steering wheel.

And there on the edge sat a perfectly pristine, white-and-blue Mallo Cup Play Money card.

6

After about thirty seconds with the Chilean consul, I started figuring that even after spending the better part of a month in Mexico, I wasn't going to be able to understand a word he was saying.

I covered the receiver and called out my open office door. "Sancho!"

Ruby's voice carried back. "He's out front, doing that interview."

"What interview?"

"I don't know, Walter." She appeared in the doorway. "Some TV thing."

"I don't understand a word the Chilean consul guy is saying, and unless we want an international incident, I think we should get the only Spanish-speaking staff member on this."

"Well then, go get him yourself." She disappeared without another word.

I pulled the phone back to my ear where the guy from the Chile Department of State was still talking. *"Por favor, señor. Un mo-mento, por favor . . ."* After hitting Hold, I stood, moved into the main office, and crossed to the stairs as Ruby eyed me. "I thought you would like me again if I had a computer."

She paused typing. "Having one and using it are two different things."

"I'm working on it."

Easing down the steps, I reached the landing and pushed the door open into Jon Rupert, the television host, whom I was fighting the urge to consider the biggest horse's ass I'd ever met, but I couldn't really come up with anyone who would give him a run for the money, so he got best-in-show.

Saizarbitoria was standing in front of the other door, and I reached out to take him by the shoulder and pull him away. "I've got the Chilean consul on the line, and evidently, he doesn't speak English."

"Oh."

"So I need you. Now."

"Sheriff, we are in the middle of an interview." The short, bald man stamped his polished loafer as the boom microphone operator and the lighting person stepped down.

"Not right now. I need my deputy."

He stepped in closer. "Well then, we can

153

finally speak with you."

I'd turned down the opportunity earlier, but I really didn't see any way around it now. Pulling Sancho through the door, I stepped out and took his place. "You've got three minutes."

The man in the used-car-salesman suit pointed a finger at the cameraman and then turned to me as the lights came back on and the mic hovered over our heads. "Jon Rupert here on the steps of the Absaroka County Wyoming sheriff's office with Sheriff Walt Longmire." He turned to look at me. "So, Sheriff, tell us about lycanthropopoly."

I blinked. "Excuse me?"

"Surely you've heard the term *lycanthropopoly* — the transformation of humans into wolves?"

I looked around at the four members of the crew, but none of them seemed to be in on the joke. "You mean lycanthropy?"

"Exactly."

I held up a hand. "Excuse me, but could you stop filming for a moment?" I turned back to Rupert, but the cameraman continued to film. "What kind of show is this?"

He feigned a state of unbelievability. "We are the highest-rated cryptozoology show on cable television, Sheriff. You've never heard of the *Rupert Report*?"

"No." I shook my head. "Correct me if I'm wrong, but isn't cryptozoology an attempt to prove the existence of entities of folkloric record?"

"Um, yes, I believe so."

"Pseudoscience."

He paused, glancing at the camera and then me. "Science."

"It doesn't follow scientific methodology, so you can't refer to it as a science."

"We are pushing the envelope of —"

He was struggling for the word, so I provided one. "Bullshit?"

The cameraman lowered the camera, and the light and sound people followed suit. "You shouldn't say 'bullshit' on basic cable."

"You're lucky my undersheriff isn't here."

"Sheriff, we're attempting to bring into question the world in which we live."

"No, you're attempting to use a man's suicide as some kind of salacious exploitation, and I'm afraid I can't have that, especially when it concerns an ongoing investigation." I started to open the door and escape but couldn't help but pile on. "Lycanthropy is the word, not lycanthropopoly, which as far as I know, isn't a real word. Clinical lycanthropy is a rare psychiatric syndrome of delusion, where the subject thinks they can physically transform

155

into some sort of animal, usually a wolf . . ." I thought about it. "Although there was a prince of Persia who thought he was a cow. There are reports of this mental abnormality going all the way back to the seventh century when an Alexandrian physician, Paulus Aegineta, attributed it to a deep melancholy. In 1563 a Lutheran physician by the name of Johann Weyer wrote that some of the symptoms were caused by an imbalance of the humors, and then in 1597, King James VI dismissed the delusions of transformation as a depression causing men to imitate the behavior of animals." I leaned back over the man. "So, in essence, your show is about 420 years behind the times."

Closing the door, I climbed the steps.

Ruby looked up as I approached. "How did it go?"

"I don't think I'm destined for cable stardom."

I crossed to my office and found Sancho on my phone conversing at a high rate of Spanish with the Republic of Chile.

I started to go, but he held up a finger and then made a few more statements before lowering the receiver back on the cradle and looking up at me. "There's a problem."

I sat in my guest chair. "When is there not?"

"Miguel Hernandez was politically active in Santiago, and now the government is afraid that his death, especially if it ends up being a possible murder, is going to lead to an uprising and martyrdom."

I squeezed the bridge of my nose in an attempt to intercept the headache that was building. "He was a shepherd."

"Evidently he was also a writer of political pamphlets."

"So, this is not a formal protest concerning working conditions?"

"Yes, it is. Well, at least that's what they'd prefer rather than a murder, which will be seen in some circles as an action by their government."

"A Chilean assassin in the Bighorn Mountains of Wyoming."

"The ambassador seems to think there is a contingent that will attempt to use the death for political gain."

"So, what do they want from us?"

"To discern whether the death was a suicide or a murder and, if it was a murder, to capture a suspect not of Chilean nationality and especially not a member of their government."

We sat there in the silence of global

stupidity. "Well, I think we're all on the same page there."

He nodded. "How did the interview go?"

"The man is a moron."

"We're on the same page there too." He glanced around. "You want me to get out of your chair?"

"No, I'm fine."

"Isaac call about the final on the autopsy report?"

"No, he sometimes forgets, so I think I'll go over there this afternoon."

"Want company?"

"I would, but somebody has to hold down the fort." I pointed toward the computer. "You want to check my email for me?"

He tapped a few keys and then gestured with a palm. "You've got mail from the server."

"What server?"

"Your internet provider, probably welcoming you to their email platform." He moved, tapped the thingamajig, and nodded. "Just a routine response."

"Nothing from my daughter?"

"No."

"Well, that's disappointing. How do we know she got it?"

"Got what?"

"The email."

He stared at me. "Because I sent it."

"Yep, but how do we know she got it?"

"It didn't come back."

I glanced at the computer like we were being rude, talking about it in third person. "They do that?"

"What?"

"Come back."

"Yeah." He glanced around. "One bit of good news, *Mickey Southern: Pervert Hunter* is not coming up today."

I took a deep breath and tried to think, for the life of me, what in the world he was talking about. "Who?"

"The internet guy who baits pedophiles — I guess he decided that our case wasn't as bad as he thought."

"Well, that is good news, right?"

"Right." He stood and glanced around. "This is a nice office, Boss." He looked at the bay window behind my desk. "With a view of the mountains. The only thing I can see out of my window is the bank across the street."

I waited a moment, but the need for him to say more was palpable. "What's on your mind?"

He leaned against the wall and looked down at me. "You've got two more years in your term — are you planning on standing in the next election?"

I studied him. "Haven't thought about it."

He laced his hands. "I've been approached by a few people in the community." His eyes came up to mine, and he started to speak but then closed his mouth for a moment. "Look, I don't want you thinking I'm trying something here, but I'm just curious as to your intentions. I mean, you talk about retiring all the time, and I know that Vic is your heir apparent, but she's told me herself that if you walk through that front door for the last time, she's going to be right behind you." He stopped and eyed the Bighorns. "Look, I just want to be open about this. I don't want to be skulking around and have you thinking ill of me, all right?"

"All right."

"So, do I still have a job?"

"Yep."

"You're not pissed off at me?"

"Nope." I stood. "I'll start giving it some thought but don't expect an answer real soon." Placing a hand on his shoulder, I dipped my head and looked under the brims of both our hats. "I appreciate you coming to me with this, and I'm not upset or anything. I honestly don't know what I want to do, but you'll be the first to know. Deal?"

He smiled. "Deal."

160

"Now you have to go say something to Vic."

"Oh, crap."

"Don't worry, I think it's already crossed her mind." I patted his shoulder and steered him toward the door. "I'm not so sure she even wants to be sheriff."

"I'll let you know." He stopped and looked back at me. "If you don't hear from me the rest of the day, you'll look for my body, right?"

"We'll do our best, but it's a big county."

Leaning on my dispatcher's counter, I waited as she scribbled down the number and handed it to me. "Donnie Lott."

I took the Post-it and glanced back at her. "Where did you get it?"

"Libby Troon. I figured if he contacted her about hiring a kidnapper that she probably had his phone number and address."

"Fort Collins."

"It's in Colorado."

"You don't say?" I started back toward my office but added, "I turned my computer on." She said nothing. "I just wanted you to know."

Sitting in my chair, I leaned back and looked out at the view Saizarbitoria coveted. Soaking in about all the high plains beauty

161

I could handle, I reached over and took the receiver from my phone just as my under-sheriff came in, closed the door behind her, and sat in my guest chair, lodging her boots on my desk once again. "Careful of the computer."

"Fuck you."

I hung up the phone. "Been talking to Sancho?"

"What. The. Fuck."

"He's just testing the waters."

"How 'bout I test his gonads with the point of my tactical boots?"

"This doesn't come as a surprise to either of us."

She sighed deeply. "I suppose not, but would it have killed him to wait another two years?"

I shrugged. "He got approached, and you know how rumors spread in a small town. He just didn't want any of us to get caught flat-footed."

"It still pisses me off."

"Amazingly, I can tell."

She raised the tarnished gold eyes up to study me the way cats watch birds. "What are you going to do?"

"I honestly don't know." Leaning forward, I rested my elbows on my desk and rubbed the smooth skin of my left eyelid with a forefinger. "I think I changed down there in Mexico."

"Well, you have. You have that great scar."

Dropping my hand from my face, I slumped back in my chair. "I just feel . . . disconnected, like I'm not sure if I should really be here doing this job anymore."

"Where would you go?"

"I don't know. Hatch, New Mexico, or Hyder, Alaska, maybe."

She let that one settle. "So, you talked to Henry."

"I did."

"That usually helps."

"Well, this time it didn't."

I reached into my pocket for the Mallo Cup candy card and held it out to her. "Did you leave this on my dash last night?"

"No." She took it and studied it, fully knowledgeable of the significance. "Was your truck locked?"

"I'm not sure."

"Well, there's an extra set of keys on the rack in the main office, so anybody could've put it there if it was, but why?"

"I don't know."

"It's in perfect condition, just like the other one." She handed it back to me. "Somebody's fucking with you."

"It would appear."

"Speaking of, how 'bout we fuck." She lowered her boots to the floor. "In case you're not keeping score, I am. We haven't had sex since you got back."

"I'm sorry."

"I wasn't asking for an apology, I'm just wondering what's up."

"I don't know."

"You wanna try it and see if it makes things better? It usually does."

"Vic . . ."

"I'm willing to take one for the team — a quick one here in the office since the door's shut?" She patted the desk and stood. "Let me know, but don't wait too long — a girl gets frustrated, you know?" She placed a hand on the doorknob and looked back at me. "For the record, I will have my way with you."

"Is that a threat?"

She turned the knob and opened the door, signaling that the personal portion of the conversation was over. "More of a guarantee."

And like that, she was gone.

Flipping the handset up, I took the scrap of paper from my desk and punched in the number, dialing Fort Collins.

It rang three times and then a woman answered in an uncertain voice. "Hello?"

164

"Hello, this is Absaroka County Sheriff Walt Longmire. I'm trying to get in touch with Donnie Lott?"

"Is this about my dad?"

"Excuse me?"

"This is his wife, Jeannie. Is this something about my dad up there?"

"Well, possibly. You're Abe Extepare's daughter?"

"Yes, God help me."

I leaned back in my chair and cradled the phone in the crook of my neck. "I get the feeling that you know why I'm calling."

"The kidnapping thing."

"Yep. Would you like to tell me what that's all about?"

"Why?"

I took a second. "It's kind of a serious charge, and I'd just like to get the lay of the land before it gets even more serious."

"Are we being charged with something?"

"Not now, but I would like to know what's going on between the two of you and your father."

She fumbled with the phone. "Oh, God . . ."

"If this is a bad time?"

I listened as she breathed. "It was just a stupid threat. Look, my father is very attached to Liam, and we sometimes have

165

trouble getting him from the old man, so Donnie called that idiot Libby Troon and asked her about getting someone to help us get our son back."

"Why didn't you call me?"

"Well, Donnie's had some difficulties with the law, and I didn't want to press charges on my dad. I mean, Abe's my father for goodness sake."

"I see."

"But my husband can be a little intimidating and so can my father, and the last time we were up there he threatened Donnie with a shotgun." There was a pause. "Look, my parents are getting older, and it's easier for them when Liam is around, and they know we'll be coming if he's there. I don't know, it's all screwed up. Family, you know?"

"It's what I deal with the majority of the time."

"Well, Donnie's going to be pissed that Dad's gotten you involved."

"Actually, he didn't."

There was another pause. "Did Libby Troon get you —"

"No, there's been a bit of a tragedy up here that involves one of your father's herders, and I happened to be over there and met your son."

"What kind of tragedy?"

"He appears to have committed suicide."

I listened as she caught her breath. "Oh no, which one?"

"A Mr. Hernandez. Did you know him?"

"No, but I know that Dad gets very attached to his herders."

"Miguel Hernandez, he was Chilean and somehow politically involved down there."

"How terrible."

"Is there any possibility that your husband knew him?"

She laughed. "No, no. Donnie doesn't want anything to do with the sheep business — the closest he ever came to ranching was buying a cowboy hat and learning to line dance. That's one of the problems between him and my father." There was a long pause, and then she spoke again. "I'm sorry, but what did you say your name was again?"

"Longmire, Walt Longmire."

"My father built an empire, Sheriff Longmire. The problem is that now that he's built it, nobody wants it but him. I don't suppose you have any kinds of problems like that in your family?"

"Actually, I still own my family ranch."

"Working?"

"Leased."

I could hear disappointment in her voice,

all the way from Colorado. "Oh."

"Ms. Lott, from what I understand, Mr. Hernandez has family down there in Greeley and we're having trouble getting in touch with them. You wouldn't happen to know them, or know how I could contact them?"

"I'm afraid not."

"Well, are you or your husband planning on coming up anytime soon? I'd like to speak with you, perhaps along with your father?"

"We were hoping to get Liam this weekend."

"Maybe I can help with that. When you get a clear picture of what your travel plans are, could you give me a call and we'll set something up?" I read her the number and then we said our goodbyes.

That's the problem with empires — they're all personal.

As I rounded the corner at Fort Street, I noticed a white Toyota pickup with Montana plates trailing me. Making the turn to go to the hospital, I pulled into the alley behind the bank and stopped, rolling down my window as Keasik Cheechoo pulled up beside me and lowered hers.

"Hey, robbing a bank?"

168

"Nope, I just saw you tailing me and thought I should see if you wanted something."

"You saw me?"

"I did."

"I thought I was being really inconspicuous."

I glanced around. "It's a small town with not much cover. Do you have something on your mind, Ms. Cheechoo?"

She nodded, parked, and, telling her dog to stay, walked over to my window. "News from the wolf front." She leaned her elbows on the sill, a little breathless. "As it turns out, 777M is something a little special."

"In what way?"

"He's native."

"I'm afraid I don't understand."

"To Wyoming, he's one of our original wolves." She smiled and continued. "Sheriff, wolf remains in the Lamar Valley of Yellowstone National Park go back almost a thousand years; wolves have always been here, but they were *irremotus* and not *occidentalis*."

"I'm not following."

"By the late nineteen thirties there were maybe a dozen wolves remaining in Yellowstone Park, and they were *irremotus,* but in the sixties they started using compound-

169

1080, sodium fluoroacetate, to virtually wipe them out. Do you know that one spoonful of that stuff can kill a hundred people?"

"No, I can't say that I do."

Ignoring my answer, she continued, "But there was a sighting in the late seventies of a dark-colored pair living in the northeast section of the park."

"So?"

"So, the midnineties was when the *occidentalis,* the Canadian wolves, were reintroduced into the Yellowstone ecosystem — a completely different subspecies."

"And the *irremotus* is the native Wyoming wolf that you say survived? How is that possible?"

She threw up her hands. "Who knows? Usually the ox's kill the irre's but some of the irre's must have survived both them and the poison." Out of basic respect, I reached down and switched off the motor on my truck. "There must've been a mating pair that produced pups that produced more pups that must've produced this guy."

"How can you be sure of that?"

"777M was tagged and collared by a National Park Service trainee before turning him loose. Well, our people did the DNA paperwork and discovered 777M is full-blood *irremotus*."

"Don't the two subspecies mix?"

"Not generally, and like I said, it's more common for the ox's to kill them because they're smaller, but not this guy if he's as big as you described."

"You've seen him too."

"Yes, but not as close as you."

I thought about it. "So, you have a throwback."

"I know, isn't it amazing?"

"Congratulations."

"Well." She stared at me. "You have to stop your wolf hunt."

"It's not my wolf hunt, Ms. Cheechoo, it's the Department of Agriculture's Wolf Management people or the predator board you need to be talking to, not me."

"But you're picking the wolf hunter."

"No, I'm not. That was Ranger Coon's attempt at a joke, since he is retiring, and one that I don't think is particularly funny. I suppose you could also talk to Don Butler of the Wyoming Cattlemen's Association, but I'd imagine that's going to be a rather one-sided conversation."

"You're not going to help me?"

"Frankly, I don't see how I can."

She stepped back and practically shouted at me. "Call off the wolf hunt!"

171

"I don't have the jurisdiction to call off anything, Ms. Cheechoo. It's the state and federal agencies you're talking about. I'm a county sheriff. Now, if you want to talk to me about the investigation into the death of Miguel Hernandez, that's within my job description, but not wolves."

She stood there for a moment more and then stalked away, headed for her truck, but turned back and stuck a finger out at me. "By the way, I read your interview in the local paper, and for my money it was one of the most shameless, exacerbating things I've ever read — you've started a full-blown wolf scare here, Sheriff."

With that, she turned away again and jumped into her truck, tires squealing down the street. I thought about going after her and giving her a citation, but for the life of me I couldn't remember if I had a ticket book in my truck.

I glanced over at Dog, who looked as shell-shocked as I felt, and then pulled out and continued to the hospital. "Let's not follow that car, shall we?"

Dog wanted to go into the hospital and couldn't understand why he wasn't allowed inside. "It's not my fault they don't allow dogs." I stood there holding the door of my truck in the sunshine as he studied me. "I don't know why you wanted to come, they've never allowed dogs."

He sat and continued looking at me, eye to eye.

"Some people are allergic . . . Or something. I don't know." I rolled down the windows a bit, and he settled, resting his mammoth head on his huge paws, and stretched out the full length of the seat as I shut the door.

Walking into Durant Memorial always gave me a slight chill, maybe because there were times when I wasn't sure if I was ever going to leave the place of my own volition. I turned the corner, waved at the receptionist, and walked down the hall to Isaac Bloomfield's office.

Knocking on the door, I heard nothing inside and then knocked again, wanting to make sure that the piles of files hadn't fallen over and incapacitated him.

"He's not in there."

I turned to see David Nickerson, Isaac's protégé — and didn't we all have them these days? "Where is he?"

"Outside. There's a picnic table in the back where the staff can eat if the weather is nice."

"Thanks." I pushed off and walked past the dark-haired young man.

"It's the other way."

I called over my shoulder. "I'm bringing a friend to lunch."

It didn't take long for Dog to navigate the grounds around the hospital building, and he now sat with Isaac's hands cradling his head, the finely boned fingers supporting the boxy muzzle as the two old souls gazed into each other's eyes.

"Maybe you should do his DNA."

"I'm not so sure I want to know what he is."

Isaac released Dog's head and reached onto the picnic table, breaking off another piece of matzo and feeding it to the beast. "Happy Passover."

I broke a piece off for myself. "Certainly seems like spring today." Chewing the unleavened bread, I did my best to ignore the thin remains of snow on the grounds, leftovers from the skiff of the other night.

"Are you all right, Walter?"

"I . . ." I thought about whether I wanted to share my symptoms with him but then figured he was the only one who was medically trained that I really trusted. "Um . . . I've been having these phases."

"What kind of phases?"

"I'm not really sure, but it's like some traumatic pause."

174

"Physically or mentally?"

"Both."

He studied me, and then his eyes went toward the trees by the creek. "You are familiar with the fight-or-flight response?"

I nodded. "Survival-oriented acute stress response."

"Yes, but have you ever heard of the fight-flight-or-freeze response?"

"No."

"You access the menace as something you can defeat or one that you must run from. Both of these responses require a burst of biochemical, such as adrenaline, that enable you to combat or flee your adversary. But what if in those nanoseconds of response time, you realize that you can neither defeat nor escape the menace." He finally looked back at me. "Are these phases happening in moments of stress?"

"No."

"Interesting. Are you alone?"

"Mostly."

"How long are these periods?"

"Vic timed one at almost eight minutes."

"It is possible that your mind is disassociating itself from the terrifying enormity of what you are facing because accepting it might rob you of your sanity."

I looked at the concentration camp survivor. "I'm getting tired of it all, Doc. I'm getting sick of what people do to one another."

"This is the first time you've felt this way?"

"No, but it's gotten to me worse than it ever has before."

He nodded. "You've been through a great deal lately."

"Maybe it's enough." He stared at me through the thick-framed glasses as I spoke to the surface of the table. "Maybe it's time to have it over with — just up and quit."

"That would be a shame."

"Why?"

He adjusted the glasses and smiled the sad smile that had aged like wine. "Because you are very good at what you do, Walter." Isaac reached under his down jacket and pulled a small plastic bag from the front pocket of his smock. He handed it to me.

I held the bag up but couldn't see anything inside.

"Mule hairs."

I sighed, thinking about how high the man had been hung. I held the bag up in the sun and could now see the short fibers and then lowered it to the table and studied the wood grain of the surface. "So, what is it I'm so damned terrified of, Doc?"

"Why Walter, I would've thought it was

obvious." He smiled his sad, worldly smile. "Yourself."

7

"Even though Chuck Coon is fur-bearing, I still don't think we're going to be able to have a hunting season on him."

Vic cocked her head at the game warden. "He's retiring, that means he's old and slow and will be easier to shoot."

"Um, I don't think the department will go for it."

She crossed her legs. "Then I guess I may have to resort to the shoot, shovel, and shut-the-hell-up plan."

I glanced at the twenty-inch brown trout on the wall above Ferris Kaplan's desk, adjusted my hat on my knee, and changed the subject. "What do you know about this Keasik Cheechoo?"

He laughed. "The wolf advocate — she's a major pain in my ass, but that's not an official department position either."

"She was quoting me some interesting findings on 777M earlier today."

178

"Like what?"

"That he's a native Wyoming wolf and not one of the Canadian transplants you guys brought down here in the nineties."

"First off, we didn't bring them down here, the Forest Service did, and second, I haven't heard anything about that." I spread my palms as he studied me and looked thoughtful, finally shaking his head. "*Irremotus.* That would be highly unlikely."

"How big of a deal would it be?"

"Huge, like finding an extinct species or the Loch Ness Monster or Bigfoot."

Vic slumped in her chair. "So, we get to be the ringmaster of an even bigger shitshow than the one we have now."

"Possibly." Ferris leaned down and opened a desk drawer. "Want a drink?" Not waiting for a response, he placed a bottle of Sazerac Rye on his blotter along with two tumblers. "You guys are going to have to share."

Vic reached for the glass as he finished pouring. "Okay, so this wolf is collared, right? So why can't you guys just track him and dart him, or whatever you do?"

Kaplan took a sip from his personal glass and leaned back in his chair. "Well, that supposes that the smart collar is operating."

I reached over and took the tumbler from Vic as she lowered it from her lips. "I take it

179

it's not?"

"Sometimes. The new collars were developed by a team of scientists at UC Santa Cruz with accelerometers like those of smartphones." He paused and glanced at Vic. "Will you explain what a smartphone is to him?"

She turned to me. "It's a phone that's smart."

The game warden sighed. "Anyway, they not only track the wolf but give us an indication of when they're burning up calories by running or conserving energy while resting, almost like keeping a diary of the wolf's activities."

"Sounds great. So, what's the problem?"

"That batch got the first-generation leftovers, and they proved to be a little finicky. Sometimes they transmit; sometimes they don't."

"The Cheechoo woman also mentioned that a trainee was the one who tested and collared 777M."

"That could've also had an effect."

Vic took the glass back from me. "Does it have GPS tracking?"

"Sometimes."

I leaned forward. "And is it true that private individuals can get transponders and track the wolves themselves?"

180

He nodded. "If the transmitter on the collar is working, yes. I've heard of cases over near Yellowstone and that could be true with 777M."

"Hey, what the hell is this 777M shit anyway? It sounds like we're talking about a U-boat — can we just name this fucking wolf?"

Kaplan shook his head and placed a hand over his bearded face. "Oh, please don't do that."

"Why not?"

"It will anthropomorphize the animal, and pretty soon we've got GoFundMe sites, Facebook pages, Twitter accounts, and Instagram pictures . . ."

"And what's wrong with that?"

He glanced at me and then back to her. "Because somebody's going to shoot that wolf, and it always has a negative effect when people start looking at large predators as Fluffy-the-dog-next-door."

Vic made a face. "So, somebody's going to shoot him."

"Most assuredly."

"Because he might've killed a sheep? Which, by the way, was not confirmed by your own lab's DNA testing."

He raised his hands in surrender. "Yes."

181

"Not because he nibbled on the shepherd?"

Ferris took a sip and then rested the tumbler on his blotter. "Surprisingly, in the eyes of the federal and state government that's less of an issue."

"Well, in the eyes of the denizens of Absaroka County, it's not." I took the glass back from my undersheriff. "Evidently there are hordes of wolves preparing to descend out of the Bighorn Mountains and run rampant through the streets of Durant."

He shook his head. "Have these people ever checked the statistics to see what the odds are of a wolf attack on human beings?"

"Somehow I doubt it."

"In modern history in the contiguous United States, we've had two deaths by wolves, and in both cases the animals were habituated to the point of not being afraid of people. Wolves generally know better than to associate with human beings in that it's always going to end badly for the wolf. It's a case of humans perpetuating a campaign of selective breeding — over the centuries bold wolves are killed and the more timid animals survive. So, if you even see one in the wild, it's quite an accomplishment."

Vic took the glass back and finished it off with one slug. "How about Larry?"

Kaplan looked at her, then me, then her again. "Excuse me?"

"The wolf, how 'bout we call him Larry."

Carrying the sawed-off shotgun through the Durant Home for Assisted Living didn't raise much of a response from the staff — Lucian Connally had had visitors bearing firearms before. Stopping at his door, I reached down, ruffled the hair behind Dog's ears, and looked at Vic. "Why Larry?"

"KYW back in Philadelphia used to have this Chiller Theater show on Saturday nights, and as a kid I was an avid viewer."

I looked at her, taking in her open flannel shirt and tight thermal she wore underneath just to distract the old sheriff. "Okay."

"My Nonna used to stay up with me, and we'd watch the movies and sleep on the sofa. I don't think she ever made it through a single one, but I felt better having her there." She reached down and petted Dog's enormous head. "They would show a triple-creature feature — you know, three Frankenstein movies or three Dracula movies. But my favorites were the Wolf Man movies with Lon Chaney Jr., and his character was named Larry Talbot."

I knocked on the door. "There are times when I think I barely know you."

183

"There are times you're right." She reached up and pounded. "You home, you old pervert?"

I glanced up and down the hallway in hopes that Lucian was the only one to receive the greeting. After a moment, the door opened and he stood there in a freshly ironed shirt, clean blue jeans, and polished Paul Bond boots, his silver hair combed and parted.

I'd told him Vic was accompanying me this evening.

"Entrée, entrée . . ." He stepped back and ushered us in with a sweep of his arm — Dog shot into the room and jumped onto his favorite leather sofa.

The place was spotless, and some sort of fragrant burbling was coming from a pot on the stove. I sat the shotgun by my usual chair. "I'm sorry, we were looking for the apartment of Lucian Connally?"

He ignored me and continued into the kitchen on his four-prong cane. "Get in here and shut the damn door." He stirred the ingredients as we slipped off our jackets and piled them beside Dog, who was already stretched out, his head on his paws.

"What's for dinner?"

"I had a friend drop off some elk tenderloin, and I used it to make what I consider

184

to be one of the finest stews I've ever created."

Looking over at the chessboard, I could see the ol' sheriff had left it the same as it was last week when I'd been here, and I was worried that none of his other players had paid him a visit. "Is that last week's game?"

He came in from the kitchen holding a bottle of Clos de l'Oratoire des Papes and an opener, which he handed off to Vic. He only drank wine when she accompanied me. "It is."

"No other games this week?"

"Nope."

"How come?"

"All my opponents are either dead or too senile to play anymore."

"So, you're stuck with me?"

Vic expertly pulled the cork on the red and handed the bottle back to him. She wandered toward the sliding glass doors and stretched her arms upward. "And me."

He allowed his eyes to linger on her, and I couldn't blame him.

"All three of you." He petted Dog and tottered back into the kitchen to collect the wine glasses and, returning, handed them out to me. "So, what're you gonna do about this wolf situation you got on your hands?"

I extended a glass, he poured, and then I

handed it off to Vic. "There is no wolf situation."

"That ain't what's in the papers." He glugged another for me — a technique that would have appalled the vintners. "What came over you, giving out with statements like that?"

"I was misquoted."

Pouring one for himself, he raised a glass. "Here's to the fourth estate."

After the three of us touched glasses, he looked thoughtful. "What the hell are the other three estates anyway?"

"Edmund Burke, 1787, referring to the three estates of the realm in the European sense, the clergy, nobility, and commoners, but in the American sense, the legislative, executive, and judiciary branches — ceding power to the fourth, the press."

Lucian shook his head. "Drink up, maybe we'll get some sense out of you before it's all over." His eyes lingered on Vic again. "How the hell do you put up with him?"

She sipped her wine and sat on the sofa beside Dog. "It's going to get worse. He's got a computer now."

The old sheriff turned to look at me, appalled. "The hell you say."

I nodded. "I haven't figured out how to turn it on, but when I do I'm going to be hell on wheels."

"Saints preserve us."

Anxious to change the subject, I remembered it being my turn and hooked in a knight from the left. "So, did you ever have any wolf problems back in the day?"

He studied my move and sipped his wine. "Define the term *problem.*"

"You know what I mean."

"Did I ever have a wolf problem . . ." His eyes came back up but paused when he noticed the weapon leaning beside his guest chair. "What? These games become so competitive that you have to come armed these days?"

Reaching down, I picked up the old shotgun and tabled it in my outstretched hands, presenting it to him. "You remember this weapon?"

He studied it up and down as Vic stood nearby with a smile playing on her lips. "Can't say that I do."

"It's the one that cost you your leg."

He stared at it. "You're shittin' me . . ." He took it, and I watched as he swung it up and stared at it almost as closely as if I'd handed him the leg they'd cut off all those years ago. "I'll be damned."

"Look familiar now?"

He shook his head, unbelieving. "Well, I

only saw it for a few seconds back in the day, and by then it was far too late." He studied it some more. "I thought it was a twelve gauge."

"Twenty."

He nodded. "By gawd, that night it took off my leg it looked like a bazooka." He studied it a bit more and then raised his dark eyes to look at me. "Remington Model 11, widowmaker, the Dillinger Gun. This little booger was easy to saw off and made it the go-to weapon for motorized bandits back in the Dirty Thirties; along with those new en block V-8 engines those ol' boys were hard to run down. Hell, this gun alone is probably responsible for the National Firearms Act of '34 — no silencers, machine guns, or anything sawed off." He studied the thing, running his hands over the metal. "You're sure this is the one?"

"Pretty sure."

"Where'd you get it?"

"Abarrane Extepare found it under one of the lambing sheds on his father's summer place. He says it was in pretty bad shape and probably had been lying under there since the act."

Lucian raised the shotgun and sighted it on the mule-deer mount on his wall just above my head, and I could see how a man

188

could be intimidated by it. "I'll be damned."

"He also said something else interesting about who it was that actually shot you. He said to give that to you and see if the *statuary limits* had run out yet."

The old sheriff lowered the weapon but continued looking at it. "Beltran was the older of the two, bigger and tougher than his little brother."

He sipped his wine.

"It took me a couple of weeks to get out of that damn hospital, but when I did I went looking for 'em. When I caught up with 'em it was down on the Middle Fork on the Powder River near the Outlaw Cave — they didn't know what county they was in, and I ain't so sure I did either. They had a sheep camp and a little dugout no bigger than a walk-in closet." He reached out and stroked the pebbly finish of the shotgun astride his knees. "They'd been down there hidin' out for a month." He shook his head. "Now, just imagine how tough you had to be to be out there livin' in a hole in the ground."

Vic held out an empty glass to him, and he picked up the bottle to refill her before setting it at the edge of the table.

"They knew I was comin', but they didn't have a weapon between 'em. Beltran come out empty-handed, and if there's ever been a man I faced that was certain he was gonna die, it was him." His eyes fell to the board and tightened, attempting to seize those fleeting moments when just one mistake might mean the end of your life. "I had my .38 out and pointed at him as he stood there between the doorway of that ol' dugout and me and said he understood if I wanted his life for what they done, but that if I could see fit to just blow off an arm or leg and leave his head attached he sure would appreciate it."

Vic laughed.

Lucian cocked his head and smiled. "Honest to God, that's what he said."

"Then what?"

"I asked him where his brother was, and I told him I wasn't gonna ask twice, and that's when Jakes come out of the dugout, also empty-handed."

I sipped my wine and waited.

"I told Beltran to step aside, but he didn't — he just stood there between me and his brother, who had those spooky blue eyes. Starts tellin' me that one of the last things he promised his mother was that he'd take care of his little brother, and he didn't see any way out of it now. He said you know how it is down there in Rawlins, Lucian. They'll eat him up and spit out a half-man

190

if he survives, and he was right — that was back in the day when that place was rough, brother. So anyway, he says, 'Why don't you just send me down there, or whatever's left of me when you get done and we'll call it even.' "

We waited for a long while as he seemed lost in his thoughts, and finally Vic stood and went into the kitchen to stir the stew as a relief from the tension or to provide even the smallest bit of privacy as Lucian looked out the windows at the darkness.

"Think about that, givin' up years of your life for somebody else."

Vic came back out and stood there, leaning against the wall with the ladle in her hands. "You let him take his brother's place?"

He glanced back at her. "Once."

She studied him. "Excuse me?"

His eyes came back to mine. "Had a wolf problem once out on Cat Creek. They'd just started puttin' collars on those things, and if you shot one you might as well have shot Spiro Agnew. They had a specialist who said they had a wolf out of the park but that somethin' must be wrong because their telemetry said that wolf was headed across South Dakota, and the last they heard, it was just outside Chicago. So, we call it in

191

and these Chicago PD boys head out to the last given location on a wolf hunt, and boy, I'd have paid money to witness that."

"What happened?"

He glanced back down at the shotgun. "They found a dead wolf in a coal hopper where somebody'd dumped it off an overpass."

"Why do you suppose he didn't want it?"

I glanced at the Remington Model 11 sitting on the floorboards. "I don't know. Maybe it reminded him of things he didn't particularly want to remember."

"Why don't you come in?"

I pulled the Bullet to a stop in front of the little Craftsman house with the red door on Kisling. "I can't. Dog and I need to go home every once in a while just to make sure the wildlife hasn't taken up residency."

"Like Larry?" I said nothing, but she smiled. "How about I go with you?"

"I don't think I'm going to be that much fun."

She studied me. "You're sure you're all right?"

"I think so." I took a deep breath and sighed. "Just listening to Lucian got to me a little bit. I guess I see him over there at the home for assisted living, and I can't help but think that that's where I'm going to end up."

She reached back to pet my companion. "Never — you've got Dog . . . And me." I smiled.

"Lucian likes being alone, Walt, he always has — I swear he likes company once a week when that granddaughter of his brings over a box of pastries and that's it. You're not like that, and more important, you have too many people who care about you, so if you're worried about being alone in your old age, I'd forget about it. They'd have to put a revolving door over at the home for assisted living." She reached across and placed a hand under my chin, pulling it toward her and gently kissing me. "There, now go home and go to bed."

Watching her get out and walk up to her tiny house, I made sure she was at the door before lowering the window so she could look back at me. "What?"

"I'm making sure Larry isn't here to attack you."

She curtsied with the container of stew.

Driving out of town to the rhythm of blinking caution lights, I couldn't help but think about my daughter and granddaughter so many miles away. I crossed under the overpass to I-25 and pulled into the Maverik gas station. As I filled my tank, I looked up at the moonlight reflecting off the mountains.

I missed my daughter, but I really missed my granddaughter. The last time I'd seen her, Henry had come down from the Rez for a reunion with Cady. When the two of them fell into a lengthy conversation, Lola and I went out for an abbreviated walk with partial carry. It was sunset, and we watched as the Bighorn Mountains turned a raging violet and then a more somber purple before darkening into blackened cutouts.

I pointed. "Mountains."

"Moontins." She reached for them, excited. *"My moontins."*

"Yep, your mountains."

At the pump, I glanced back at the overpass and the inviting on-ramp that led south. I could just hop on the highway and be in Cheyenne in five hours, but I hadn't received any response from my first and only email, so . . .

Hanging up the handle, I looked across the parking lot and could see an animated conversation going on inside the Maverik convenience store: a powerful looking man in hiking pants and a fleece jacket appeared to be arguing with the attendant.

I held a finger up to Dog and started

across the lot, hoping that I could draw this confrontation to a quick close and get back on my way.

When I pushed the door open the man was leaning on the counter and yelling at the attendant in the de rigueur red vest, but he pulled back and stopped at the electronic tone that announced my entrance.

I waited for him to turn around and look at me from under the brim of a North Face cap. "What the hell do you want?"

I glanced at the employee behind the counter. "Is there a problem?"

The customer stepped closer, and I noted he was smaller than me, but not by much, and looked to be in remarkable shape. "I asked you what the hell you wanted."

"Well, first of all, I'd appreciate it if you'd lower your voice and change your tone."

He leaned toward me. "You got some kind of problem?"

"That's what I'm trying to find out." Stepping to the side, I addressed the clerk again. "Is there something going on here?"

He seemed relieved that I was there. "His credit card didn't work, so he came in here, but I tried it and it still didn't go through."

The man pointed at the card machine, the jacket's horsehair zipper pull swaying with the effort. "There's nothing wrong with that card. Run it again."

"I've tried it four times. Do you have another one?"

He threw his hands in the air. "Look pal, I don't know who you are, but I know people around here and the local sheriff is a family friend."

I stood there for a moment, letting that one settle. "Is that so?"

"Yeah, so if you don't want any trouble you should just lay off."

"Really?"

He stepped forward, thrusting his face in mine. "What, are you hard of hearing?"

Carefully opening my jacket, I pulled my badge wallet from my pocket and flipped it open displaying the six-point star for him. "I'm a pretty good friend of the sheriff myself." The color kind of drained from his face as I put the hardware away and hiked my jacket back to incidentally reveal my Colt. "How about you show me some ID so that we can all get acquainted."

"Um . . ." He glanced around, licking his lips, and then pointed at a black, four-door Jeep Wrangler with Colorado plates out by the pumps on the opposite side from mine. "It's in my wallet out on the dash of my car."

Reaching over and taking his credit card

from the attendant, I handed it back and gestured toward the lot. "Well, let's go take a look."

Following him out to the vehicle, he began backpedaling a bit. "So, you're a deputy here in Absaroka County?"

Evidently, he hadn't read the ID card that accompanied my badge very carefully. "Something like that."

Reaching the door, I watched as he took the wallet and pulled out his Colorado driver's license, handing it to me. "Well, I do know the sheriff, I mean, he knows my family."

I read aloud. "Donald Lott?"

"That's not the family name, the family here in Absaroka County, that is."

I looked up at him. "Extepare would be the family name here in-county, and Abarrane Extepare would be your father-in-law?"

He looked surprised and a little confused. "Um, yeah, but how do you know?"

We sipped our Styrofoam cups of coffee as his tank filled, courtesy of the Absaroka County Sheriff's Department fleet credit card. He was embarrassed and not wanting to talk, but that was too bad, because I did. "I spoke with your wife, Jeannie, and she said you weren't driving up until this com-

197

ing weekend."

He watched the numbers go by as the tank filled; anything better than making eye contact with me. "I had a change in schedule."

"And what is it you do, Mr. Lott?"

"IT for Western Banking and Trust down in Denver."

I nodded, proud of having just learned the term. "I can see why you aren't too excited about the sheep business."

For the first time he smiled, placing an expensive-looking hiking boot onto the concrete of the pump island. "Abe told you that?"

"He said you and his daughter were less than excited about the prospect."

The pump stopped, he hung up the handle, and turned to look in my general direction. "You ever work sheep?"

I leaned on the fender of his car and shook my head. "Nope, my family were cattle people, but I think the romance is about the same after you've done it for a couple thousand head."

He turned and laughed. "I'm from Mississippi. I didn't know anything about sheep, but I was trying to impress Jeannie. If I never see another sheep again in my life it'll be too soon."

"Sounds like your wife pretty much feels the same way."

"Maybe worse."

"How about your son?"

He froze up a bit but then peeled the top from the cup of coffee I'd fronted him and took a sip. "Oh, he thinks it's a grand adventure every time he comes up here."

"He and your father-in-law seem close."

He nodded, keeping his nose in the cup. "They are — maybe a little too close."

"Meaning?"

He sipped the coffee some more and then turned to look at me. "Look, Sheriff, I don't know how much you know about what's going on here?"

I lowered my own cup and studied him back. "Enough to know that you tried to hire a good friend of mine or me to kidnap your son."

He expulsed a lungful of air and acted as if I'd hit him. "Now, wait a minute. It wasn't anything like that."

"Then what was it like?"

"Look, I just wanted my son back, and I didn't want it to turn into a big legal hassle, so I was talking to Libby Troon down in Cheyenne and she said that she knew people up here that —"

"And if you don't mind my asking, how

do you know Libby?"

"My bank sometimes finds itself in situations when we need a bail bondsman, and in cases that concern Wyoming, it's often best to have one from in-state, and Liberty Bail Bonds fits the bill. Anyway, I was just venting to her, and she came up with the idea."

"Libby did?"

"Yeah, but I don't want to get her into trouble or anything. She was just trying to help me."

"Why didn't you simply contact my office?"

He dipped a shoulder in a modified shrug. "Jeannie said her family had a history with the sheriff's department up here and that it might not be for the best."

"She also mentioned that you might've had some run-ins with the law?"

"She said that?" He paused for a moment. "Just some stupid stuff from back when I was a kid . . . Good grief."

"But then you were going to try and hire me to kidnap your child?"

He shook his head. "I didn't know it was you. For goodness sake, if I was going to hire somebody for an illegal kidnapping I wouldn't hire the local sheriff. Tell me, is Libby Troon some kind of moron or what?"

"She can be" — I considered my word choice carefully — "eccentric."

"I just wanted to get my son back — you can understand that?"

"I suppose so, but you can't go around kidnapping people and transporting them across state lines, even family — the law has some strong feeling about that kind of thing."

"I know, I know. Look, I apologize, it's just that I found myself in a difficult situation and was trying to find some way of solving the problem and made a few bad choices."

"Okay."

He stood there for a moment more. "You were out there, at the ranch? About the dead shepherd?"

"Yep."

"That's horrible."

"Did you know him?"

"I may have met him once, but I don't remember. Sometimes I'd ride along with the camp tender, Jimenez. I know him, but the others, what with the turnover rate and the few times I saw any of them, are just a blur."

"Any idea why he might've killed himself or somebody might've killed him?"

"You're serious?" He stared at me. "Somebody killed him? You mean actually killed him?"

"It's a potential, and we're duty bound to investigate all possibilities."

"The murder thing I have no idea, but you said maybe suicide?"

"Yep."

He crossed one muscled arm, hugging himself, and looked around, saying the next words carefully. "Well, Abe is kind of hard on those guys sometimes."

"How hard?"

"Look, Sheriff, I don't know how much of this I should be talking about."

"You don't have to talk about any of it."

He sipped the coffee. "He beat on one of the shepherds one time while I was there; practically beat him to death."

"Miguel Hernandez?"

"No, this was years ago. I mean he smacked the guy until he was trying to hide under the wagon and then went around kicking at him. I'd never seen anything like that in my life."

I sipped the last of my coffee and then tossed the cup in the trash can. "I suppose that has something to do with your concerns about your son?"

"Oh, I don't think Abe would ever hurt Liam. It's just . . . He's got a temper, comes from a line of tempers, and that's just not something I'm acquainted with, if you know what I mean."

"Western Banking and Trust doesn't have a bare-knuckle Friday?"

"No, not that it might not be a good idea." He sighed and then tossed the remains of his own cup into the trash. "Will you excuse me for just a moment?"

"Sure."

I watched as he crossed the parking lot to reenter the Maverik and speak with the clerk at length, and then I watched as the two of them laughed. They then shook hands, and he returned to where I stood. "Sorry, just something I needed to do."

"No problem." I watched as he climbed in the Jeep and fired it up. "You still owe the Absaroka County Sheriff's Department forty-three dollars and forty-two cents."

"Oh, shit." He started fumbling for his wallet on the dashboard. "I can write you a check?"

I waved him off. "Just drop it at my office sometime — I'll be interested in how the meeting with your father-in-law goes." I glanced around. "It's getting kind of late. I'm thinking you should maybe grab a motel room rather than drive all the way out there tonight."

He nodded. "I agree."

"Do you need a loan?"

"A broke banker, pretty ridiculous, huh?" He flushed a little. "I think I've got enough cash if I don't need to pay you back to-night."

"That's fine."

He extended a hand. "Sheriff, please don't judge me too harshly from my behavior this evening. I'm a little upset about my son, and sometimes the pressure of all of it just gets to me. Please accept my apology?"

I shook the hand. "Certainly."

He took a last look at me and then pulled the Wrangler into gear. "I just want to see my child, you know?"

With that, he pulled out, making a U-turn and waving at the convenience store at-tendant and then wheeling across the street to the Best Western as I started for my truck and Dog, my eyes drifting back to the pool of light that illuminated the southbound ramp of I-25.

"Yep, I do."

8

"It says I have a message."

Ruby's voice trailed in from the outside office. "Well then, answer it."

"How do I find it?"

"It should be right there on the left."

I studied the screen. "What left?"

She appeared in my doorway. "It is in no way helpful for me to have to come in here and assist you in the simplest tasks." Crossing my office, she turned and looked at the computer. "You don't have a screen saver?"

"That's going to be my next email."

She pointed. "See that little icon down there on the bottom?"

"Which icon?"

"The one that looks like a stamp." Grabbing the thingamajig, she moved it and a little arrow magically appeared. "You just left-click it and it'll open your emails."

"Left-click?"

"The mouse, you left-click the mouse and

it opens your email."

"What if I right-click?"

"Don't."

"Okay."

"Any more questions?"

"Why do they call it a mouse?"

She left without answering, and I moved the thingamajig as she'd instructed, very careful to left-click.

An entirely new screen appeared, and I could see an abbreviated version of my email response boxed in the left-hand corner. I shouted to the outer office. "It worked!"

Ruby's voice came back in response. "We're all so proud of you, Walter."

"What now?"

"Left-click the email you want."

"Right." I did as she said, and the thing grew to encompass the screen so I could now read my daughter's four-word response:

I love you too.

"It worked again!"

"Hallelujah."

"What now?"

There was a moment and then Ruby appeared in my door like the magic arrow, making a beeline for my seat and then grabbing the thingamajig and manipulating it again. "You just hover the curser at the top here and click on the arrow facing this direction and then type your response."

"What if I click the arrow that goes in the other direction?"

"Don't."

"Right."

She left, and I stared at the screen, composed a response and a request before placing my two middle fingers over the keys. When I was finished, I called out again. "How do you send it?"

There was another pause, and then she appeared once more, walked to my side, and pushed my hands away. "See the little paper airplane up here in the left-hand corner? You just click on that, and it sends the email."

"Paper airplane, that's clever." She stared at me. "Left-click?"

"Always left-click, until otherwise notified."

"Right."

Ruby disappeared, and I sent my email, feeling very proud of myself. "Hey, that wasn't so bad." There was a ding, and I looked at the screen. "I got another email!"

There was no response, and I carefully

left-clicked the box and was rewarded with a magnificent photo of my daughter and granddaughter sitting in the back of a hay wagon, Cady looking to the side with her striking profile and Lola looking straight at me with those deep-souled eyes.

I remembered taking that photograph.

"Wow."

Another face appeared in my doorway, and Saizarbitoria glanced around. "Is it safe to come in?"

"Safer than it is out there." I gestured toward the computer, my new pal. "Hey, I can do emails."

"That's great, Boss." He stepped in. "There's a bit of a problem."

"What?"

"Did you go off on some tirade about werewolves with Jon Rupert?"

"The TV idiot?"

"Yes."

"No. I had a tirade on clinical lycanthropy, a condition Jon Rupert couldn't even pronounce much less understand, but that was after they stopped filming."

"Evidently not, because it's being included in the episode they're airing tonight."

"I said 'bullshit,' and they said you can't say that on the air, so I assumed they'd stopped filming."

He sat in my guest chair. "Boss, when was the last time you checked the FCC rulings on profanity? 1964?"

I laced my fingers in my lap. "I might be a little behind the times."

"You can now say the word *shit* on television."

"Even broadcast television?"

"There is no more broadcast television, Boss."

I thought about the TV set back at my cabin that I hadn't turned on in a long while. "I wondered why mine had stopped working."

"Well, they've got you spouting off about the most detailed aspects of clinical lycanthropy — did I say that right?"

"Yep."

"So, they say there's some kind of cover-up going on with the sheriff's department."

"And what are they basing that on?"

"Your knowledge of clinical lycanthropy. Look Boss, I know you, so it doesn't seem strange to me, but most sheriffs wouldn't be able to tell you what clinical lycanthropy is if their lives depended on it." He looked out the window. "What do you want to do about it?"

"Nothing."

He turned back to me. "Nothing?"

I shook my head. "Until Joe Meyer, the state attorney general calls, there really isn't anything to do. They got me talking about a psychiatric condition that has nothing to do with the death of Miguel Hernandez, so if they want to air it, feel free."

"Okay." He shrugged. "Where are we on the Hernandez case anyway?"

"Isaac found mule hair traces on his jeans, which explains how he got up high enough to hang himself."

"So, he used a mule to commit suicide?"

"The mules were tied up when I found them at his camp."

"Oh."

"The mules couldn't have tied themselves."

"So, it's a murder." He stood to go. "Which is why you don't give a crap about this stupid werewolf story on cable television."

"Can you say the word *crap* on television?"

As he departed, he called back. "I'll check on that."

Ruby took his place and held a Post-it out to me. "Abarrane Extepare called and said that his camp tender, Jimenez, was in town getting supplies and that if you wanted to speak with him and not have to drive up the mountain or out to the ranch, it might be a good time to catch him."

"How was Abe's English?"

"Exemplary."

I took the piece of paper with the camp tender's cell number. "Did he say anything about his son-in-law?"

"No, why?"

"I met him at the Maverik station on the way out of town late last night, and he said he was on his way there to collect his son. I just thought he might've mentioned it."

"We don't have enough to do besides keeping tabs on the familial affairs of the broader Extepare family?"

"Hey, Ruby, could you c'mere?"

I gestured toward the photo on my screen. "How do I make that my screen saver?"

She reached across, manipulating the mouse thingamajig and left-clicking the living daylights out of it as two of the most important things in my life expanded on the screen. "How do you want to set the sleep settings?"

"I don't know."

"When do you want the photo to go away?"

I glanced at the two faces, the one looking back at me. "Never."

211

■ ■ ■ ■

I always loved the old SETTINGS FOR YOUR TABLE sign that had stood on the roadway outside the IGA since I was a kid. The giant crossed spoon and fork made shade for Dog who was always happy to go to the grocery store because, as far as he knew, that's where they keep all the ham.

I'd called the number on the phone and left a message for Jimenez. It went straight to voice mail, so I figured he hadn't gotten in range just yet. My supposition was confirmed when I saw an elderly Hispanic man in a do-rag wheeling into the IGA parking lot probably talking to Ruby back at the office on his phone.

I walked toward him as he finished the call. He looked to be about a thousand years old with wrinkles on his wrinkles, but handsome nonetheless even with a prodigious and colorful black eye.

"Howdy."

He cracked open the door of the early eighties Dodge D100 with more rust holes than body. "*Hola, hola,* Sheriff. How you doing?"

"I'm good, how 'bout yourself?"

"Okay, okay." He shut the door behind

212

him and smiled, a striking set of what I assumed were dentures sparkling white in the sunshine. He shook my hand like an irrigation pump. "More work these days, but work is good."

"Agreed." I spotted a bench on the sidewalk in front of the grocery store where we might be able to talk without being overheard. "Let's have a seat over here."

The small man followed, and we sat. "Plenty of snow still up on the mountain, and I am thinking that we will have good spring."

I unzipped my jacket and nudged my hat back. "We already are."

He nodded. *"Sí, sí."*

"Seen any wolves up on the mountain?"

He shook his head. "No, no. I no see no wolves." He smiled again. "You sure you see one and not some dog?"

"Yep, I saw one, but only one." Having passed the pleasantries, I got down to business. "Do you mind if I ask you a few questions about Miguel Hernandez?" He nodded. "How well did you know him?"

"Not too well, not too well. He work for us a couple of years now."

"What was he like?"

"Moody, he was moody man — read too many books."

213

"Do you know if he had any problems here in town with anybody?"

"What kind of problem?"

"I don't know, arguments he might've had, fights or anything?"

He laughed, fingering the discolored swelling around his left eye. "He up on the mountain, who he gonna argue with, the trees?"

"I heard he was in a fight at the Euskadi Bar in town."

"I don't know nothin' about that."

"What about Abarrane, did he ever argue with him?"

He studied me. "They have arguments sometime, sure."

"About what?"

"Money, time, the sheep — same stuff everybody argue about."

"How big were the arguments?" He shrugged, saying nothing. "I was told recently that Abarrane is a little tough on the hired hands."

"Who tell you that?"

"I'm not at liberty to say at the moment."

He stared at me some more. "I work for the man for twenty-three year now — you think I stay with him he not good to me?"

"That's not what I asked, Mr. Jimenez."

He huffed and puffed a bit. "Why you try

214

to blame this on Mr. Extepare?"

"I'm not blaming anyone, but there's a man who's been killed and I'm trying to find out who did that."

"Not Abarrane."

"Then who?"

He stood, smoothing his wool bibs. "I no talk to you no more."

"Begging your pardon, Mr. Jimenez, but we can either have a nice chat here on this bench out in this lovely spring air or we can go over to my office — either way this conversation isn't over until I say it is."

He stood there for a moment and then sat back down. He didn't say anything but crossed his tattooed arms and looked out into the parking lot.

"Thank you." I waited a moment and then continued. "So, am I to understand that Abarrane has a bit of a temper and has physically abused his hired help in the past?"

Begrudgingly, he responded. "Not like you talk."

"Then what?"

"These men, the new ones, they no good, no good. They no want to work. We come there, and the camp all gone to hell and sheep scattered all over the mountain — that no good."

"You mean Miguel Hernandez?"

He gestured openly. "All of them."

"Let's confine ourselves to Hernandez. Did you ever see him arguing with anybody besides Abe?"

"Yes, he argue with everyone — he rather argue than breathe."

"He ever argue with you?"

"Yes."

"About what?"

His head dropped, but then he looked away. "He sometime stick his nose where it no belong."

"Concerning?"

"I . . . Not at, um . . ." His eyes returned to mine. ". . . liberty to say."

I let that one sit for a spell. "Is it true that he was hurting himself, cutting his arms with a knife?"

He nodded his head and looked away. "Sí, sí."

"Just one more question." He continued to study the parking lot as I leaned forward, examining his face. "How did you get that black eye?"

"If you can throw together a couple of sandwiches for me too, that'd be great."

Ronnie, the deli guy, started cutting the meat on the slicer and looked up at me. "Nobody cuts ham this thick, Sheriff." He

216

grinned. "What are you doing, feeding a wolf?"

"Watch what you're doing before you lose a thumb."

He finished wrapping up the pound of ham and then went about making my sandwich. "Horseradish?"

"Absolutely."

Knowing my habits, he reached back and grabbed a bag of salt and vinegar chips and an iced tea, depositing them in a white paper bag, and then began making the next one. "Philly hoagie?"

"How did you guess?"

He chin pointed. "She's standing behind you."

I turned to find my undersheriff. "Howdy."

She cracked open a Diet Coke I was sure she had purloined from the cooler. "Hey. Any luck?"

"The camp tender said there was another herder up on the mountain range, Jacques Arriett, and that there had been some problems between Hernandez and Arriett and that I might want to go speak with him."

"How do we find him?"

I patted the breast pocket of my shirt. "I have a map Jimenez drew for me."

She sipped her soda. "So, we're going on

217

a picnic?"

"A jug of wine and thou . . ."

Ronnie nodded at Vic and held up some peppers. "Hot and sweet?"

"Yeah, just like me."

She leaned against the glass and looked up. "Anything else?"

"Jimenez was sporting a beauty of a black eye."

"That's the camp tender, right?"

"Yep."

"Who clipped him?"

"He kind of intimated it was the other herder, Arriett."

"Basque?"

"French-Basque, the genuine article. Think we should get Sancho to go with or instead of us?"

She made a face. "Why does he get to do all the cool stuff? Besides, he's got an abandoned vehicle, a lost dog, and somebody stole one of the CLEAR CREEK TRAIL signs."

"Spring is officially upon us."

Ronnie winked at Vic and then handed me the entirety. "You can pay here — save you time at the checkout line."

"Deal." I handed him some bills, took my change, and we started out through the automatic doors. Figuring that since I had

Dog we'd travel in my truck, I made my way and climbed in as the beast gave up riding shotgun and jumped onto the backseat. Vic climbed in and buckled up.

"Where's the infamous shotgun?"

"I gave it to Jimenez to give back to Abarrane since Lucian didn't want it."

She nodded. "So, what's the story on all the animosity between cattlemen and sheepmen?"

I started my truck and backed out, took a right, and headed out of town. "Transhumance."

"Is that some kind of LGBTQ thing?"

"I don't think so." Settling in, we raced across the foothills and then began the long climb crisscrossing the canyon that leads to the high country. "It's a type of herding that goes back to the old-world methods of pastoral migration, moving large herds of sheep from the lowland plains to the mountains where there's enough grass to fatten the herds."

"So, what was the problem?"

I gestured out the window. "It's not easy to explain but private land ownership and fences to make it simple. The old style called for vast areas where sometimes thousands of sheep grazed across the checkerboard of public and private land. There was always and maybe still is competition between the cattlemen and the sheep owners for that grass. You add the homesteaders into the pot, and you historically get trouble."

"So, it was all about grass?"

"Some, but I suspect there was a little more to it than that."

"What?"

"Bigotry. Most cattlemen and cowboys were white, while most shepherds were Hispanic, Mexican, Native, or Basque. The cattlemen looked down on the sheepmen — they saw them as meek individuals who didn't have the gumption to seek independence like the cowboys had, and both cattlemen and sheepmen looked down on the homesteaders."

"That's stupid."

"I'm not saying it wasn't, but you have to remember that period of the American West was a time of great racial identification and suspicion of different peoples."

"Was it really violent?"

"In 1903, the Sheep Shooters, a group of antisheep cattlemen, tallied between eight thousand and ten thousand sheep killed on the open range. Hell, hooded riders used clubs to kill thousands of them here in Wyoming and Montana."

"When did all that foolishness stop?"

"World War I, when we all got the Germans as a mutual enemy. It's still a difficult business to be in. The sheep industry has bottomed out in many ways. There are fewer sheep in this country than there were two hundred years ago and only a tenth of the number that there were in the forties. There are now a little over five million sheep, mostly located on land that can't support cows."

"Who has the most sheep?"

"China, with about a hundred and forty million."

"How come we're not getting shepherds from China?"

"Good question."

She sat up as I turned right onto the gravel roadway. "Where, exactly, are we going?"

"The road at Hunter Corral and the access path on the other side of Paradise Guest Ranch."

"So, the other side of paradise." She lodged her boots on the dash as she always did. "Sounds good to me."

Clay Miller, the head ramrod at Paradise Guest Ranch, said we were free to use their road to the park where Extepare had one of his herds, and he even invited us to lunch — I had held up my white paper bag.

221

He cocked his stained cowboy hat back on his head and nodded. "Arriett's up in that North Park section, but he comes in here every week or so."

"For what?"

"Wine — he's French after all."

I nodded and started my truck as Clay squinted an eye at me. "So, what are we doing about this wolf problem?"

Playing into the old joke, I made something up. "I think the Game and Fish are capturing them, neutering them, and then releasing them."

"They do understand that the problem is the wolves eating the sheep and not screwing them, right?"

"Have a nice day, Clay."

Laughing, he pulled back from my window and waved us through the open gate. "Don't get bit."

Bouncing along the dirt road, we entered the tree line and watched as the forest closed around us. There was a small amount of snow on the ground where the drifts had been, but it was obvious that winter was in recession, and before long the brimming reservoirs would be sending the life-giving water down the mountain to the pastures and irrigation ditches below.

"I love it up here."

222

I turned to look at her. "Really?"

"There aren't any people."

"Oh." I waited a moment before adding. "You know I have a cabin up here."

She turned to look at me. "What?"

"A private lease with the Forest Service that my family has had since 1904."

"Where?"

I gestured in a vague direction. "Oh, back that way."

"And you never told me about it?"

"Its formal name is Ranch 34 of the National Order of Cowboy Rangers — a fraternal order of cowboys that started up before the turn of the century whose *lodges* were referred to as *ranches,* and the one here in Absaroka County was my family cabin, Ranch 34. Back before World War I, these groups were mostly organized to provide life insurance and burial rates, but the NOCR was infamous for one more thing."

"What's that?"

"Stealing the body of William Frederick Cody, aka Buffalo Bill."

She turned in the seat to stare at me. "What?"

"January 10, 1917, Buffalo Bill Cody died of kidney failure in Denver, Colorado, and for four months lay in state until they could

223

blast enough ground away to bury him at the top of Lookout Mountain, there near Denver. The American Legion and other groups in Wyoming responded by joining together in a reward for the return of the body to Cody, Wyoming, which resulted in the state of Colorado placing the body under armed guard until it could be interred under four feet of concrete in June of that same year."

"So, Wyoming and Colorado fought over the body?"

"Yep."

"And this National Order of Cowboys and Indians . . ."

This time I said it a little more forcibly. "National Order of Cowboy Rangers."

"They went down and tried to steal the body?"

"Yep."

"But they didn't?"

"There's a lot of conjecture on that."

"But Buffalo Bill is buried on Lookout Mountain in Colorado, right?"

I drove along in a modicum of silence. "I don't know, is he?"

She continued to study me. "Oh, you fucker." After a moment, she slumped back in her seat. "I want to see this cabin."

I nodded. "If I can remember the combination."

"Then you can tell me the rest of the story." She pointed to the ridge in the wide meadow. "Sheep."

Sure enough, there was a broad band of off-white at the ridge, so I wheeled up the dirt road and slowly bumped our way to the location about a half-mile distant.

The sheep wagon was backed into the trees at the very top of the ridge, which provided viewing access to both sides of the vast field of what would become green grass. Pulling my truck up a respectful distance, I parked and we both got out. I didn't see any dogs or livestock other than the sheep, so I allowed Dog the luxury of stretching all four of his legs.

The beast jumped out and trotted toward the wagon, choosing a chocked wheel to lift a leg.

There were about a hundred head milling about, looking for new grass and bathing in the warmth of the spring sun, as I knocked on the door of the wagon. "Jacques Arriett, are you home?"

There was no response.

Walking around the wagon, I could see where a horse or mule had been tied up in the shade, but the water bucket was still half-full and the stake line hung limp to the ground. "He must be out on his mount."

"Rounding up wine?"

"Maybe." I looked around but couldn't see any sign of the man. I smiled. "I guess we could've called ahead."

"Uh huh." She knocked on the door again. "You think he hung himself too?"

"I hope not, and just for the record I don't think Miguel Hernandez hung himself either." Glancing toward a copse of aspens near the wagon, I walked over and ran my hand over the trunks, studying the signs and images that had been freshly carved in the tender bark.

"And this breakthrough in the big case is based on what?"

Pulling out a small notepad from my jacket, I drew a pencil from my pocket and quickly sketched the images as best I could. "Mule hair on the inside of Hernandez's pants."

"That means somebody could've used a mule to hang him."

I continued to study the symbols. "And the mules were tied up when we found his camp."

"Holy shit, you're right."

"I guess I'd be more worried if this Jacques guy's mule or horse were here."

Folding her arms, she leaned against the

wagon. "Walt, why the hell would someone be running around killing shepherds?"

I took in the entire area but could see no sign of Arriett. Finally folding my field notepad closed, I turned to look at her. "I wish I knew."

The place hadn't changed much since the last time I'd seen it almost fifteen years ago. Some of the footers on the front porch were starting to rot along with the exposed rafter ends and the purlins. The old asphalt roof was missing a few tiles, but the tarpaper underneath appeared to be holding up, at least until I could get inside.

Feeling along the top of the doorframe, I finally found the old commercial-style key. I turned to see Vic leaning against the railing looking through the grove of quaking aspens to the beaver pond below. "This is beautiful."

"Not bad, huh?"

"Why do you never come up here?"

I looked around, taking a deep breath and slowly letting it out. "Strong associations with my grandfather." I turned back toward the door, hoping that Tom Groneberg, the manager of my familial properties, hadn't changed the lock.

Luckily the key turned like I'd been here

only days before.

Standing there in the doorway, I inhaled the old air that my grandfather had at one time exhaled and my feet felt frozen to the porch.

"You all right?"

"Um . . ." I glanced inside. "Yep." I took a step. The place looked exactly as I remembered. The room was dominated by an old moss-rock fireplace, barrister bookcases, and old Mission furniture. From where I stood I could see the massive moose mount on the far wall and the old Navajo rug that covered the floor where the weathered leather sofa stretched across the room.

"Hey."

I turned and looked down at her.

"We don't have to go in here if you don't want to."

Turning back, I could see the opening that led to the bedroom and the string of black and white photographs that I knew by heart on the log wall, the closest one of my mother and father standing down near the pond maybe sixty yards away.

There was a noise, a persistent noise, that came rushing at me, and all I could do was stand there and listen as it grew louder. It was like something was calling out to me from a long time ago, something that had to be answered now.

Opening my mouth, I could feel a constriction in my chest and couldn't seem to speak as I turned toward Vic again, who stood just a little away, talking on her cell phone; a miracle in itself that there was service. It took a minute, but I caught my breath and smiled as she hung up and turned to look at me.

"That abandoned vehicle Sancho was going to check on? Well, it belongs to that guy you met the other night."

"Which guy?"

"Abarrane Extepare's son-in-law, Donnie Lott."

9

"Did you check the room?"

"No, I talked to the woman at the front desk who reported the car and then came up here and knocked on the door, but nobody answered."

Pulling the magnetic card from the paper sleeve, I held it in my hand as I rapped on the wooden surface of room 214. "Mr. Lott, it's Walt Longmire, the sheriff." There was no answer, so I knocked again. "Mr. Lott?" I slipped the card through the lock mechanism and pushed the door open wide.

The room was clean, but he'd been here.

The bed had been slept in, and there was a sports duffel sitting on a chair; a laptop on the desk nearby. Taking a few steps farther, I walked into the bathroom and could see that his personal items and a Dopp kit were on the shelf above the sink. He'd taken a shower, a damp towel still hanging over the edge of the tub.

Turning around, I could see Sancho taking a closer look at the nightstand. "Something?"

"A notepad with a local number written on it."

"Mobile phone?"

"Nope."

"We'll have to check if he made any calls through the front."

He gestured toward the desk. "What about the computer?"

"We'll look at it, but only after we're sure he's really missing."

"Want me to phone the number into Ruby and find out who it is?"

"I've got a suspicion, but go ahead."

He got out his cell and followed me as I vacated the room, careful to close the door behind us. Walking down the steps, I stopped at the front desk and spoke with the perky young woman there who was inordinately excited to be in on the crime of the century. "He only paid for the one night?"

She nodded enthusiastically. "Yeah, but that's not unusual. Sometimes people aren't sure what they're doing and then pay for another night. Housekeeping knocked on the door, but there was no answer, so they opened up and saw all the personal items

231

and immediately closed it."

I propped an elbow onto the counter. "When was the last time you saw him?"

"I didn't, but Bobby checked him in last night. I came in at eight this morning, but I never saw him at the breakfast buffet or anything."

"Is Bobby around?"

"No, but I can get him on the phone." She reached for the receiver and dialed. "Normally I don't make much of a fuss, but the car had been there all day and I was getting worried, so I kept calling up to the room and when nobody answered . . ." Her attention returned to the phone. "Bobby, the sheriff is here, and he wants to talk to you."

She handed me the phone. "Hey, Bobby, Walt Longmire. You checked Mr. Lott in last night?"

The voice was young and sounded tired. "Uh huh."

"And what time was that?"

He thought about it. "Late, like after midnight."

"Did you ever hear or see anything of him after that?"

"No, not a peep."

"Okay. Well, if you think of something, could you give me a call?" I handed the phone back to the young woman. "Thanks."

"What are you going to do?"

"Nothing, for now."

"Nothing?"

"Well, he took a shower last night and slept in the bed and all his stuff is still in the room with no sign of foul play or anything else for that matter. His vehicle is still parked outside, so I'm guessing that he'll show up. Maybe he went for a run and turned his ankle or something. We'll check the hospital and the out-clinics and then we'll just keep an eye open."

She seemed disappointed. "That's it?"

"I don't want to put out a full-blown manhunt and call in the bloodhounds and then find out he's eating a sandwich over at the Co-Op."

"We have bloodhounds?"

"One. Well, he's a hound, although I don't think he's into the blood thing." I turned to look at Sancho and started out the door. "C'mon, let's go look at the vehicle." Rounding the building, I spotted the four-door Wrangler parked alongside, which was easy because it was the only vehicle there. "What, they were worried about parking space?"

Sancho smiled. "She's a criminal justice student at Sheridan College."

233

"Oh."

"She says the instructors over there use some of your incidents as case studies."

I pulled up to the black Jeep. "Oh, boy."

The doors were locked, and there was the usual detritus of highway travel — an energy drink in the cup holder, an open bag of cashews, and a map of Durant and the Bighorn Mountain area with a highlighted section that was the Extepare ranch. "I'm assuming that the phone number was the Extepare place?"

"Your assumption would be correct."

I pointed through the glass. "Well, his cell phone is on the center console, so if he made a call he did it from here or returned his phone to the car, although the night manager said he never saw him."

Saizarbitoria nodded toward a door at the middle of the building. "He could've come that way, then the kid would've never seen him."

I gestured toward the dark globes at the corner eaves of the building. "They've got security cameras. Do you want to ask Pepper Anderson in there if we can run through the tapes from last night?"

"Sure."

"You want to loan me your cell phone and dial the Extepare place for me?"

"Sure." He did and then handed me the phone. "It's ringing."

As he walked away, I held the thing to my ear and glanced around at the surrounding area, including the sidewalk that led under the interstate overpass and back toward the center of town.

The phone rang five times and then an answering machine with a prerecorded message asked me to leave a message, so I did. "Abarrane, this is Walt Longmire, and I'd like to speak with you about your son-in-law, Donnie Lott. If you could call me back at the office I'd appreciate it. Thanks."

Hitting the red button, I stood there looking up at the passing vehicles on the highway and then back at the only vehicle in the parking lot, noticing the wallet on the dash where he'd had it last night. "Where did you go, Donnie, my wandering boy?"

"He hasn't heard anything from him?"

Ruby pulled the phone from her ear and looked up at me. "That's what he said, duly noted in the Post-it I just handed you."

"Didn't even know he was coming to get his son?"

"As near as I can tell, no."

"I guess I need to call Colorado."

"I guess you do." She went back to talking

235

on her phone. "No, that would be the predator board you need to talk to . . ."

Entering my office, I sat and hit the space bar on my computer and drew warmth from the two smiling faces on the screen. "How are you guys? Me, I'm doing pretty well. Have I told you about the dead sheepherder? Nope? Well, he hung himself, but then they found mule hairs on his pants —"

"Am I interrupting something?"

I looked up to find Vic staring at me. She sat and glanced at the computer with which I'd just been in conversation. "So, have you finally gone off the proverbial deep end?"

"I'm in the shallows."

"Hell, that's where I live. The son-in-law is missing?"

"As of the moment. I guess I'm calling Colorado, but I got distracted by my computer and we were having a conversation."

"You know they don't talk back, right?"

"I hadn't noticed." Pulling out my Rolodex, I flipped through to Extepare and noted the other number I'd scribbled on the margin. I called it and was rewarded with the voice of Jeannie Lott.

"Hello?"

"Ms. Lott? This is Walt Longmire, the sheriff up here in Absaroka County?"

"Oh, thank God."

"I'm assuming you're aware of the situation?"

"Do you have my husband there with you?"

"Not at this time, but I do have his belongings and a vehicle at a motel here in Durant."

There was a pause as she readjusted the phone and sighed. "What are you talking about?"

"Were you aware he was coming up here last night?"

"Well, he was upset about Liam and said he was going for a hike and left in the Jeep, but when he didn't come back, I had a suspicion he might be heading that way. I've been calling his cell, but there's no answer."

"So, you haven't heard from him since he left?"

"No, and what do you mean by belongings and abandoned vehicle?"

"He appears to be missing." There was a very long pause. "And his phone is in the center console of his car along with his wallet on the dash."

"He never goes anywhere without his phone."

I waited a moment before adding, "It may be that he's just out taking a hike, but with your permission, I'd like to open his vehicle and get his wallet and phone to see if they might help in locating him?"

"Yes, of course."

"Needless to say, if you hear from him, would you give us a call?"

"Certainly, and Sheriff?"

"Yep."

Her voice was low. "Do you know if he's had any interaction with my father or Liam?"

"Not yet, but you will be the first one I will contact." I hung up and looked at my undersheriff. "If Abe doesn't call back soon, I'm going out there."

"Oh, joy. But wait, there's more — two pains in the ass for one."

"What?"

"Ferris Kaplan has arranged a town meeting concerning the wolf problem at the firehouse this evening with the Large Carnivore Response Team." Her expression changed to one of disbelief. "Who knew the Duck Detectives had a Large Carnivore Response Team?"

"That's short notice."

"I think that's the idea, so that they can say they had a public meeting about shooting the wolf without the inherent difficulties of dealing with the public. You know how troublesome they can be."

238

"A wolf?"

"No, the public."

"So, a stealth meeting."

"You got it."

"And we have to attend?"

"Ferris said he would appreciate us being there. You know, strength in numbers?"

"Right."

She studied me. "What's wrong?"

"Nothing." I stood and came around the desk. "You want to call up Ted's Towing and tell them we'll meet them over at the Best Western to haul the vehicle here and then jimmy the Jeep so we can check Lott's stuff?"

"Sure. Then we can go to the clandestine wolf meeting?"

I raised a fist. "The pack."

Ted already had the Jeep open by the time we got there. I signed the receipt for the towing service, handed the clipboard back to the driver, and turned toward the Wrangler in which Vic sat in its driver's seat. She was going through Lott's wallet.

"He's got seven dollars in here."

"Yep, he was running out of money when I met him last night."

She reached for his phone, pulling it from the console and holding it up to her face.

"Eight calls from the wife in Colorado and one local call late last night."

"Extepare?"

"Yeah." She stared at the screen. "Nothing after that." Her eyes came up. "Okay, worst case scenario — he calls ol' Abe, who what, comes out here and gets him? Why?"

"I don't know."

"And then does what with him — shoot, shovel, and shut the fuck up?"

"Leaving his possessions and vehicle at the Best Western — doesn't make for very nuanced criminal activity, does it?"

"No." Placing the phone in a plastic bag and sealing it, she glanced down in the space between the seat and the console where entire universes are devoured. Sliding a hand between, she pulled a business card from the floorboard. "MICKEY SOUTHERN: PERVERT HUNTER?"

"Saizarbitoria mentioned this guy, said he'd been in touch and was coming up from Denver to speak with us about a situation here in-county."

"You think Lott's been in contact with him?"

I stared at the card on my desk. "I'd say it's a good bet."

"So. . . ." She pointed at the card. "This

240

guy hunts perverts?"

"I guess. Sancho said he had a show on the internet or something, outing pedophiles."

"There's no contact information, no email, no phone, nothing." Turning the business card toward her, she studied it and then straightened from it as if it were giving off a bad smell. "Walt, there's only one reason Donnie Lott would be in touch with this guy."

"I know."

"You think he confronted Abe and things went sideways?"

"I don't know."

"This is getting creepy." She took the card and came around my desk, moving me aside with a hip. "Well, let's check out the pervert station, shall we?"

"How do we do that?"

She typed, her fingertips driving the keys almost as hard as I did. "Easy — we just put in 'Mickey Southern: Pervert Hunter' — I'm afraid of what will come up if we just put in 'Pervert Hunter.' " A string of photos appeared on the left of a hooded individual with street scenes in the background and graphics emblazoned across the top that read MICKEY SOUTHERN: PERVERT HUNTER. "Holy crap, this dude is a cottage industry — he's got over fifty episodes of this stuff."

She clicked the thingamajig, and the screen filled with the hooded guy, with a mechanically altered voice, talking about texting with an individual in Denver who thought he was communicating with a fourteen-year-old girl. The quality was rough, and you never saw Mickey Southern's face, which led me to believe that he was the one running the camera. Each episode was about ten minutes in length and showcased the Pervert Hunter confronting pedophiles or suspected pedophiles on the street, in cars, and in a house I assumed he used as bait into which he could lure the targets.

Each episode ended with Southern facing the camera and giving the lowdown on his activities and reporting to authorities the individuals he was outing in the same mechanically altered voice.

Vic stopped the onslaught of episodes and turned to look at me. "Wow."

"Yep, seems dangerous for a private citizen to be doing this kind of thing, not to mention illegal."

"I can't believe somebody hasn't shot the guy."

"Maybe nobody really knows who he is."

She stood, folding her arms, and then reaching down typed in more information. "Obviously, people get in touch with him about situations with predators that they know." Hitting a final keystroke, she gestured with a hand. "His website with a contact email. I guess that's the only way to get in touch with him."

"Understandable. I can see how a man like this might have enemies."

"So, what do you want to do?"

"I want to know if Donnie Lott has been in contact with him and concerning what?"

"In an official capacity?"

"Ours, yep. We've got a missing person, and I want to know what this pervert hunter knows."

She began typing and after a moment sent off a message. "There, but I don't know when we'll hear something — if ever. I don't know what this guy's relationship is with law enforcement, but I didn't see any cops in those videos."

"But he said he contacted authorities to report these predators, right?"

"Right."

"So, to whom did he report them?"

"I can track the provider that's used by the website domain, that I imagine is in Denver, and then give the local police a call

243

to see if they've ever had any contact with this guy."

"Tell them we have reason to believe that this Mickey Southern, if that's his name, has communicated with a missing person and we're tracking all the leads. Also, Sancho said that this Southern guy had been in touch with him — I'm assuming through email — so you might want to see if it's the same email as the website."

She stood there, smiling at me. "You're getting so tech savvy."

"Thanks."

"There's only one problem."

"What's that?"

"It's seven o'clock at night, and Sancho has gone home."

"Oh."

"And we're going to be late for the wolf meeting."

I slumped in my chair. "I forgot about that."

She glanced at the Seth Thomas on my wall. "We're already two minutes late."

Gathering myself, I stood and then walked into the main office where Dog was lying at the top of the steps, taking advantage of the cool metal treads that had resided there since 1909. "I think we should take a wolf to the wolf meeting, don't you?"

She regarded the beast. "He's not really White Fang — more Buck from *Call of the Wild.*"

I shook my head as I followed her down the steps, turned off the lights, and saluted Andrew Carnegie before locking the door behind me. "Do you have the rock?"

"It's Sancho's tonight."

We piled into my truck and drove to the town bypass, approaching the modern firehouse complex at the edge of town.

"You know the difference between fire-fighters and Boy Scouts?"

"What?"

"Boy Scouts have adult supervision." She leaned forward to look at the mammoth amount of parked cars. "Oh shit, there goes the clandestine part of the public meeting."

Wheeling through the crowded lot along-side one of the quasi bypasses in our tiny town, I spied an opening alongside the dumpster, which was close to the building. "I think maybe we should leave Dog in here, just in case anybody gets the idea of shoot-ing him."

"Agreed."

Inside I was confronted by a crowd in the anteroom and what looked to be standing room only in the event area visible through the open doorway. There was a small platform set up at the south end, and I could see Ferris Kaplan standing on it attempting to get people to stop shouting and yelling.

Moving through the logjam at the doorway, I gently shouldered through toward the stage. Ferris looked relieved to see me and gestured for me to step up with the other men from Game and Fish. I gave Vic a hand. She joined us, muttering, "What a clusterfuckectomy."

Ferris raised his hands and tried to hush the crowd, but he failed. I was about to raise my own voice when there was an ear-piercing whistle that literally shook the windows of the meeting room. I turned and could see Vic with the pinkies of both hands at the corners of her mouth.

"Thanks."

"No problem."

Turning back to the hundreds of people who packed the room, I raised my hands. "Folks, if you don't let Ferris speak, then we're not going to know what's really going on. So, if you would, please leave your comments and questions until he gets done, okay?"

The grumbling died down quickly, and I turned to look at the poor, besieged man from Game and Fish who reclaimed his voice. "Ladies and gentlemen, I know you're all pretty concerned about this wolf that's been spotted in the Bighorns, and I just want to assure you that from our knowledge this is a singular wolf that's split off from one of the Yellowstone packs." He took a breath. "We've got some folks here from Wildlife Services that can answer your questions about the wolf better than I can . . ."

"There's more than one up there."

I turned and stared at Les Harris in the bright-orange hunting cap that he always wore, in hopes that he'd pipe down, and he did, which was good because I could feel a pain growing in my side and creeping up into my head.

Vic noticed the look on my face, and her eyes narrowed. "You okay?"

"Yep."

Ferris continued. "This is Jim Towles from Predator Control and he's got some facts for you."

A trim-looking individual wearing the traditional red shirt and green ballcap, Jim Towles raised a hand and the crowd grew quieter. "There have been a number of questionable reports that there are a large number of wolves in the mountains, but with the information we have it looks to be a singular wolf that was fitted with a smart collar and is being monitored by the Forest

Service." Jim turned toward me. "Walt, you've actually seen the wolf, and he was alone, right?"

I nodded, even though my head hurt. "Yep, he's an adult male, older . . ."

"Why didn't you shoot him?"

I turned to look at Harris. "Not my job, Les."

"Not your job to protect the people and property of Absaroka County?"

I stared at him for a moment. "From the number of applicants I've received, there appears to be no end of individuals who want to shoot this wolf . . ."

"But not you."

I continued staring at him. "As you know, Absaroka County and the Bighorn Mountains are predator zones, which means that, like coyotes, anybody can shoot that wolf on sight."

"But not you." Emboldened, he glanced at some of his buddies. "Seems to me you've been gone from the county so much, you don't know what your job is anymore."

I said nothing, but the silence in the oversized room was now palpable.

Towles, sensing that we needed to move on quickly, added, "The wolf may have killed domestic stock and is in the process of being dealt with swiftly, but there are no signs that this is a breeding pair or that there are even any other wolves on the mountain."

"What about the dead sheepherder?"

I turned back to Les. "I don't think that the warden is finished."

"Thank you, Walt." He shook his head. "It would appear that there's been a suicide in the mountains, but the two events are unrelated . . ."

Another man in the crowd asked, "Didn't this wolf eat a guy?"

"No, that appears to have been the result of scavenging and not predation. Analysis shows that the Yellowstone wolves have quite a variety in diet including ungulates, rodents, vegetation —"

"And shepherds," a voice cried out from the crowd.

There was a roiling of laughter as the poor man continued. "Wolves most often hunt in packs, and since this is a singular wolf, he's more likely to take advantage of whatever meals might come his way."

"Like sheep." A different voice.

There was more laughter as the game warden continued. "And domestic livestock, which is why the animal will be swiftly dealt with."

"Dealt with in what way?"

I glanced around and finally spotted

Keasik Cheechoo.

Jim folded his arms and looked at her. "The wolf will be killed."

"By whom?"

Jim glanced at me again, but Ferris stepped forward and spoke. "Well, we've had a number of applicants, but Absaroka County is somewhat unique in that we don't rely on state predator board hunters but rather private individuals within the county with whom we have contracts."

She moved closer. "Why?"

"Well, because it falls to the county commissioners and the predator board to —"

"No, why kill the wolf?"

"Because those are the rules in a predator zone."

She stepped closer, and you had to admire the hutzpah it took to show up at a meeting like this one. "How do you know this wolf killed the sheep?" She held up a sheet of paper. "I've got a report from the wolf conservancy that states the kill was actually by a mountain lion."

The game warden stepped forward, holding out a hand. "Can I see that?"

"No, you may not. It's the only copy I have."

He glanced at Jim and then continued. "Well, I'm not going to respond to an unofficial report that I haven't seen, but I seriously doubt that it's going to counter official, scientific results from the state authorities."

She waved the piece of paper some more. "It also states that the wolf in question is an actual Wyoming wolf and not an Arctic transplant."

Ferris shook his head and then approached the edge of the stage. "The department's position on those *irremotus* wolves is that there were possibly a few back in the nineties but that they've pretty much gone extinct, especially with the introduction of the larger Canadian species. As far as I know, there's no data supporting the existence of those animals here in Wyoming."

She continued to hold the paper up. "And yet, here he is."

"Look, Ms. Cheechoo . . ."

She shook her head and then pulled the paper down, folding it and stuffing it into her down coat pocket. "Game and Fish tranqued and collared this animal, this innocent animal, and now you people are attempting to drive up a witch hunt . . ."

"Ms. Cheechoo, all we're attempting to do is discover the facts and appease all parties that are involved."

"Appease? What about the wolf? What are

251

you doing about his right to live?"

My head was killing me, but I stepped forward. "Jim, in your estimation, how many wolves are in the Bighorn Mountains?"

He glanced around at the packed room for effect. "One, two at the most at any given time."

"Doesn't exactly constitute a pack, does it?"

"No, like I said, we've seen no denning activity or mated pairs in the Bighorns. The singular wolves we've seen are young males that have either been kicked out of their packs or simply moved out in search of a life in a place that no longer exists." He glanced at me. "But from what Walt has told me, this guy is a pretty big boy and old, which means he probably was challenged by another, younger male and driven off from his pack in Yellowstone."

"And we've got a sheriff who's too chickenshit to shoot him." Harris glanced at Vic. "Or maybe he's got other things on his mind."

His words hung there in the air for so long I wasn't even sure he'd said them. Suddenly I was now off the stage and standing in front of him and there were words coming out of my mouth, words I didn't even recognize. There was emotion in the words even though I felt completely removed, and it was like I was watching someone else's life unfolding in front of my disinterested eyes.

"Wow." Vic sat in the truck next to me and readjusted the louvers in the heat vents. "Just, wow . . ."

We sat there quietly until the silence overtook me and I had to ask. "I'm guessing my response was a little over the top?"

"Wow."

"All right."

"Wow." She turned and smiled a wicked little smile. "I have been waiting for that for years."

"Pretty bad, huh?"

She stared at me, more than a little nonplussed. "You don't remember any of it?"

"No. Honestly. It was like a fit."

"It was a fit all right." She blew air from her mouth like a modified steam whistle and shook her head. "I thought you were going to kill him."

I glanced down at my lap and felt the heat from my face and the stillness in my hands finally fading. "Did I touch him?"

"No, but your chin was about an eighth of an inch from the bill of his cap."

"Les is almost as tall as me."

"He wasn't by the time you were finished."

She leaned back in her seat. "Granted, he could've stepped up onto that pile of shit he let go down one of his pant legs by the time you were done with him."

"Did anybody else hear it?"

"Oh, yes." She nodded. "Everybody in the place heard it. By the time you were done, I'm pretty sure everybody in Wyoming heard it."

"Did I threaten him?"

She started to speak and then turned to give me a priceless look of incredulity. "Oh . . . Oh, yes, you most indeed threatened him."

Raising a hand to my face, I rubbed some feeling into it, and felt a twinge from the scar that bisected my eye. "So, I guess I need to find him and apologize?"

"I think we're well beyond the realm of apology."

"Great."

"I didn't even know you knew some of those words." She studied me. "You really don't remember any of it, not a word?"

"No."

She kept her eyes on me for a while more and then quickly changed the subject. "Well, it doesn't look good for Larry."

"Who?"

"Larry the wolf." She reached back and

ruffled the hair behind Dog's ear in species-specific sympathy.

"777M."

"Whatever." She turned back. "Who are the contracted county killers?"

"Heck if I know; of all the scat that is hitting the fan, that particular load of feces is not my problem." Wheeling out of the fireman's complex, I took a left and started south toward the Extepare place. "Do you want me to drop you off at home, or do you want to go see a sheep ranch?"

She pointed south. "I feel I should know where our victims are coming from."

"It's not as exciting as you might think."

"Neither is soccer." She studied the road ahead. "You really think ol' honest Abe has done something drastic to his son-in-law?"

I thought about it. "It's just odd. I mean why wouldn't Extepare just wait for Donnie to come out there in the middle of nowhere to do something rather than leaving the car and personal belongings at the motel?"

"Passion strikes at inopportune moments."

"Yep."

"And then we have the dead shepherd."

"Yep."

"This is all sizing up with Abe as the bad guy."

"Yep."

255

"Is that all you've got to say?"

"Yep."

We made the gravel cutoff that leads underneath the ranch gate and the sign that read EXTEPARE. "Jeez, this place really is out in the middle of nowhere." She leaned forward as we drove on, looking for some signs of life in the sprawl of outbuildings. "And don't say 'yep.'"

Pulling to the left, I circled the empty sheep paddocks and parked in front of the dark house. I figured they were in bed as with all good ranchers, but the ever-present Travelall was missing.

Dog jumped into the front and watched as Vic met me at the steps. She unsnapped the safety strap on her sidearm. "If he comes out with a shotgun, I'm leading his ass."

I reached up and knocked on the wooden screen door, the screening strong enough to hold back a wildebeest. There was no response, so I knocked again.

We waited, and then I saw a light come on to our right. After a moment, Wilhelmina arrived through the living room and unlocked the door, carefully opening it wide.

Slipping off my hat, I leaned in. "Wil, it's Walt Longmire."

Pulling her nightgown tighter around her

256

neck, she peered up at me. "Who?"

"The sheriff."

"Is there something wrong?"

"We're looking for Abe — is he around?"

She glanced back toward the bedroom. "He's in bed."

"Can we speak with him?"

Her tired eyes came back to me. "He's awful worn out."

"I'm sure he is, but I still need to speak with him, if I could?"

She stared at me for a moment more and then turned and disappeared as Vic leaned against the other side of the door. "She gonna go get the shotgun?"

It seemed to take an inordinate amount of time, but Wilhelmina, now wearing a bathrobe, finally came to the door again and looked up at me. "I can't find him."

"You mean in bed?"

"Yes."

"Is there some other place he might be?"

"I don't know." She glanced around. "Is it lambing season?"

"I don't think so."

"I get confused."

"Yes, ma'am."

"He sometimes sleeps in the lambing shed during lambing season."

I nodded and reached out and placed my

257

hand on hers to calm her. "Mrs. Extepare, have you seen Liam?"

Her face brightened. "Liam, he's my grandson."

"Yes, ma'am, have you seen him?"

"He sleeps with us."

"Is he with you now?" She began looking around, so I specified. "In your bed — is Liam in your bed now?"

Without another word, she turned and trundled off only to return a few moments later. "He's not there either."

Vic and I looked at each other. "So, both Liam and Abe are missing?"

Wilhelmina's eyes tightened. "Abe is missing?"

I glanced at Vic again and sighed. "Mrs. Extepare, do you mind if I use your phone?"

10

"So, I hear you almost pounded the living crap out of Les Harris last night at the wolf meeting."

I snugged the receiver a little closer to my ear. "And where did you hear that?"

The Basquo laughed. "Oh, pretty much everywhere, but mostly from his wife, who came in here to lodge a formal complaint."

"Sarah."

"Yeah, that's her." There was a pause. "Say, isn't he the one that dropped an elk out of season over in Washakie County last year?"

"Yep."

"Probably trying to feed that wife of his. Boy, she was pissed, Boss."

Sighing, I turned and watched Vic and Wilhelmina playing cribbage. "Well, in the meantime, run the plates on Abe's International and get them out to the highway patrol in adjacent counties."

"Will do."

I hung up the old rotary dial phone and smiled at myself. "How's the game going?"

"She's cheating."

Wil looked up. "I am not. She just doesn't know the rules."

Vic accepted another card and smiled. "Evidently the rules change west of the Mississippi."

I sat in the empty chair. "Mrs. Extepare, are you sure you don't know where Abe and Liam might've gone?"

"Hah!" She moved her peg, displaying some more cards for Vic's benefit. "They go fishing."

I glanced up at the old wall clock, a tarnished starburst model from the seventies that indicated it was creeping up on midnight along with the next century. "Kind of late for fishing."

Chuckling to herself, she drew another card. "They like to get an early start."

I sighed and took a cookie from the plate on the table — oatmeal raisin, one of my favorites. "Where do they go fishing, Wil?"

She waved a hand. "Down south, near one of the sheep camps."

"Powder River?"

She studied her cards. "Uh huh."

Realizing we'd be searching an area

roughly 19,500 square miles, I attempted to narrow the field. "North Fork?"

"Nope." She hooted, laid down more cards, and advanced her peg on the antler board. "No fish up there."

"Middle Fork then?"

"Yes, but they go all over." She glanced at me. "Do you like fish?"

"Um, sure."

"I don't — tastes fishy to me."

Realizing she wasn't joking, Vic and I shared a look. "Right."

"Don't like the bones either."

"Wil, as much as I hate breaking up the game, I'm afraid that Vic and I are going to have to be going." She looked crestfallen, but I continued. "So, you don't have any idea where they might be, or any way to get in touch with them?"

"No."

"And you haven't seen Donnie either?"

"Who?"

"Donnie, your son-in-law."

"No." She took a cookie for herself. "He's a good boy, our Donnie. He brings me pecan log rolls from the Howard Johnson."

"But you haven't seen him recently?"

She glanced at me, confused. "Howard Johnson?"

"No. Donnie, your son-in-law."

"He's a good boy."

"Yep." I stood. "Wil, have you got somebody who comes and stops by when the boys are out fishing?"

She nodded, still munching on the cookie. "Mrs. Reynolds, the hired woman, she'll be here at eight. I don't like having people in my home." She snuck a peek at Vic. "Unless they play cribbage."

We whistled south on the highway at an even hundred. Vic glanced out the window at the darkness, intermittently broken by my revolving blue lights. "So, do we call Double Tough and get him out of bed?"

"Nah, let him sleep."

She reached back and petted Dog. "What, he needs the shut-eye?"

I shook my head at the bad joke. "Powder Junction is only ten miles ahead, and I figure as crazy as that ol' Basquo is, he wasn't likely to navigate the canyon at night with his grandson in that old Travelall."

"Great place to hide a body."

"With the kid in the car?"

She shook her head. "Doesn't make much sense, does it?"

"None of this does."

She numbered off a finger. "One, we've got a dead shepherd, Miguel Hernandez,

262

who was killed."

"Possibly killed."

"Who tied up the mule then?"

"He hangs himself and the mule wanders off as mules have a habit of doing and goes back to the wagon where his buddy is and some Good Samaritan ties him off."

"The fuck." She studied me, more than a little incredulous. "Nobody would've come forward with that information after all the stuff that's been in the press?"

I veered into the passing lane with lights and siren at full force and effect and then swept back into the right-hand side of the road. "Mountain folk are different."

"Can we at least agree that the shepherd in question is dead?"

I shrugged.

Another finger came up. "Next, we have a missing father from Colorado who is related to the rancher who employed the shepherd."

I shrugged again.

Another finger came up. "The same rancher who has a habit of surreptitiously running off with his grandson."

I shrugged yet again.

"From a family who is known to take target practice on law enforcement."

Tired of shrugging, I grunted.

"None of this looks good for ol' Abe. I

mean the dad had a card from the perv-hunter in his car, and the granddad has a history of running off with the kid. Anyway, I'm thinking the shepherd found out about ol' Abe and got whacked and then the son-in-law found out about it and got whacked."

"That's a lot of whacking for an old man."

"Hell, I'm expecting Larry the wolf to get whacked by ol' Abe at any minute." She slipped a cookie from her duty jacket and began gnawing on it before splitting it in two and handing half back to Dog, who sat with his head hanging between the front seats. "So, what do we do when we find them?"

"Separate them and bring in child services."

"That doesn't help us with the missing father."

I studied the road ahead. "So, we think the father is dead?"

"We haven't found him. Where the hell could he be?"

"It's a big county."

"He's dead, Walt. Like you always say, 'Buried in a shallow grave and shit off a cliff by a coyote.' "

"If he is then, whoever killed him doesn't care if we know it — as a matter of fact they might as well be advertising the fact by leaving his car, never mind his personal items all over the motel room."

"Meaning?"

"They're desperate."

"Who's desperate?"

"Good question, but whoever it is it makes them even more dangerous."

I took the exit at Powder Junction and was surprised to see one of our vehicles parked at the base of the ramp along with a Wyoming Highway Patrol cruiser on the other side. Pulling to a stop between them, I rolled down my window and glanced at Double Tough. "What, are you guys having a convention?"

He got out and came over, leaning on my door. "Saizarbitoria called in, so I got up and came over." He gestured with his chin toward Scott Kirkman, the HP currently assigned to Absaroka County, who now fully occupied Vic's window. Double Tough's wayward glass eye looked a little skyward. "Scott was passing through when the call came in, so we took up a post in town but then decided to come up — been here for about an hour, but so far, nothing."

Reaching in behind my seat, he swiped at Dog's nose, who reciprocated by grabbing his hand and holding it. "All right." I leaned forward and nodded. "We'll head up the

Middle Fork and see if we can spot that old International parked at any of the access trail heads." I looked back at DT. "You guys stick it out here."

He tried pushing off but couldn't move. "Roger that."

"We'll eventually take the main road up to Hazelton and then double back off the mountain into Durant. If you don't hear from us in a couple of hours, we've spotted them and parked, so somebody come in and back us up."

"You're sure he's on the Middle Fork?"

"It's what his wife, Wilhelmina, said . . . well, sort of."

DT glanced over the top of my truck toward the Bighorns. "Still a lot of snow up there."

Vic interrupted. "And?"

"Lot of runoff from the snow melt — the fish are going to be fighting for their lives in that current and you'd need a beacon on your fly to get 'em to bite."

She glanced back at me. "Translation?"

"It's doubtful that they're fishing."

"Right."

Turning back to Double Tough, I nodded. "Anything else?"

He smiled his goofy, lopsided smile, and I could still see the fire damage on his face.

"Could you have Dog let go of my hand before you drive off?"

Vic leaned back in her seat as we made the turn and headed west. "The color of DT's eye still looks fucked up."

"Vic."

"What?" She glanced out the window. "So, Middle Fork?"

"Pretty much."

"I would've thought ol' Abe would've had more imagination than that."

"There's good fishing down here when the water isn't like a tsunami."

"So, other than to hide — why here?"

"Sometimes that thing a man is looking for when he goes fishing is fish, sometimes not."

Trailing red dust in the darkness behind us for a few miles, we rounded a number of curves and hit a straightaway before slowing at the first turnout where a metallic-green International Travelall was parked near a scrabble field with only a minimal piece of footpath visible, leading down into the howling darkness of a gaping canyon.

Vic turned and looked at me. "You've got to be kidding."

Aiming my spotlight, I played it across the vehicle and then the rim and into the darkness, so vast it swallowed the light. "Outlaw Cave Canyon."

"Well, you'd have to be an outlaw to want to go down there in the dark." She pulled out her cell phone, looked at it, and then held it up and out the window in a futile search for a signal. "Nothing."

I nodded, turning my spotlight back and switching it off. "The actual cave is on up, not too far from where the old Smith cabin used to be."

"Smith."

"I know, imaginative, huh?" We climbed out with Dog, and I met her at Abe's vehicle. I aimed the Maglite inside but didn't see anyone.

"So, who were the outlaws?"

"Nobody knows. Some say Butch Cassidy and the Sundance Kid, but there's no irrefutable proof as to who was actually there, just some old rawhide beds and a few broken sticks of furniture."

"And that's the Hole-in-the-Wall?"

"Not exactly."

She walked to the edge and looked down as Dog sniffed around the International. "So where is the Hole-in-the-Wall?"

"Some say it's an opening in the Red Rocks a little north of here and some say it's just a small depression on the rim out on Willow Creek Ranch where the gang used to run stolen cattle."

"Which one do you say it is?"

Joining her at the rim, I looked into the darkness along with her. "The one on the backlot at 20th Century Fox."

She extended a hand. "Gimme the flashlight, smart-ass."

"Why?"

"I'm going down there."

I folded my arms, knowing how fast her hands were. "Not without me, you're not."

She gestured toward the slope. "What is that, about a mile down, and then a mile back up? You're in no shape to do that." I didn't move, and she unsnapped her holster, pulling her sidearm and aiming it at my foot. "Gimme the flashlight or I'm shooting you in the foot."

Dog barked and head-butted her.

"No, you won't."

"Walt."

Starting off, I slapped a thigh for Dog to follow and then played the beam on the narrow trail. "C'mon, if you want."

I could hear the water of the Middle Fork down below, that and the breeze that fluttered the new, chartreuse leaves of the cottonwood trees that had just broken free a week ago. The leaves flickered an almost radioactive color green and twirled like a kaleidoscope caught in the light of the flashlight, sending me back to a time when I was a kid, fishing with my father, and was first getting to know this canyon.

"What are you reading, son?"

I lowered my book and looked at him. *"The Outlaw Trail — A History of Butch Cassidy."*

He threw out another graceful cast, one that it seemed to me any trout in the ten-mile length of the Middle Fork of the Powder River would've been happy to lay into, even this early in the season. "The Charles Kelly book?"

"Yes, sir."

He nodded, his gray eyes following the fly as it drifted near the opposite bank on a cool March morning with the melting snow wetter than a well, the hanging droplets clinging to the undersides of the bushes. "Good book. He wrote it when there were still people around who knew the Wild Bunch, primary research material being the best."

"Yes, sir."

"Is that my signed first edition?"

"Yes, sir."

Giving up on the cast, he stripped the five-weight line in and prepared to present

270

another to the finicky fish. "You'll make sure to keep it dry and that it returns to my study undamaged."

"Yes, sir."

Watching the ripples that swept just under the skim ice of the water where the sun reflected like a jewel case, I kept wondering why we were here. I guess because it was uncommonly warm for the time of year and my father had gotten one of his wild hairs and decided we should go fishing. We'd tromped through the snow and broke a trail down to the river, where he stood and I sat, having scraped the snow from a boulder.

He flicked the rod tip forward, but just as he did the wind came up, and carried the Gray Hackle Peacock into the bushes on the other side. "March in Wyoming is a useless month where all you can do is wish the wind would stop blowing." He yanked, but the fly stayed stuck. "Little wonder to me that Spurinna the haruspex warned Caesar of the ides of March." He yanked again, but this time the leader broke, the gossamer line falling to the water without the lure. "Damn."

He pulled another fly from the small wool patch on his vest as I asked about the outlaw. "He never killed anybody?"

"Butch Cassidy?" Sliding his glasses onto

his nose, he slipped the leader's tippet through the eye of a fresh fly, expertly tying a clinch knot and clipping the tag end with a small tool that hung from his vest. "Nope, and he said he never robbed an individual, just banks and railroads that he said had been robbing people for years."

I watched as my father flipped his arm back to a ten o'clock position, the line looping out behind him and then suddenly forward, sending his hand-tied fly across the stream and under a large bush that hung over the fast-moving water.

"But he robbed banks, and banks are where people keep their money."

"I guess he didn't think of it that way." He adjusted, playing in a little and mending the line, keeping the arc upstream. "Anyway, he went to jail for that, but at his parole hearing he promised the judge he'd never rob another bank in Wyoming."

"Did he?"

"No, he went and robbed banks in Utah and Nevada, so I guess he was a man of his word, of sorts."

I glanced around the canyon. "And they used to be here?"

My father nodded his head upstream. "One of their hideouts, a cave, was over there — or so they say."

"Can we go see it?"

He turned toward me. "I thought we were here to fish?"

"We are, but . . ."

"Maybe after we catch a few. We come back to camp empty-handed and that mother of yours is going to think we were just here to take a nap."

"Yes, sir." Dutifully placing his book in my rucksack, I picked up my rod and, pulling a few yards of line from my own reel, draped it out in the water and flipped it forward, rolling the line out about a yard from his.

"Poacher."

Our lines danced to the right in the vibrant water. "Do you think they were bad men?"

He thought about it as he stripped his line in. "Well, it's debatable as to whether Butch killed anybody, but at least three of the others did."

Feeling a tug on my line, I lifted and watched as a twelve-inch brown trout arched and spit my fly back at me. "Darn."

"I've told you, don't pull up to set the hook, go sideways and preferably upstream so the current does some of your work for you."

I moved past him and redirected my cast.

He had pulled his own line in and then threw it, and I watched as the gentle loop played out on the surface of the water, an even larger brown snapping up the fly, my father steadily hauling it in.

I watched as he netted the fish, carefully taking it and slapping its head against a nearby boulder before flipping open his fillet knife, cleaning him out, and placing him on the dampened moss in his willow creel.

"But Butch and Sundance never killed anybody?"

He stood, towering above me. "That's the story."

"So, maybe they weren't such bad guys. Maybe they just rejected the rules of society and wanted to make up their own game."

His voice took a different tone. "They were thieves, Walter. They took things that didn't belong to them, intimidating and harassing people all over this country. The amount of effort they put into stealing and hiding . . . Think what they could have accomplished if they had turned their efforts toward an honest life? Gunned down at forty years of age, they were men of low character and they all met bad ends."

Quietly stripping in my line, I waited and then watched as he moved up the bank.

He turned and looked back at me.

"There's a tendency in our society to romanticize the exploits of outlaws and gangsters, an insistence that they're Robin Hood–type characters, that they have more in common with us than the people whom we hire to protect us and enforce our laws. I don't buy that. I think that when you pick up a gun and use it to take things away from people, it doesn't matter how clever or charming you are — you're just a thief, plain and simple."

I nodded.

He studied me for what seemed like a long while. "You want to go look at that cave?"

"Yes, sir."

He started off as I secured my line and stumbled after him with a hidden smile. "How do you get low character anyway?"

He called back. "By not listening to your father."

"I guess you can't call it daydreaming at night, so are you sleepwalking?"

Surfacing from my memories, I caught myself about to miss a switchback that would've sent me tumbling down a scree field and into the canyon. "I guess."

She watched as Dog went ahead. "See anything?"

"No, but with this heavy tree canopy, they

275

could have a bonfire going down there and we'd never see it. It'll be another quarter of a mile before we get to the tree tops."

She sighed, having stopped at the switchback slightly above me. "If I can't shoot you, can I shoot myself?"

"No. C'mon, this is good exercise."

She started after me. "Drop dead."

Starting to feel the stitch in my side, I mumbled to myself, "I may."

"I heard that."

We finally reached the tree tops but still couldn't see any sign of life other than a group of mule deer Dog must've spooked. Chances were good that if Abarrane and Liam had made it down here before dark, they were holed up in a pup tent somewhere snoozing soundly in their sleeping bags.

I found it hard to believe that Abe was abusing his grandson, and even as inherently dangerous as the family was, I doubted he had killed his son-in-law. I guess I thought I might get answers to some of the questions that had been mounting up, and so I did what I did best in these situations and placed one foot in front of the other.

The canopy gave way to a boulder field, trailing into a rock shelf that ran diagonally down the canyon and tapered back around a cornice where Dog stood looking back at us. I waited as Vic caught up and then continued along the edge until it cut back and the sound of the rushing water filled our ears.

She gestured toward the beast. "You think he knows where they are?"

"More than we do." Zipping my jacket, I cast the beam eastward toward Powder Junction. It was colder down here, a product of the stream's humidity having been ice and snow only days ago.

"Now what? And don't say we should split up and cover more ground, because in the movies that's how people die."

"We should split up."

She made to unholster her sidearm again.

"We don't know which direction they went, but I don't think they could've gone far, so just head down that way a couple hundred yards and if you don't see anything come back."

"And you?"

"Dog and I'll do the same in this direction. Eventually one of us will find them and when we do we just stay put till the other comes back, got it?"

"Who gets the flashlight?" I started to hand it to her when she held up her phone and illuminated the ground in front of her. "Just kidding, Squanto."

Watching her go, I turned upstream and followed Dog toward the mountains. Realizing they could be anywhere, I played the beam up the hillside, figuring that if they made camp they might've made it on higher ground. It would take a hell of a rain to flood the canyon, but stranger things had happened.

Lifting my face, I looked out from under the brim of my hat and was pleasantly surprised to see a few stars in the sky.

The water was roiling and the chances of catching a fish were relatively slim, something Abe would most certainly have been aware of; but maybe, as I had said, he was looking for something beyond fish. I'd been a disappointment to my father, who'd been a maestro with a fly rod, because I always brought one of his books with me and settled in a shady spot to while away the hours as he actively fished, providing the fresh fillets for my mother's cast-iron frying pan.

Food had tasted better then and the air had seemed sweeter, but maybe it was just the memories that made it so. There is no sweetness without loss. What I would give for five minutes to ask all the questions I hadn't and listen to all the answers I'd ignored.

Continuing on, I caught a flash of metal to my right and stepped closer to the stream so that I could shine the flashlight beam toward the water, the light revealing a broken bamboo rod and a maroon South Bend Oren-O-Matic fly reel.

I balanced on a boulder and reached down with my free hand, lifting the tackle up and studying it. It was about the sixties vintage that I would assume Abarrane would carry, fly fishermen being almost as superstitious as ballplayers and cowboys about giving up their worn-out tools.

I glanced around and could see where a large swipe of moss had been scraped away under the surface of the rock where I stood. It was a deep tub, and if you fell here, you were getting wet. Playing the beam around, I hoped that was all that had happened. There was nothing on the opposite bank, so I played the flashlight on the hillside behind me, hoping to see a tent or at least a nest of sleeping bags, but there was still nothing.

I was at a large V with the buttress of the canyon thrusting straight up a good thousand feet toward me, and I was pretty sure this was the spot where my father and I had usually fished. Glancing back over my shoulder, I could see the abutment where a rock formation I knew pretty well stuck out, and the scree pile where the notorious cave was hiding.

I thought about how much effort it would've taken, after falling in, to climb up there. "You crazy old bastard . . ." I whistled for Dog and then carefully laid the rod across the path so that Vic would find it, pointing the tip toward the Outlaw Cave.

The wind was picking up a little, and it felt like a front was moving in, but nothing that would change the weather much other than to raise or lower the temperature some twenty degrees. I could see the vague glimmer from Vic's phone and figured she must've already started back, having found nothing in that direction.

I took another breath and stretched, immediately regretting it, then bowed down to try to make the stabbing pain go away. I placed a hand out on a boulder and found the rhythm of my breathing. Slowly standing, I turned and looked up the slope and could've sworn I saw something move just as Dog barked. Starting after him, I slipped in the scree but found a clearer pathway that led off to the left and steadily rose up to the cave.

I could see a bit of light as if from a dying campfire flickering off the cave's rocky mouth above a few bushes that I didn't remember, which blocked the opening. Funny how things changed in a half-century.

I reached a hand up, grabbed the nearest bush, and pulled myself the rest of the way, taking handfuls as I went like a longshoreman pulling a ship to the wharf. Standing at the opening, I could see that Dog was sniffing around someone lying on a sleeping bag on the other side of the dying campfire.

Huffing my breath in and out, I caught up with myself, took a few steps in, and glanced to the right, seeing a pack, another rod, and some supplies stashed against the wall. It was Abe in the sleeping bag, and I was about to step around the small fire and stoop to him when I heard something in the back of the cave just as Dog growled and bristled. I couldn't see anything even with the flashlight. "Liam?"

Nothing.

Dog barked.

I had the sense that someone or something was there watching me. I rested my hand on my Colt, just in case. "Liam, remember me? I'm the sheriff who came and visited you and your grandfather a couple of days ago at his ranch?"

Nothing.

"Don't worry about Dog, he's friendly."

Nothing.

"Liam, my deputy Sancho gave you a badge — a deputy's star that makes noise."

Nothing.

I'd just about given up when I heard the siren.

Dog barked again but then wagged and moved forward.

I smiled. "That's it, Liam, that's the toy. Remember me? I'm here to help you and your granddad."

There was some movement in the back of the cave, and the young boy stepped out from the shadows. He blew the whistle again and, without another word, walked toward me and Dog, who gave him a broad lick in the face. Liam sat at Abe's feet on the other side of the fire, petted Dog, and breaking green twigs, fed them into the tiny blaze.

I angled to the side. "You need drier wood."

He raised his face to me, shiny with tears in the flickering light.

I nodded. "Don't worry, I'll get some." Glancing at Abe, I lowered my voice. "Is your grandfather asleep?" I waited a moment. "Liam?"

He shook his head, swiping at the tears, and hugged Dog.

11

His pulse was very faint and his skin was frigid, but the tough old buzzard was still alive, if barely. I turned and looked at the boy as he stood against the rock wall, one palm pressed flat against the stone, his arm around Dog. I decided to lie. "He's going to be okay . . ."

Dog barked again, and a light shone in on us from the mouth of the cave. "You find Batman and Robin?"

"Over here."

Vic crossed toward us and, with a glance at the boy, knelt down. "Hi."

He nodded but still said nothing.

Vic felt Abe's pulse and then pried one of his eyelids back before turning to look at me, her own eyes widening before turning to Liam. "Honey, what happened to your grandfather?"

The boy just stood there.

"Did he fall? In the water?"

He nodded.

She leaned forward and, after placing an ear against the old man's chest, glanced back at me, lowering her voice to a whisper. "Severe hypothermia with dysrhythmia."

I sighed. "Yep."

"We've got to get him out of here."

Running the topography through my head, I couldn't think of a single spot where we could possibly land a medevac helicopter.

She interrupted my train of thought. "We're going to need help."

"I can carry him out."

"Are you nuts? There's no way."

"You take Liam and get back up to the rim, drive to where you can get a signal, and get Double Tough and Scott out here — maybe get Casper to send a helicopter and land it at the pullout topside with full setup."

Her laugh was a bitter bark. "And what, you just waltz out of here with him on your back? In your condition?"

"My condition is fine. I'll start out with him and then when you get in touch you can send those guys down to get him. It's not like I'll get very far."

She barely whispered. "And two dead guys are better than one? Why not wait?"

"You felt his skin and listened to his heart, he must have a core body temperature of about seventy-five . . ." I lowered my own voice even more. "The farther I get him the better shot he has at surviving." I gestured toward Liam. "Now, get him out of here. The faster we move, the better."

"We can't risk moving him, he's an eyelash from being dead."

Leaning into her, I gave out with the old ER saying, "They're not dead until they're warm and dead."

She glanced down at Abe, reached out and placed her fingertips at his throat before looking back at me. "I'll go, but only if you promise to just stay here with him, and no carrying him out there in the dark up a cliff."

I nodded.

"Walt . . ."

"Go."

She shook her head and then turned to look at the boy. "Hey, Liam, you wanna take a walk with me?"

He didn't move.

"I've got candy in the truck, and we can go for a ride and drive real fast and blow the siren and flip on the lights. You wanna do that?"

He still didn't move.

"Gotta be better than sitting around watching your grandfather take a nap, huh?"

This time he nodded.

She stood and went to him and reached down to take his hand as Dog followed after them. "We need to get going, what do you say?"

I watched as she led him to the opening and looked back at me, gesturing as if to a dog. "Stay."

Dog sat.

"Take him with you."

"No, I think if you're going to need any backup, he's it."

Dog looked at me, and we listened as the two of them made their way down the scrabble field into the boulders, Vic talking to Liam the whole way.

Pushing on my side, I couldn't feel any pain and figured I had a fighting chance of getting the old man out of there. It wasn't like I had to make it to the top. I just needed to get him as far as I could, or possibly more out into the open where they might be able to lower a gurney.

Looking down at him, I shook my head. "Old man, what were you thinking?"

Listening to Vic's voice as it grew fainter down the canyon, I assessed my situation. I figured the smart thing was to do as she'd said and just stay put; then I heard the little voice that had gotten me in trouble my entire life, telling me that my side wasn't hurting that bad, that Abarrane wasn't that heavy, that the climb out wasn't that steep, that I didn't really need the flashlight.

I told the little voice to shut up.

It didn't. I lumbered to a standing position, stamped out the dying fire, and thought how lucky I was that Abe was a small man.

Taking a deep breath and blowing it out through my lips, I peeled the sleeping bag back and carefully lifted him up against my chest until I could get an arm under his shoulder. Then I crouched down and held the one arm as I lifted him from the ground with Dog watching me. "You know, if you were just a little bigger I'd have you do this."

Taking another deep breath, I shrugged him up a little higher and then stood there testing the weight. He was heavier than I thought, but nothing like other men I'd carried and the conditions were better.

I figured I'd make it.

I took the first step, slid on some rocks, and just stood there for a moment attempting to not second-guess the decision. "So, Abarrane, how 'bout you tell me the story of your life — and just skip the part up until a few hours ago."

I could see through the trees that the sky was still clear and that a sliver of moon had sliced through, giving out with a little more illumination. "Thank heaven for small favors." Dog swept past and took point as I slowly began the descent to the stream below with the unconscious man draped over my shoulder in a fireman's carry.

Having dropped about thirty pounds during my recent adventures in Mexico, I was lighter on my feet, but my energy hadn't fully returned, probably because I hadn't had either the inclination or time for any form of exercise or rehabilitation. Still, what mass I'd lost certainly made it easier on my joints, and I had to admit that I really didn't feel so bad and was almost enjoying stretching the dormant muscles.

It was about then that the stitch in my side spoke up.

Pausing for a second, I took another deep breath and looked ahead to Dog, who was watching me from the next switchback. "I'm okay. Honest."

He waited there until I started off toward him again.

There was still a dull ache from my side, but it didn't feel like somebody was poking me with an icepick, so I allowed my mind to wander back to Henry's potential fishing trip to Alaska. Maybe it wasn't such a bad idea after all. Maybe a vacation was just what I needed to jolt me from my malaise. Then I remembered the more pressing issue involving a high school basketball player and remembered that I hadn't been back to Henry about that.

I followed the white on Dog's tail like it was a flag. "Don't get too far ahead of me now."

I hadn't been to Alaska since the early seventies, and that had been on the very North Slope where I'd provided security for an oversize oil rig. I drank too much then, and a bear had tried to eat both Henry and me.

I wondered if girls high school basketball was really safer.

Stumbling over a brick-sized rock, I caught myself and stood there for a few seconds to get my bearings. We'd made it down from the embankment leading to the cave, and the stream was to my left. The ground was flatter down here, but there was less light, so I just wanted to allow my eyes to adjust. I could pull my Maglite from my belt, but then I wouldn't have a hand free to catch us if we fell.

Taking another step, I tripped over another

rock, so I pulled out the heavy-duty flashlight, and clicked it on, realizing I was now losing any hopes of night vision, not that it was doing any good anyway.

Dog was up the trail getting another drink of water before turning and looking at me again.

"I'm coming."

Assured, he turned and started up the path with me following a little slower this time. I took a few more steps when I noticed that Dog was simply standing in the trail, looking up the long ascent to the pullout. It was strange how he stood without moving, and I figured there had to be something or somebody there — probably more mule deer. The last thing I needed was to be out here in the dark carrying a man and wandering around looking for a lost dog. "Hey, don't even think about it."

In another second, he was gone.

"Dog!" Barking his way up the trail, I listened as the noise echoed off the rock canyon. "Dog!"

He was making good time up the switchbacks, and all I could do was sigh. Maybe he'd heard Vic or Double Tough or the highway patrol pull up at the top and had gone off to meet them. Either way, I needed to get going and shrugged Abe farther up onto my shoulders.

Stepping off again, I made good time and, as near as I could tell, it was just about another quarter of a mile to the top. I had caught my breath and had reached the last scramble before making it topside when the stitch in my side came back with a vengeance. I'm not sure what was going on in there, but it was like something had blown apart and my tires were trying to run flat.

Swallowing, I lowered my head and trudged on, bending my back a little in an attempt to relieve the pain. I dropped the flashlight near the trailhead and watched as it bounced off the rocks and whistled into the darkness with a clattering finality.

I averaged at least one of the things per year.

I took the last few steps into the clearing at roadside, and there was Dog sitting beside the International Travelall, wagging his tail and looking up at the same wolf I'd seen on the mountain, who now sat on the roof of the vehicle, centered in the luggage rack.

"What the hell?"

The wolf turned to regard me but made no other movement.

At second look I could make out a little more detail and could see he was indeed darker than the other specimens I'd encountered but with the gray around his muzzle more evident. Whether it was in comparison with the beast known as Dog, or just being closer, I could see he was even larger than I had thought.

I figured he must've gotten Dog's attention and then realized what he was dealing with and decided that vertical was the better part of valor — but climbing on top of a vehicle? That couldn't be normal behavior for any wolf.

"Howdy."

He didn't move, and neither did I.

"Dog." He turned his head to look at me, but he didn't make any move to abandon his post either. Patting my leg, I called out. "Dog."

Reluctantly, he rose and sidled in my direction.

Mostly because I couldn't hold the weight much longer, I carefully knelt down and pulled Abe from my shoulder, laying him on the ground. I was relieved he was still breathing, but he showed no sign of consciousness.

Glancing up, I could see that 777M was still sitting there, watching the three of us.

Slipping off my jacket, I placed it over Abe in an attempt to make him as comfortable as possible. Having done the best I could, I sat beside the old man and studied the wolf, which studied me in return. "I tell you, Larry, you are one strange animal."

The ears perked a bit, but that was all.

"There's going to be a bunch more like me here in a short time and maybe even a helicopter, so maybe you want to get out of here while the getting is good."

He continued to study me, apparently unconcerned.

"Look, I'm not giving you Abe. First off, he's not dead, and second, you need to get out of the habit of snacking on people. It's bad enough that you ate a sheep, if it was you that did it."

His luminescent eyes never left me.

"What do you want?"

He glanced up the road toward Powder Junction.

"Are they coming?"

Dog barked and started to move back toward the vehicle.

"C'mere, you." He turned to look at me, longing to ignore my command, but then paced over and sat where he'd been. "Stay."

The wolf rose up on all fours and even deigned to stretch but continued keeping his attention toward the road, where I could now see flickers of headlights and hear the angry howl of a siren.

Forcing myself to stand, I reached out and grabbed Dog's collar, holding him fast as my truck's emergency and off-road lights became visible, along with a few other vehicles just behind. They were closing fast, and I could hear the distant but steady thumping of my least favorite form of transportation coming from the south.

When my eyes returned to the top of the International, in that instant, he was gone.

Glancing around, I felt like I was looking for an apparition I'd summoned up. Walking forward, I continued to hold onto Dog. I peered into the bushes around us and up and down the road, but it was as if he'd never been there.

Dog lurched, and I lost my grip on him as he darted around the Travelall and back to me. Dropping his nose to the ground, he circled the vehicle again, swinging his great bucket head side to side in an attempt to pick up the scent.

With another stab of pain I felt a little woozy, so I placed a hand on the International. "You . . . you can't track him?"

He sniffed the ground a few more times and then raised his head and whined — perhaps for the first time in his life.

"It's okay, honest." I petted his broad head

and glanced up the road at the approaching lights, lots of them, and started laughing. I laughed so hard I threw my head back and the next thing I knew I was lying on the ground looking at the left front tire of the Travelall.

Dog was barking and sniffing at my head as I lay there, having difficulty breathing. Dust clouds were broiling up everywhere, and I felt completely disoriented, so much so that I reached out and clung to the tire in hopes that I wouldn't blow away into the canyon.

The engine of the helicopter and the sirens from the vehicles were deafening, but I could hear voices and called out even though I was pretty sure no one could hear me. I felt something blow against my jacket sleeve and released the tire long enough to grab ahold of whatever it was. The noise and wind had died down a bit, so I risked opening one eye. The dirt was still swirling, but I held the paper close and chuckled into the darkness as I read the blue-and-white card in my hand — CASH PRIZES, MALLO CUP PLAY MONEY 5 POINTS.

"Motherfucker."

"Nice to see you too." I raised a hand but found an IV there and so let my hand drop back onto the small, tidy bed. She started to speak again, but I interrupted. "No, wait. I have to say this . . ." Putting on my best most confused and melodramatic voice, I spoke with a dreamy quality. "Where . . . Where am I?"

"Motherfucker." I turned and looked at her, running a hand through the raven hair. "You're at the Ass-Kicking World Finals and you're first in line."

"Abe?"

"Alive, but still unconscious in a drip sedation coma in an attempt to stabilize his body temperature. He's in the ICU of Wyoming Medical Center in Casper, because it was their helicopter." She glared at me. "And you are in Durant Memorial, because I wanted to stab you with a pencil the whole drive back."

"I feel a little sore, now that you mention it."

"Mother. Fucker."

I glanced around the room, noting with relief that she was the only one there. "Where's the doc?"

"He's not talking to you, and he says he's never taking care of you again."

"Uh-oh."

"He's pissed, Walt, just like the rest of us." She leaned back in the chair and shook her head at me like a hanging judge. "Stupid."

"I know."

"Rookie stupid."

"Yep."

"Arrogant stupid."

"Yep."

"Just plain stupid."

I nodded silently.

"Motherfucker."

"Okay, all right, I get it."

"You had an abscess, a dangerous one that set up a wall that wouldn't let the antibiotics get to the infection, and it finally burst."

I felt around on my side and immediately found the source of discomfort. "That's what was hurting?"

She threw her hands in the air. "Who knew it was hurting at all, you asshole?"

"This has pretty much shot you to the top of the office pool, huh."

With hands on hips she bent from the waist, really rearing back for this one. "Motherfucker!"

"So, is this a result of the stab wound in Mexico?"

"Maybe, or possibly some new and cataclysmically stupid shit you may have done since then." She started to turn away but then whipped back. "What if you had died? Lying out there somewhere with Abe-sicle on top of you?"

Sighing, I self-consciously looked around for my hat — it usually made things better. "I knew we had to get him out of the cave and also knew it was going to take a long time hiking down there with a gurney and then hauling him back out — I figured by that time he really would be dead."

"So, once again, two bodies would be better than one?"

"I didn't know I had a problem . . ."

"You've been in pain for weeks, most people take that as a sign that something's wrong, you idiot."

"They'll have to fix it."

"They already have, you moron. Half of it, at least."

"Hmm . . . Is it a nice scar?" I peeked down the neck of my gown, attempting to see the repaired area, but it was heavily bandaged. "Is everybody as angry at me as you?"

"Angrier, but I'm the one who gives a shit about you enough to sit in here for hours to see if you'd wake up. It's obvious to everyone that you don't care whether you live or die, so why should they?"

"Is Liam all right?"

"Yes."

"Dog?"

"Yes, except for Abe maybe, everybody is all right except for you."

"How long have I been out?"

She went over to the window. "All night and most of the morning."

"Any sign of Donnie Lott?"

"No."

"I saw Larry."

Annoyed, she turned back to me. "Who?"

"The wolf. 777M. Larry."

"Get the fuck out of here."

"He was sitting on top of Abarrane's International when I got to the rim."

"You imagined it."

"Dog saw him too."

"Get the fuck out of here."

"Honest."

She reached into the breast pocket of her duty jacket and pulled out the Mallo Cup Play Money card, holding it out to me from the foot of the bed. "And that explains this?"

There was a knock at the door and Henry Standing Bear appeared, his dark hair hanging down at the sides of his face. "I brought you a Whitman's Sampler, but the head nurse took it."

"Very thoughtful."

Vic interrupted. "This is no ordinary wolf."

"No, I don't think most eat Mallo Cups."

"Interesting." The Bear entered the rest of the way, reached over and took the card from Vic before slumping down into the guest chair.

I nodded at him. "Long night?"

"For the owner of the Red Pony Bar and Grill, it is always a long night."

"Uneasy lies the head that wears the crown." I glanced at Vic. "Do you know Sancho quoted Shakespeare to me last night?"

"Taking your job a little seriously, isn't he?"

Henry looked up. "Am I missing something?"

"Saizarbitoria has been approached by some citizens to stand for sheriff."

"Really?"

Vic folded her arms. "Motherfuckers."

The Bear examined the card. "Unlike the other one, this one appears to be relatively worn." His eyes came up to mine. "Where did you find it?"

"It found me as I was hugging the tire of Abarrane Extepare's International trying to keep from blowing into the canyon. And by the way, the wolf was there too."

"The same wolf?"

"Yep, on top of Extepare's car."

Vic leaned her thighs against the foot of

300

my hospital bed as Henry handed the card back to her. "Strange behavior for a wolf, if you ask me."

Henry suppressed a smile. "The more I hear of this wolf, the more I believe that he may be extraordinary."

She tossed the card onto the bed. "You mean other than him popping up all over the Bighorn Mountains?"

"That is not particularly notable in that wolves are known to travel a hundred miles a day or more."

"He's not a ghost, Henry. Dog saw him."

He perked up at that information. "How did Dog react?"

I thought about it. "Strange, he acted strange. He took off after him while we were on the trail and when I got to the top, he was sitting there looking at the wolf as it sat on the car."

"On the car?"

"Right up on the top between the luggage rails."

"Dog was not barking?"

"Not much, no."

"Then he knew this wolf, *if* it was a wolf."

"Well, the wolf didn't seem too concerned about us, it just sat there until Vic and the troops arrived."

"Then what happened?"

"He disappeared."

"How do you mean . . ."

"I looked away for an instant, and when I looked back he was gone." Shaking my head, I added, "Also . . . Dog tracked around the truck twice and never picked up his scent."

"Nothing?"

"Nothing. Now, he's no bloodhound, and it's possible that he was more worried about me . . ."

The Cheyenne Nation reached down and picked up the card again. "Is there a child endangered in this case?" He stood and walked toward the window, but I was sure he wasn't seeing the landscaped scenery there. "Virgil White Buffalo seems to appear when there are ramifications for children, and didn't Libby Troon mention something along those lines?"

"She did."

"I am not saying the wolf is Virgil, but it is possible that this wolf is a totem or messenger animal being used as a mediator between the spiritual forces and temporal beings here in the physical world."

"Well, I don't think we have anything covering that in the Absaroka County Sheriff's handbook."

"What I am saying is that he may be here

to help."

Vic laughed. "He wasn't much help to Miguel Hernandez."

"He is still a wolf."

I sighed. "The better part of a week on this case, and I don't think we're any closer to finding out who killed Hernandez or even if he was murdered."

Vic came around, sat on the bed, and reached through the blanket to pull the toe she sometimes used as target practice. "Maybe Larry tied the mule back up."

I sighed, feeling the only thing I always felt when I was in a hospital, the need to get out. "There's still something odd going on in the Extepare family, and if we can find out what that is, then maybe we can get some traction." I glanced around the room. "Now the important question: where's my hat?"

"No, the important question is . . ." The Bear looked between the two of us. "Who, pray tell, is Larry?"

"How come there's nobody at the office?"

"If by 'nobody' you mean Ruby, it's Saturday night."

"Oh." I sat at the top of the stairs as Henry followed in with the pizza, trying to pretend it was my idea. "Where's Dog?"

"With her." I watched Vic pull a depleted four-pack from the commissary refrigerator. "I guess she decided that if you were going to take him out cavorting with wolves that you weren't a responsible guardian."

"She's probably right."

The Cheyenne Nation handed out paper plates and plasticware and opened the box. "You know, this place takes on completely different environs at night."

"Really?"

He dropped the first slice on my plate. "Yes, much worse."

Sitting my plate on the stoop beside me, I took the can Vic proffered and opened it, taking a deep draught. "I needed that."

Vic examined her slice. "You didn't get anchovies on this, did you?"

"I procured exactly what you ordered." I took another sip before attending the lesser need. "Anyway, how come you get to decide?"

Making use of the oversize canine tooth, she took her first bite. "Because I'm Italian, and you two are heathens who would put pineapple on pizza."

Henry shook his head in mock outrage. "I would never do that."

"So, no sign of Donnie Lott?"

"No." She shrugged. "It's been twenty-

304

four hours, not that that makes any difference. Who talked to his wife yesterday?"

"I did."

"And?"

"She seemed concerned, but in a strange way. She said that he sometimes goes for long runs."

"Twenty-four hours?" She pointed at the slice on my paper plate. "You gonna eat that pizza?"

Knowing her penchant for poaching, I picked up the piece and took a bite. "Where the hell could he be?"

The Bear folded his slice, taking half of it with one bite. "With friends . . . nowhere . . ."

Vic made a face and took another. "What's that supposed to mean?"

"Very few people can completely disappear without help."

"So, you think he has an accomplice?"

"Difficult to say, not knowing his motivation in this situation — is he attempting to retrieve his son, trying to get at Abarrane, something to do with the wife? These affairs of the heart are always the most difficult — or there is the more simplified answer."

"Which is?"

"Dead people are much easier to make disappear, especially in parts." He reached down and picked up another piece. "Slice?"

"Very funny."

"Going back to this wolf, if it is a wolf. Everything has a voice, but you will not hear it unless you listen." He leaned back with one of his wide hands covering his knee. "Human social interaction is more closely akin to that of wolves than to the primates your Darwin saw as our ancestors. We could do worse than to see ourselves affiliated with the master hunter par excellence." He looked up at me. "Virgil White Buffalo was a shaman, but there are older terms such as the *sheven,* or spirit helper, but that description is misleading in that it is sometimes the animal spirit that picks the shaman to embody . . ."

Vic looked doubtful. "Doesn't the person have anything to say about that?"

The Bear shook his head. "Not really. To deny the spirit helper is to invite madness or death." Dropping the piece of pizza on his plate, he looked up at me again, his voice echoing off the high ceiling of the miniature rotunda. "I have another question."

"Go ahead."

"Do you still have the ring that Virgil White Buffalo gave you in the mountains a year or so ago?"

I sat there looking at him. "I do." Reach-

306

ing under my collar, I pulled out the dog-tag chain that held the massive ring, which looked more like a pipe fitting in the reflected light of the old library's entryway fixtures — the turquoise and coral wolves flashing as they chased each other in the silver in a never-ending pursuit.

12

"Liam is in good hands?"

"Child services has him until his mother gets here from Colorado, then I think she's planning on taking him back there. I thought I would see if I could get them to use Dave and Sally Anders; they're good people." Ruby leaned on my doorway, sipped her coffee, and studied me. "Are you thinking what I'm thinking?"

"I don't know. What am I thinking?"

"She doesn't seem overly concerned about her missing husband."

"She seems more concerned with getting her son back, which I suppose is normal." I stared at the black dormant screen on my computer, matching my mood in every aspect. "Any word on Abe?"

"Still unconscious in Casper." She gestured with a Post-it. "You did get a phone message from Clay Miller that a Jacques Arriett was at Paradise Guest Ranch picking up some wine, and Clay can point you to where his camp is on the mountain."

"Well, that's something."

"Who is Jacques Arriett?"

"Another of Abe's shepherds who was probably on the mountain when Hernandez was killed."

"A person of interest."

"For lack of anybody else."

She studied me. "How are you feeling?"

"Fine."

She studied me with her searchlight blues. "Really fine or Walt fine?"

I reached out, tapped the space bar, and watched Cady's and Lola's faces appear. "Somewhere between."

"You're not thinking of going up the mountain, are you?"

"Maybe."

"Walter, the doctors said for you to rest."

"I am resting, besides it's just a ride in my truck. It's not like I'm climbing up there with a pair of crampons and an ice ax."

"One never knows, does one?" She shook her head and disappeared, only to be replaced by the Basquo.

"We have a problem."

"When do we not?"

"ICE."

"What, the refrigerator is broken?"

"Immigration and Customs Enforcement — part of Homeland Security."

Evidently, my funny bone was in need of a little fine-tuning. "What about them?"

"They want Miguel Hernandez."

I leaned back in my chair. "Well, tell them they're going to have to get in line behind the Chilean authorities and the man's family back home."

"You don't understand. They want him alive."

"I'm sure that's what we'd all prefer, but it's a little late for that."

"I'm sure it's pushback from the U.S. embassy in Chile."

"Did you tell them he's dead?"

"The guy I was talking to didn't seem to get it."

I stared at him. "What part of 'dead' did he not seem to get?"

"That they couldn't take Hernandez back to DC and interview him there."

"Well, they're welcome to take him back to DC, but the interview is going to be a disappointment."

"He wanted to talk to my supervisor."

"Your what?"

"Supervisor." He nodded toward my phone. "Line two."

I stared at the red light. "You're kidding."

"I wish I was."

I picked up the receiver and punched the button. "Walt Longmire, Absaroka County Sheriff and Supervisor."

There was fumbling and then someone spoke on what sounded like a speakerphone. "Sheriff, this is Agent Steve Phelps of the Enforcement and Removal Operations."

"I thought you were Immigration and Customs Enforcement?"

"I'm both."

"ERO and ICE?"

"Yes, sir."

"Sounds confusing."

There was a pause. "Sheriff, do you have Miguel Hernandez in custody?"

"In a way."

"Well, we want him."

"Why?"

"Because he's a war criminal."

Of all the things I was expecting to hear, this was not one of them, and I took a moment to reassess. "Excuse me?"

"Alfredo Rafael Anaya is a former agent of the now disbanded Columbian DAS, or Departamento Administrativo de Seguridad. He's wanted back in his home country for countless murders, including three journalists, a sociologist, and his own body-guard."

"Wait a minute, we are talking about a shepherd by the name of Miguel Hernandez, right?"

"An alias that Alfredo's been using for about four years now. We got intel from the attaché in Bogotá and the Human Rights Violators and War Crimes Center — the HRVWCC identified Anaya as being involved with war crimes, persecution, extrajudicial killings, and recruitment of child soldiers."

Vic, ever with her antenna alert, appeared at the other side of the doorway from Saizarbitoria and watched me questioningly.

"How did you connect this Anaya fellow to Hernandez?"

"The Colorado Department of Labor has all their international employees fingerprinted and one of their people pointed out some anomalies in Hernandez's papers, and when they supplied the prints to us, Anaya popped up. With all these human-rights violations the Columbians want him bad."

"When was this?"

"The violations?"

"No, the notification from Colorado."

"About two weeks ago."

"And it took you this long to find him?"

Long pause. "You're not exactly on the beaten path, Sheriff. As I'm to understand it, he was posing as a Chilean national and was a sheepherder in the Montana wilderness?"

"Wyoming." I glanced at Vic, who sat in the chair across from my desk. "Can you send us the information you have on this case?"

"Certainly. Can you hold him till we can get there? We'll start the deportation process here in DC and then take custody of the prisoner within twenty-four hours."

"I can hold him for as long as you want, but you better get in touch with the Chilean consul in that they're pressuring us to return him to them."

"We can take care of that."

"There's just one more detail you should probably be aware of."

"I'm listening."

"He's dead."

"Excuse me?"

"Miguel Hernandez or Alfredo Rafael Anaya or whoever the heck he is. He's dead."

"Dead?"

"As Kelsey's nuts."

"You're sure of that?"

"Pretty sure, yep." I glanced at Vic, who cocked an eyebrow. "We've seen dead out here before."

The longest pause yet. "That's inconvenient."

"Imagine how Hernandez/Anaya felt about it."

"How did he die?"

"Suicide, possible murder."

"Murder?"

"Possibly."

"That's going to complicate things."

"Not for Hernandez/Anaya it's not."

"It is with the Columbian government."

I leaned back in my chair and looked out the window and resigned myself to the thought that the case was about to get a lot more complicated. "So, what do you want to do about this, Agent?"

"I guess we have to come and identify the body and then have the remains shipped to Columbia. Do you have photos, and is the body intact?"

"Besides a general autopsy and a little wolf nibbling, yes."

"Excuse me?"

"I'm sure our medical examiner has photos."

"Can you have those sent to me?"

"My dispatcher or the hospital can. Hold on just a moment." I cupped a hand over the receiver and called out. "Ruby!"

"What's the nearest airport there in Montana?"

I uncovered the receiver. "Wyoming. Gillette, Casper, Sheridan."

"So, our Chilean shepherd was some kind of covert Columbian badass?"

Vic was sitting outside on the bench in the back of the courthouse; she had decided to accompany me in neither the peace nor the quiet as we sat there in the warmth of the early afternoon. "According to the U.S Immigration and Customs Enforcement."

"Homeland Security."

I leaned my head back and nudged my hat up, enjoying the sunshine on my face. "Yep."

"Aren't they supposed to know where the airports are?"

"Evidently they don't know where Wyoming is."

"What are the chances he's one of the assassins that Bidarte hired?"

"It crossed my mind, but why the heck would he be shepherding up in the Bighorn Mountains — pretty deep cover if you ask me."

"Just a thought."

"No, I think it's pretty straight up — he was a war criminal hiding in the farthest region he could find." I shrugged. "If he hadn't been killed, we wouldn't have been made aware of him."

"So, who killed him?"

"That is the sixty-four-thousand-dollar question, now isn't it?"

"Somebody he had a run-in with in his previous life?"

"Possibly, but I don't see a wide range of suspects, besides . . ."

Even with my eyes closed, I could sense hers on me. "Besides what?"

"His literary tastes, what Keasik said about him . . . It just doesn't match with the kind of brutal thug that the agent was describing." Shrugging again, I swiveled my head and looked at my undersheriff. "But I could be wrong."

"Why don't you go home."

"With a murder investigation and a missing-persons case looming?"

"Speaking of, the Lott/Extepare woman is supposed to be here this afternoon to pick up Liam."

"I know, Ruby mentioned it — any idea what her plans are?"

"Nada."

"Ruby also pointed out that she seems somewhat unconcerned about her missing husband."

"She hasn't exactly burned the roads getting up here."

I nodded. "Well, I want to stick around long enough to speak with her, but I was thinking about heading up the mountain to talk with Jacques Arriett, the Basque shepherd who may or may not have had contact with Hernandez."

"Or Anaya?"

"Whichever." I shook my head. "It just doesn't make sense."

"Name me something about this case that does."

I stood and stretched my back, pulling at my abdomen where I now had a spanking new surgical drain and padding, which felt like a sidecar taped to my ribcage. "My side hurts."

She stood facing me, hands on hips. "Good, I hope it keeps you up at night."

"That's not very nice."

"I'm at the top of the office pool."

I nodded and reached out, placing a hand on her shoulder. "Okay, how about you stay here and get an interview out of Jeanie Lott and I take Saizarbitoria and head up the mountain and meet up with the Basquo herder?" She started to interrupt, but I continued. "That way if anything happens, Sancho shoots to the top of the charts and

317

you get off the list."

She thought about it, trying to find a flaw in my logic but failing, in a sense. "On one condition."

"What's that?"

She hugged me gently, avoiding the apparatus taped to my side. "You make it a small altercation."

Turning to walk back into the office, I noticed a familiar Toyota pickup pulling into our parking lot. "Uh-oh . . ."

"Is that the Choo-choo woman?"

"I believe so."

"Good, I wanna talk to her."

"How 'bout I talk to her first?" Catching Vic's arm, I urged her toward the office. "I want to see her response to the latest information on Hernandez/Anaya."

"What, and I'll get in the way?"

"You might punch her, besides I think she'll be more open if I talk to her myself." Horrifically, she couldn't find a fault in that logic either.

"Fine." I got the full hand flap with that one as she made her way up the steps without looking back.

Keasik Cheechoo crossed the parking lot with Gansu and studied me as I leaned against the steel railing and raised my hands. "No wrestling, I've got a new drain

318

in my side."

She stopped, looking concerned. "Was that my fault?"

"No."

She approached but then leaned on the opposite railing. Folding her arms, she looked at me disapprovingly. "What'd you do?"

"You know, I'm really getting tired of being asked that question by all the women in my life, even the ones I barely know."

"Sorry." She smiled. "You looked pretty good last night at the wolf meeting when you threatened to throw that hunter out the window."

"That's what I hear."

"I guess you don't respond like that very often?"

"No."

She continued smiling. "Well, that explains why the whole crowd looked like they didn't know what to do."

I smiled back, happy to change the subject. "Keasik, how much do you know about Miguel Hernandez's history?"

Her smile faded. "What I've told you, why?"

"Santiago, Chile, with a wife and kids?"

"Yes."

Ruby poked her head out from the heavy

glass door and glanced around, spotting me. "Walt, sorry to interrupt, but child services took Liam over to the Anders place on Parmalee Street."

"I thought they lived on Fetterman?"

"They moved; people do."

She disappeared as I turned back to Keasik. "And you got that information about his family life from Hernandez himself?"

Watching Ruby go, she turned back to me. "Why are you asking me these questions?"

"It's a possibility that he's not who he says he was."

"I don't understand."

I pulled the report from my pocket, unfolded the single sheet, and handed it to her. "I got a call from the Immigration and Customs Enforcement folks in DC, and they gave me a report on Mr. Hernandez that doesn't match up with the information you gave."

She studied the piece of paper and then looked at me. "Who is Raphael Anaya?"

"They say it's Hernandez."

She studied the page anew. "This doesn't make any sense — I've seen pictures of his family and even spoken with his wife in Chile."

Stooping down, I smoothed her dog's

320

ears. "Is it possible that he went there after Columbia?"

"He has children."

I straightened and ignored the pain in my side. "How old?"

"Two and three."

"So, he could've had them after escaping."

She looked at the paper again and then back up at me. "This really doesn't make any sense . . . This is not the person I knew."

"The ICE agent seemed to think the fingerprints made the case pretty irrefutable."

She continued reading but then looked at me again, her eyes beginning to well. "This can't be Miguel."

"Well, they're going to be here tomorrow to collect the remains — that is if they can find Wyoming — and I'm sure they're going to want to speak with you."

She straightened. "Why?"

"You knew him, and you were one of the last people to see him before he . . ."

"Was killed."

"Yep."

She handed me back the paper. "How did they become aware of Miguel's existence and whereabouts?"

"Your own Colorado Department of Labor."

She looked stymied. "How?"

"Anomalies in the fingerprints threw a red flag."

"We don't fingerprint people at the Department of Labor."

"Somebody did. Would you mind getting in touch with them and finding out what's going on from their end? And in the meantime, I'd appreciate you talking to Agent Phelps when he arrives tomorrow."

"I can't."

"Why not?"

She turned and looked at her truck, and for a moment I thought she might make a break for it. "I need to get back to Missoula."

"Because?"

"Work, I need to get back for work."

Folding up the paper, I stuffed it into my pocket again and gave her my most suspicious look, which I'm sure was amplified by my nifty new scar. "That's sudden, what about the wolf conservancy and 777M?"

"I need to make a living while saving the world, you know?"

"Well, I'm afraid I'm going to have to ask you to not leave town until you speak with this guy from DC."

"I'm telling you I can't."

"Ms. Cheechoo, we're talking about a homicide investigation here. I'm sure I don't need to impress upon you the importance of acquiring as much evidence as we can about Miguel Hernandez in our attempts to try and bring his killer to justice."

"Look, I understand, but . . ."

"But?"

"I need a shower."

"Excuse me?"

She glanced at the Toyota. "I've been living out of my truck for about a week now, and I need a shower."

"That's what this is all about?"

"I stink."

"I hadn't noticed." As I studied her, she avoided my eyes. "We've got a shower in the jail downstairs."

"I'd rather not."

Reaching for my wallet, I started to pull out some bills. "Seeing as how you're a primary witness, I think the county can —"

"No."

I sighed. "You're not leaving me many options."

"Where do you live?"

"About fifteen miles out of town."

"Is there room to park my truck?"

"Well, there's plenty of room, but . . ."

"When you get through today, I'll follow you out and take a shower at your place, then I can just sleep in my camper."

"I don't think that's such a good idea."

"It'll be a great way to keep track of me till the Immigration people get here, right?" She pushed off toward her vehicle, gesturing for the dog, who gave me one last look and then followed. "I'll be back at five o'clock."

"Um, Ms. Cheechoo . . ."

I watched as she jumped in and pulled out, wheeling into traffic and disappearing as Saizarbitoria came down the steps to peer after her along with me. "So, we're going up the mountain?"

"Sure." I brushed past him. "I could use some air."

Turning the piece of paper in his hands, Sancho attempted to get oriented. "You know, this would be a lot easier if Clay Miller had put a compass reading on here — like something indicating north or south?"

Glancing over as I drove on the Forest Service road, I thought I spotted a geographic marker and pointed. "Is that South Rock Creek, that line there?"

He steadied himself with a hand on the dash. "I thought that was the road we were on." He turned his face back to Dog, who was panting in the back seat. "Can you make it out?"

Not waiting for Dog's response, I ventured an opinion. "I don't think Clay has a future in cartography." Rounding the top of a ridge we both spotted what looked like the opening to one of the larger areas on the left. "There's the park."

"How can you tell?"

"The X beside the squiggly line." He studied what passed for a map as I eased off the road, switched into four-wheel-drive, and continued along in the thick grass toward the gigantic meadow. As we drove, he glanced around, pulling my Bell & Howell binoculars up to his eyes. "So, what happened with Les Harris the other night?"

I sighed. "He got mouthy, so I guess I got mouthy back."

"You guess?"

"I don't particularly remember."

"There are a lot of people talking about it."

"Yeah?"

"Yeah." He lowered the binoculars and pointed. "Top of the ridge along the tree line."

I turned the wheel, diverting my course, and began the long climb across the high pasture before making the ridge and seeing the sheep wagon for myself, along with a hundred head of sheep and a man on a mule, fording the sea of baaing wool to reach us.

Pulling up by the wagon, we waited as he made his way. I held my hand on the door to block Dog. "Let's wait and see how friendly his dog is, okay?"

Glancing around, I took in the breakfast dishes drying in the grass, a clothesline with fluttering garments, and the general detritus that usually accompanies camps in the high country. This wagon was a little worse for wear compared with the one Hernandez had been occupying and even had a wheel jacked up where repairs had been started but had evidently fallen short.

Wandering to my left, I spotted a copse of aspens near the wagon and fresh carvings that bordered on the pornographic.

Sancho joined me, looking at the impromptu artwork. "Must get lonely up here, huh?"

I pulled out the drawing I'd made from the tree near Hernandez's camp. "Know much about this stuff?"

"Just what I mentioned before, they're arboglyphs. Kind of a private language among Basque sheepherders and not really meant for public consumption."

I looked at one of the more graphic depictions on one of the nearest trees. "I can see why."

"They're usually around the *kanpo handia,* or main sheep camp." Turning, he raised a hand toward the sheepherder who now approached us trailing behind an Australian shepherd. *"Kaixo!"*

The other Basquo tipped his beret, returned the salute, and continued to approach. *"Euskaraz badakizu?"*

Sancho nodded. *"Bai, bai."*

"Bai ote?" The herder stopped his mule a little ways away and smiled shyly as the dog circled us but kept her distance. *"Nongoa zara?"*

Sancho glanced about. *"Hementxe."*

Suddenly laughing, Arriett glanced at me. "I don't think this young feller is from around these parts, but I know you are, big man. How are you?"

"Good, how are you Mr. Arriett?"

"I'm good, but you don't remember me, huh?"

I studied him and then shook my head. "I'm afraid not."

"You hauled me out of the Century Club for dancing on the bar."

"Oh." I tried to remember. "When was that?"

"Seventeen years ago."

I nodded. "Must've slipped my mind." I gestured toward my truck. "You mind if I let my dog out?"

He leaned forward on the horn of his saddle and peered at Dog. "We got a wolf here, but he looks about as big — sure, go on."

I opened the door, and Dog leapt out, at first standing still but then noticing the Aussie and walking over to it. Arriett's dog dropped down but then bolted away only to turn and look at the brute again.

"She wants to play."

"I'm not sure how good he is at playing."

"She'll teach him." He lowered himself to the ground, and I noticed a single-action .45 on his hip. Seeing me spot it, he shrugged. "Alone up here, I like to have a gun."

"Sensible."

I gauged his height at just over five feet as he placed his hands on his hips and reared back on his heels. "Yep, you're every bit as big as I remember. I hit you one in the chin when you arrested me."

"Did you?"

He laughed. "Yeah, you didn't notice

328

much then either."

"Well, I was younger then."

He glanced at Saizarbitoria. *"Gose?"*

Sancho smiled. "I could eat — what've you got?"

Jacques grinned a dazzling smile, turning it toward me. "Best damn mutton on the mountain, my friends!"

With the adroitness of a trained chef, the Basquo moved around in the wagon's limited space and produced heavy bowls of rich stew with chunks of mutton, green peppers, and potatoes along with homemade bread and thick slabs of Amish butter.

He handed us small, ornate glasses and, pulling a wine bag from beside the door, squeezed us each a serving before tipping his head back and shooting a strong stream into his mouth. Lowering his face, he smiled again and wiped his lips with the back of a tanned hand. "That's the only thing I miss up here, movies. When I get off the mountain I go down to Abarrane's lambing shed, and I stay there. He's got a big-screen TV with a satellite dish that gets every movie in the world. You ever see that *Thunder in the Sun?*"

I swallowed the first spoonful of stew and discovered I was famished, then devoured the bread, all the time thinking about how different this camp was from the last I'd visited. "Nope, can't say I have."

"Worst movie you ever saw; had Jeff Chandler and Susan Hayward in it . . . Story about this Basque wagon train." He began laughing. "Had these Basques jumping out of trees onto the Indians." He glanced at Saizarbitoria. "I recorded it if you want to see it sometime."

"Mr. Arriett, how well did you know Miguel Hernandez?"

He turned his head to look at me, a little annoyed that I'd interrupted. "The Mexican?"

"Chilean, or possibly Columbian."

"Moody man." He studied me. "I heard he killed himself?"

"Possibly, or somebody killed him."

The shepherd nodded. "That's what I heard all right." He glanced toward the sheep. "Lonely life this high."

"So, you think it was suicide?"

He turned to look at me, his eyes extraordinarily dark, like oil stains in his head. "No."

I stopped chewing and took a small sip of the wine, smoky and biting. "Got any theories?"

"Not really, but he was difficult, and it

330

doesn't surprise me."

"The camp tender said the same thing and that he had a habit of sticking his nose in other people's business. Do you have any idea what he might've meant by that?"

"No, he didn't say it to me." Arriett sat on the steps of his wagon and watched as his Aussie continued to try and get Dog to play. "Most don't take this job to get into other people's business, but sometimes it just happens."

"Meaning?"

He motioned toward the bowl in my hand. "You gonna eat that stew?"

"Are you going to answer my questions?"

He took another shot of the wine and ignored me.

Setting the bowl down on the stump he used for a serving table, I reached into my pocket and pulled out the drawing, unfolding it and holding it so he could see it. "Recognize this?"

He ignored me again but then turned and looked at the paper and the few designs. "Mostly it is names and dates, but the pictures are a way of getting past the barrier of language."

Saizarbitoria lowered his spoon. "For communication purposes?"

The shepherd nodded. *"Bai."*

"All the way out here in this godforsaken place?"

Arriett shook his head. "And have you seen God, back there in that place where you live?"

I pointed at one of the designs — the one of the two figures. "What does this mean?"

"Man, child . . . Ancestors, possibly."

I pointed to the one below. "And this, the floral one?"

He glanced at Sancho and then turned back to me. "Wards off evil — it is for protection."

"From what?"

He shrugged. "Who can say?"

I lowered the paper and glanced at it. "I'm not much of an art critic, but the carvings are very good, almost Picassoesque, wouldn't you say?"

He stared at me, unblinking.

I shot a look over my shoulder and held the paper to compare the drawings to the carvings. "Very much like the ones over here on these trees. As a matter of fact . . ." Looking back at him, I picked up my wine and downed it in one gulp. "I'd say they were carved by the same artist, wouldn't you?"

13

"Leaned on him a little heavy, didn't you?"

Driving out of the Hunter Creek cutoff, I watched the ice at the edges of the creek and the frozen shelves that were thawing in the afternoon sun and thought about the substance of things and how the surface changed but the layers were still there. "He wasn't answering my questions, and I seem to have a lot of them lately — more than I do answers." I turned in the seat to look at Sancho. "What was your read on the whole thing?"

"He wasn't nervous, if that's what you're asking."

"No, I could see that, but anything else?"

"No, I mean he spoke English the whole time . . ."

"But his body language, tone?"

The Basquo thought about it. "He actually seemed a little pissed off, not angry that

we were asking questions . . . Something
else."

"How would you categorize it?"

"Like we weren't doing our jobs. You
know, the I-pay-your-salary kind of thing."

"Odd, I thought so too."

"What do you want to do next?"

I buckled my seat belt as he accelerated,
now that we had reached the paved road.
"Get some answers." Looking out the side
window at the scenery, I could tell we were
in a temperate zone, where the aspens
proliferated in the small valley. "Nobody is
answering my questions, and it's not so
much that as it is *how* they're not answering my questions."

"I don't get it."

"En masse, almost as if they're all in it
together."

"Everybody?" He laughed. "Chances of
that are kind of slim, aren't they, Boss?"

Hitting the big loopy-loops as we crested
the ridge and left the national forest, leaning back in the passenger seat of my truck, I
felt antsy and not just because I wasn't driving. "Wanna go through it?"

His eyes twinkled, and he smiled. "Happy
to."

I studied him, thinking about his taking
over as sheriff but then wondered what that

really meant for me on a day-to-day basis. I liked the kid, and maybe it was time to hand over the reins. "We've got a dead shepherd."

"We do."

"Who may or may not be who we think he was." We passed the truck runaway ramp, and my attention was drawn through the main canyon to our small town in the valley below. "We have a missing person, the son-in-law of the man who employs the shepherd and the father of the boy on whom the grandfather is fixated."

"Yes."

"There are rumors of abuse."

"Yes."

"Though warned, the grandfather absconded with the boy after the father went missing, endangering them both."

"And our sheriff."

I shrugged. "There is a woman involved who was in a relationship with the shepherd."

"Yes."

"There is a strange wolf in the mountains."

There was a pause in his response as he continued driving. "Care to explain that particular piece of information's bearing on the case?"

"Not sure yet, but I thought it should be included since he ate part of the victim and he keeps showing up."

Sancho thought about it. "Any idea why he keeps showing up?"

"Nope." I sighed, lowering my window just a touch to let some air in for Dog. "Henry says I'm waiting for a vision, but that I'm not ready."

"A vision?"

"Yep."

"Well, you're the only one who's actually seen him most of the time."

"Meaning?"

"Maybe it is some kind of mystical sign." He glanced at me. "That what you're going to tell the ICE guy when he gets here?"

"Probably not."

Carefully negotiating the switchbacks, he shifted down, allowing the motor to do some of the braking. "I'm not a big believer in that stuff, Boss, but I've got to tell you that, since I started working here, I've come to the conclusion that there might be more to it than I originally thought."

"Well, it's good to keep an open mind."

"It's more than that."

I eyed him. "What?"

"I've been having these dreams. Wolf dreams." He paused but then continued.

"It's strange, but it's like a merry-go-round where these red and blue wolves are chasing each other in a circle."

"A carousel?"

"Yeah."

"Red and blue wolves?"

"Yeah, not real wolves but old wooden ones, and they're just running in circles and going up and down, chasing each other. Not like they're hunting or anything, more like playing."

Pulling at the chain around my neck I unthreaded the massive ring from under my shirt, bringing it over my head and holding it out. "Look like this?"

Slowing my truck, he pulled to the side and reached over, holding the silver ring with the coral and turquoise wolves chasing each other around the band. "Holy shit . . ." His eyes came up to mine. "Where did this come from?"

"When I went after those escaped convicts on the mountain a couple of years ago I found this, and I know it belonged to Virgil White Buffalo because I saw it on him when we had him in custody."

" 'Belonged,' as in past tense?"

"I was hoping to give it back to him." I hedged my response. "Nobody has seen or heard from him since then."

"Just like my dreams." Sancho continued to study the ring. "Wonder what it means?"

He handed it back to me, and I hung it around my neck, stuffing it back under my shirt. "Maybe the Old Cheyenne or Virgil are starting to tune in to you."

He grew silent as he pulled onto the road and started off again, finally going back to the case at hand. "Well, knowing your pattern in these types of investigations, I'm assuming you're going to want to go back and look at the evidence, which includes the card from Mickey Southern, the Pervert Hunter?"

"It had crossed my mind. If this Web guy has evidence of wrongdoing on somebody's part then I'd like to know who and what."

"Vic was on that?"

"She was, and we can also find out what Jeannie Lott had to say."

"Are we calling in search and rescue on the Lott guy?"

"I suppose so — we've seen neither hide nor hair." I thought about it. "I'm also going to want an update on Abarrane. As soon as he's out of that medically induced coma, I'm going to want to talk to him." Reaching back and petting Dog as much for my sake as his, I glanced at the Basquo. "Did I miss anything?"

"That ring is totally weirding me out, Boss."

"She's a piece of work."

I leaned against the dispatcher's counter. "That's your professional opinion?"

Vic turned to Ruby. "Was she a piece of work?"

Ruby looked up at me. "She was a piece of work."

"So, we have a general consensus that she was a piece of work."

My undersheriff sighed. "I don't know where in Fort Collins she lives, but she was dressed to the outdoor nines and had on enough jewelry and makeup to sink the *Andrea Doria*."

"Sounds like the People's Republic of Boulder or Bozangeles up there in Montana."

She groaned at my boorishness. "You're a funny guy, you know that?" Moving to my side, she took a breath before continuing. "There's something more."

"I'm listening."

"She was beat up. I'm not sure when, and she did a good job hiding it with the makeup, but she was beaten at one point, I'm sure of it."

"Did you ask her about it?"

339

"No."

"Then I will." I sat on the lower part of the counter to give my side a rest. "So, where are we?"

"She's got a motel room out on the strip, and the foster folks, the Anders, say she can come by and get Liam at their house this evening. She's going to spend the night and then head back with him in the morning."

"Did she mention her husband?"

"No, but I volunteered the standard information about how people usually turn up and that there's no sign of foul play, blah-blah-blah-blah-blah . . ."

"Did she ask about her father? I mean she'll be driving by the hospital in Casper twice."

"No."

"Odd."

Ruby nodded, continuing to type away on her keyboard. "A piece of work."

"She does want her son back though, right?"

"Yes."

"Well, that's a relief. Any word from Casper on ol' Abe?"

Vic shrugged. "They're unsure of his neurological status, but they've decreased the sedation and are waiting to see if he shows any signs of recovery. He's still on an endotracheal tube and a cardiac monitor along with a Foley catheter."

"So, he's not going anywhere soon." I glanced around the main office in the old Carnegie building as if the high ceilings and marble tread at the top of the steps might hold clues. "Why would he risk his life taking his grandson fishing?"

"Maybe it was a pattern, something they just did."

"Possibly, but that doesn't help me solve the case."

"Which is, remind me?"

"The murder of Miguel Hernandez."

"Maybe the two aren't connected."

"That doesn't help me either."

"Sometimes this shit doesn't tie up like a nice bow on a wrapped package, you know?"

"I'm getting that." I leaned back to my dispatcher. "Any word on search and rescue?"

She stopped typing. "Three rustic young men with struggling beards came by and looked at the vehicle and the evidence and then said they would stop back and check in with you later this afternoon."

I looked at the clock on the wall, which actually did hold clues, at least to what time it was. "It is the afternoon."

"Later this afternoon."

"Anything more from the ICE guy?"

"He found the airport in Sheridan."

"Maybe they're more capable than we thought."

"He will be here tomorrow morning."

"Early or later?"

"He didn't say."

The front door opened, and the three rustic young men with the struggling beards and a lot of Gore-Tex climbed the steps like mountain goats. "Later in the afternoon it appears." They all stopped at the top of the stairs, a little unsure of themselves. "Hi, guys."

"Hey, Sheriff." The lead one extended a hand. "Mike Burgess, I'm the new head of S and R."

"What happened to Colin Ferriman?"

"He got married, and his wife told him he had to quit."

"Oh."

"Can we show you what we've got?"

"Already?"

"Yeah."

I stood. "How about right here on the counter?"

"Sounds good." He pulled out a quad-sheet from under his arm and unrolled it. "Other than being abducted or just strolling down the road, he could've followed Clear

Creek either in or out of town. Now, following west he could've hooked up with the trail and then he's gone into the mountains, but we checked that pretty well. He could, of course, have gone the other way toward Bull Creek and Stockyard Trail, which goes both south and north toward the rodeo grounds and the airport."

"Any signs?"

"Nope, but that was more of a hit-and-run anyway." Burgess looked at the others. "We thought that with the snow skiff there might be prints and we got a pretty good one from the interior of the Jeep, but so far — nothing."

"Okay."

"One more thing?"

"Yep."

"If you decide to auction off the Wrangler, we'd like first dibs."

I stared at him. "Anything else?"

"Nope. We thought we might check Stockyard Trail again just to be sure."

I nodded. "Let me know if you find anything."

He saluted, and they trooped back down the stairs as I turned back to Vic and Ruby. "Think the piece of work would like to sell the Jeep?"

■ ■ ■ ■

"I want to talk to this Mickey Southern fellow."

Vic leaned on my doorjamb and crossed her arms. "Well, he's not responding."

"What about the Denver PD, have they got anything?"

"They say the only contact they've had with him is on the internet, but it's pretty straightforward what he does with this show of his."

"We've written him emails?"

"There's a contact tab on his website that I've sent him messages on four times."

"No address, no phone number?"

"No."

"Any way we can get in touch with the people that run his website and get them to give us some kind of contact information?"

She shook her head. "Given the nature of his outing perverts, I think he's well insulated — you might as well be talking to the trees."

Punching the space bar, I watched as the photo of Cady and Lola reappeared. "I'm about ready to."

She came in and sat in her usual chair and peered around the computer at me. "You know, if all you're going to do is look at that one photo, they have these electronic frames that rotate pictures so you can have more than one."

"Saizarbitoria is having dreams."

She stared at me, cocking her head. "That's nice."

"Wolf dreams."

"And what does this have to do with the case?"

"Nothing, I guess, but the dreams are about red and blue wolves chasing each other on a carousel."

She stared at me some more. "What the fuck, is he on drugs or something?"

"I don't think so, but it sounds remarkably like Virgil's ring, doesn't it?"

She thought about it, puckering her mouth. "I guess — has he seen the ring?"

"Not that I'm aware of, at least not till I showed it to him today."

"That's weird." She scooted the chair over, giving herself a clearer view. "So, what's up with the other shepherd, Jacques Arriett?"

"He was a little antagonistic."

"He's Basque, right?"

"I think it might be more than that." I pulled out the drawings I'd made and handed them to her. "These are remarkably similar to the carvings in the trees that were near Hernandez's camp."

She pulled out her phone and held it up. "You do know that we have these things called cell phones that have these nifty cameras in them?" She put her phone away and studied the drawing. "So?"

"The ones on the other side are from Jacques Arriett's camp."

"Your artwork is improving marvelously, and I think you're ready to draw Winky the Deer from the back of a pack of matches." She flipped the piece of paper on my desk. "I repeat: so?"

"I think Arriett carved both."

"Did you ask him if he'd been to Hernandez's camp?"

"He says he's been all over the mountains."

"That's helpful."

"I intimated that. He also said he's not the only one who does the carvings and that some of them are forty, fifty years old, which is about the lifespan of the aspens."

"But the ones you saw were fresh?"

"I asked him about that too, and he said that all the shepherds do it."

"You think he's trying to hide something?"

"I'm not sure, but it seems like everyone is these days." Leaning back in my chair, I looked at the ceiling. "I asked him about Abe and whether he had a temper, and he said that he wouldn't work for a man who didn't have one; that it showed a lack of passion." I spread my hands. "And what is life without passion?"

Vic reached down, turning the sheet of paper on my desk and studying it. "I'm starting to like this guy more and more." She looked up. "What's the name of the camp tender, the one with the black eye?"

"Jimenez."

"Right." She studied the drawings. "Look, I hate to be a conspiracy theorist, but what if Abe has all these guys working with him and poor Miguel was the odd man out?"

"It's crossed my mind, but what's the motivation?"

"Hernandez found something out and the others zotzed him?"

"Zotzed him?"

"I'm trying to use verbiage from your era. I was bored the other night and watched a gangster double feature, both of them starring John Garfield."

"But what's the motivation for killing Hernandez?"

She leaned back in the chair and crossed her arms. "Well, if ol' Miguel was as big of a walking, talking, Columbian asshole as

347

ICE appears to think he is, then there are all kinds of reasons to blip him off."

"Blip him off?"

"You know, roast his chicken."

"Now you're just making those up."

"Look, anybody that did the things the Immigration and Customs people said this guy did deserved killing. Jeez, Walt, he tortured and murdered people, even his own bodyguard."

"But what does that have to do with shepherds in the Bighorn Mountains?"

"I don't know, maybe he got drunk and mouthed off to the wrong guy and they decided to lend justice a hand."

"So, either Arriett or Jimenez?"

"Or Abe." She leaned in. "Let's not forget that the son-in-law, Donnie, is still missing."

"Now I want to talk to the folks down at the Department of Labor in Colorado."

"I bet they answer their phone."

I started to call for Ruby but then thought better of it. "Can I find the Colorado DOL phone number on the computer?"

She smiled. "Faster than you can roast a chicken."

Vic reappeared in my doorway and listened while I continued my conversation with the lady at the Colorado DOL.

"So what kind of vetting process do these folks go through when they register with the DOL?"

"Department of Labor *and* Employment." The nice woman from the Department of Labor and Employment was having a good time talking to me on the speakerphone, so much so that I got the idea she didn't know many real sheriffs. "Are you the guy from Wyoming that was down in Mexico a few months ago?"

Or then again, maybe she did. "Um, yep, that was me . . ."

She laughed. "I read about you in the papers — you're something of a loose cannon, aren't you?"

Vic smiled at that one, and I cleared my throat. "Not usually."

I listened as she settled herself in. "Well, in answer to your question, we do a cursory interview, but if the individual has a clean working record with no felonies, then they're free to apply with a work visa attached. To be honest, we're not talking about rocket scientists here. Shepherds and agricultural workers like fruit pickers or even cowboys are in such demand at certain times of the year, that if they're breathing and willing to work for ten dollars an hour, then they get in."

"Do you normally fingerprint the applicants?"

"No."

"Then how did Hernandez's end up over at Immigration and Customs pitching red flags like it was a new continent?"

"I really couldn't say unless they were included from his native country."

"I think if Columbia had had those prints they would've never let him leave."

"Possibly." She sighed. "I'm sorry, Sheriff. I know I'm not being very helpful here, but I really don't have many answers for you. Most of our contact with Mr. Hernandez was through the enforcement branch that deals with working conditions, fair labor practices, and injuries."

"And that's where Keasik Cheechoo comes in?"

"She's wonderful, isn't she?"

"I don't know — you tell me."

There was a pause. "Have you had trouble dealing with her?"

"She's very passionate about her work whether it's the Department of Labor," I quickly added, ". . . and Employment, or the welfare of wolves."

"She has lots of causes." The woman took a deep breath and then continued. "She does a marvelous job in the more outlying areas that we really can't police — but I'd imagine you know about that? There's a lot of abuse in the industry, and I'm afraid the poor workers bear the brunt of it."

"Miguel was abused in an earlier case that Ms. Cheechoo mentioned?"

"Oh, it was horrible, maybe one of the worst cases we've ever had. The employer actually beat his employees, didn't pay them, and practically starved Mr. Hernandez to death."

"There was a physical altercation between the two men?"

"From our reports, yes."

"And that was a rancher down there in Colorado?"

"It was, yes. Why, have there been others?"

I shook my head, rested my elbows on the edge of my desk, and glanced up at Sancho. "It just doesn't make sense."

"Excuse me?"

I looked down at the piece of paper on my desk. "If Miguel Hernandez is actually this Alfredo Rafael Anaya, it just doesn't add up. Anaya tortured his people, killed them . . . He murdered his own bodyguard. This sounds like a dangerous man, if you ask me. So how does he get to the point where he's getting beaten up by a rancher down there in Colorado and was in another altercation up here where he didn't even raise his hands in defense?"

"Was that another work-related situation?"

"No, it was in a bar, but it still doesn't make sense, does it?"

"No, it doesn't."

"Do you have any idea who could've relayed those prints to Immigration and Customs?"

There was another extended pause. "I wish I did, but they seem to have come out of nowhere. I mean the prints are legitimately in his file, but we have no idea who could've forwarded them to the immigration people."

"Was that done electronically?"

"By email, yes, but it was just our general IP address at the office."

"No way to trace it?"

"I'm afraid not."

"Well, I'll ask the ICE guy about that. In the meantime, can you forward that same file to me here in Wyoming?"

"It's all electronic, so I can send it to you via email."

"No more manila folders, huh?"

I read her the address and bid a fond farewell to the Centennial State. I hung up

352

my phone and looked at my undersheriff. "What's an IP address?"

"Internet protocol. It's assigned to each computer as a formal designation."

"And nobody there can track it down?"

"You can find somebody's location and such, but in an office of that size I'm betting it wouldn't do any good, because they probably have communal computers that a lot of people use. Besides, who cares where the information came from if this guy is a fucking war criminal?"

I stood and stretched, looking at Seth Thomas for some guidance. "It's five o'clock?"

"Yep, and you have a visitor."

"Who?"

Her voice took on an odd innocence. "The Cheechoo woman is out here waiting for you — something about a shower?"

"She needs a hose connection for her camper."

She batted her eyelashes at me. "A hose connection?"

"Um, yep."

"Why doesn't she just go to one of the RV campsites."

"I already suggested that, along with the shower downstairs, but she said no thank you."

"So, she's staying out at your place?"

"She's hooking a hose up to her camper out at my place and then coming back into town is how I understood it."

"You might want to discuss that with her, because she's out here with her blankie and her dog."

"My truck broke down."

I stood on the stairwell with Dog, the previous sheriffs staring at me with grim faces from the 8 × 10 frames on the wall. "Then maybe you should get a motel room instead?"

"I don't have the money."

I fished in my pocket for my wallet again. "Well, how about we treat this as a ministerial aid and the county loans you enough to get a room?"

"I don't want charity." She adjusted the Tibetan *dharma-chakra* hat, the tassels swaying. "Besides, Gansu doesn't like motels — she tends to bark."

Vic stood at the top of the steps looking down at me, obviously enjoying herself.

"Hey, you've got a shower, don't you?"

She folded her arms and smiled. "Broken."

"Your shower is broken?"

"Yeah."

I took a look at the toes of my boots and

then back to her. "Since when?"

"Yesterday."

"Yesterday."

"Yeah." She gestured toward the office at large. "Besides, I've got the Rock."

I turned back to the wolf woman. "Look, Ms. Cheechoo . . ."

She glanced at Vic and then back to me. "C'mon, Sheriff, give a working girl a break? I'll sleep on your sofa."

"He doesn't have a sofa."

Keasik glanced up at her. "Really?" About that time the phone rang at Ruby's desk and Vic disappeared to answer it. "I've got nowhere else to go."

I sighed. "All right, but the cots in the holding cells here are really comfortable. I've slept on them more than I have my own bed, of which there is only one, so you're going to be stuck in the recliner my daughter bought me about five years ago."

"Sounds comfy."

Vic reappeared on the steps. "Those goofballs from search and rescue are on the line and say they found something over on the Stockyard Trail — do you want to talk to them before you head out to your little bed and breakfast?"

Frowning, I headed back up the stairs and passed her at the landing. "Your shower is broken my ass." Continuing on, I picked up the receiver and grunted, "I'm assuming it's not a body."

"No."

"What, then?"

"A receipt for gas from over at the Maverik on Route 16. Isn't that the last place you said you saw this Donnie guy?"

I nodded. "Yep."

"Well, the receipt is charged to the county, and I remember you saying you had to pay for his gas?"

"I did."

"Then he must've come this way, because the prevailing wind is in the opposite direction."

"Where are you guys?"

"Out near the parking lot at the fairgrounds, on the trail beside the creek."

I glanced at the two women and decided I was just as happy to have somewhere else to go. "I'll be there in a couple of minutes."

"Any word on the Jeep?"

"Excuse me?"

"Can we put a bid in on his Jeep?"

"We may have to hold off on that for a bit."

I started to hang up but stopped when I heard him say, "Because there's blood on the receipt."

14

"Looked like blood to us."

I lifted the Ziploc bag and peered at the piece of paper, stained with a hole in the middle. "Where, exactly, did you find it?"

He gestured down the trail toward a large sprig of silver sage. "Stuck on that one."

I walked over, knelt down, and pulled out my Maglite. Shining it about, I couldn't see any other clues. "Impaled on one of the dry branches?"

"Yeah."

I handed him the bag. "Do me a favor and run this over to Isaac Bloomfield at the hospital and have him test it, please."

"You sure he's there?"

"He's always there, so get a move on."

"What're you going to do?"

Standing, I looked around at the dying light. "Have a look around."

As I walked with them toward the parking lot, Keasik cracked open the door of my vehicle. "Something?"

"It's a receipt from the other night when I met the man who's disappeared."

"The father of the boy?"

"Yep. Look, I'm wanting to take a walk along this trail and search for myself, so you can catch a ride back into town with the search and rescue guys. I'll pay for a motel room and . . ."

"I'll wait."

I stared at her.

"Honest, I'm fine." She pulled her dog closer in her lap. "We're snug as a couple of bugs in a rug."

I nodded. "Well, I'm going to take one of the bugs with me." Circling around, I opened the driver's side door and released the beast from the back. "C'mon, you."

"Is he a police dog?"

I shrugged. "He's a dog, and I'm the police, so I guess he's the closest thing we've got." I started to close the door but then added, "Not officially, but his nose is better than mine."

"About forty times better." She smiled, accenting the broad cheekbones and wide jaw — too expansive for a typical beauty but in the long run devastatingly good-looking, even if she did need a shower. "Three hundred million olfactory receptors

358

in comparison to our six million. To put it into perspective, we might notice if a spoonful of sugar has been added to our coffee, whereas canines could detect a teaspoon of sugar in a million gallons of water or two Olympic-sized pools."

"That good, huh?" I closed the door and pulled a stocking cap that I'd taken from Lott's Jeep and held it out to Dog, who took it in his mouth. "I don't think that's what you're supposed to do." Taking it back, I held it out again and he sniffed at it and then sat and looked at me. Finally giving up, I stuffed the cap back in my pocket and started for the trail by the creek. "C'mon."

The path was well marked and in good shape even after the winter. A lot of the locals walked or ran on it through the year, so looking for specific tracks really didn't make much sense. Taking Dog out of the truck and expecting him to suddenly become a bloodhound didn't make much sense either, but here I was with the light dying and the cold coming on, standing by a creek with my pal. "So, what do you think?"

He wagged.

"I bet if we were looking for a ham, you'd find it."

As if in response to the insult, he dropped

his head and snuffled around, slowly making his way to the left and away from town, toward the fairgrounds.

Following along behind him, I pulled my Maglite and shined it toward the looming grandstands of the rodeo arena, looking pretty unsettling with nobody in the seats. When I glanced back, Dog had moved farther up the trail and had turned to see if I was following, which I was.

I had to admit that it was good to be out of doors even with the drainage apparatus stuck in my side. Still, what did I think I was doing? Maybe avoiding going home with the strange woman — and why hadn't Vic stepped in and done something to help me out?

Dog turned again and then quickened his pace.

"Hey, don't run off and leave me, okay?"

Ignoring me, he continued on, breaking into a soft trot.

"Hey!" He disappeared around the next bend, and I shouted again. "Hey!

"Hell." Pushing off with a little more urgency, I made the bend in time to see him head toward the back of the grandstands. "Damn it."

I followed up the slight grade as quickly as I could toward the long backside of the rodeo chutes and the tower leading to the announcer's booth. Darting through the open gates, he continued at a quick pace and I lost him.

There was a main gate that I took, allowing me a more direct route to a walkway where the contestants could load into the chutes. Instinctively, I pulled my sidearm and glanced around, finally seeing Dog's hind legs as he shot up the steps. "Dog!"

Hustling to the far end, I found another stairway that connected to the one he'd climbed and hauled myself up to a landing overlooking the arena as some snowflakes blew from the grandstand across the open area; swirling devils that danced and then melted away in the breeze.

Dog barked. He stood by a closed door that led into the announcer's booth.

I hoisted myself up, keeping my Colt to the side, figuring there wasn't any sense in scaring the daylights out of a couple of amorous teenagers who might be looking for an exclusive place to neck.

Dog turned to look at me but stayed close to the door as I played the beam over the glass, still seeing nothing inside. Stuffing the flashlight under my arm, I turned the knob and opened the door, immediately feeling the heat.

Dog darted inside. I traced the beam of the Maglite over the room. There was a counter to my right with scattered papers, clipboards, and other refuse from the summer rodeo season. To my left, a table, a few folding chairs, and the loudspeaker equipment in the far corner, but nothing else.

Other than Dog snuffling around, the only noise was the rhythmical hum of the baseboard heater underneath the counter attached to the front wall. Kneeling down, I placed a hand over it and felt the warmth. Before I turned it off, I looked around for water lines, a sink, or anything else that might require heat during the winter and the fall and spring hip seasons. Seeing nothing, I reached over, dialed the knob down, and turned the thing off, watching the red light diminish and finally go black.

Standing, I turned and leaned on the counter and looked at Dog. "I sure wish you could trade a few of those olfactory receptors for vocal cords and tell me what the hell is going on."

When we got back to the lot by the picnic tables, Vic's unit was parked alongside the passenger side of mine. The windows were down, and the two women were talking.

My undersheriff leaned out as I approached. "Liam is gone."

Walking between the two vehicles, I wrapped an arm around her rearview mirror for support, both physical and psychological. "Gone?"

"Jeannie Lott went to pick Liam up at the foster home, and he was missing."

"Missing?"

"Are you going to keep repeating the last word of my sentences?"

I fumbled for some originality. "What happened?"

"They put the kid in his room to rest before his mother got there, and when they went to get him, he was gone. The entire group is still over at the house with Saizarbitoria, but I thought I better come and get you since you weren't answering your radio, although Keasik finally did and filled me in."

Retreating, I made my way around to the driver's side of my unit. "We'll follow you."

Opening the door, I allowed Dog to jump in the back and then climbed in, firing up the V-10 and spinning the wheel to catch the rapidly disappearing aged unit ahead of me.

"Anything?"

Full lights and siren — I watched as Vic skidded out onto the paved road and floored

363

it, correcting her drift and jetting into town. "The heater was on in the announcer's booth at the rodeo grounds."

She shrugged. "Crime of the century?"

Making the pavement, I too turned and hit the accelerator. "I turned it off to save the county money."

"Thrifty." Bracing a hand against the dash, she reached over and snapped on her seat belt. "That poor little boy . . ."

Weaving right onto the 196 bypass that led south of town, I watched as Vic's brake lights stabbed on and her taillights made a right, stopping just after the lumberyard. She pulled into a driveway that already held another of our units as I slowed and parked at the curb. I climbed out and turned to Keasik. "You stay here."

She saluted as her dog climbed back in her lap. "Okay."

Rushing up the driveway, I noticed a BMW SUV with Colorado plates parked at the curb. I got to the porch where Dave Anders was waiting. "Walt, we have no idea what happened. I took Liam in the back bedroom, because he was falling asleep on the sofa watching TV, and he couldn't have been there for more than ten minutes before his mother came and I went back to get him and he was gone."

"Have you looked through the entire house?"

"We were doing that now."

He led the way into the house, where Sally was trying to comfort a woman who sat on the sofa and was crying, and through a short hallway to a guest bedroom, where Sancho met us coming up from what I assumed was a basement near the kitchen. "Nobody down there, Boss."

Continuing through the house, we ended in the bedroom where Liam had been sleeping where Vic now stood studying the window. She turned and pointed toward the heavily painted molding. "I haven't touched it, but there's no way that kid got out of this window by himself."

Stepping in closer, I could see where the paint had been scraped as the thing had been forced open by somebody. Turning to Dave, I asked, "Does this window open?"

He nodded. "Kind of — with a lot of force you can get it partially up."

Glancing back at Saizarbitoria, I started toward the door. "Continue to go through this house, and if you don't find anything come out and join us."

He was already on his hands and knees looking under the bed as Vic joined me in the hallway. "Circle the vicinity in your unit, and I'll start searching the outside." I stopped and turned back. "And call the Highway Patrol."

Pulling out her cell phone, she passed me as I knelt down in front of the crying woman. "Mrs. Lott?"

She raised her head a bit and sobbed. "You lost my son."

I studied her face and could see the abrasions and bruises beneath the makeup that Vic had noticed. "We're going to find him, Mrs. Lott, but I have to ask you if you have any idea who might've done this?"

She caught her breath and screamed in my face. "You're the one who lost him!"

I studied her for a moment more and then stood, turning toward Sally. "What was he wearing?"

She seemed confused but then answered. "Yellow pajamas with little cowboys and horses all over them."

"No shoes?"

"No, but there was a blanket on the bed, and that's missing too."

"What kind of blanket?"

"Um, fleece, buffalo plaid, red and black."

I walked quickly to the door and called out the description to Vic, who was standing on the sidewalk talking to the Highway Patrol.

I pulled my Maglite and continued to the back of the house, working my way around a hedgerow that jutted out from the building. I could see that the window was easily accessible from ground level. Shining the beam under the hedges and then in the tree, I finally stepped toward the window but could see no prints or any other sign that told me if the boy had been taken through there.

Edging in closer, I finally saw an indentation in the wood at the bottom, about the width of a screwdriver or tire iron.

Reaching up to the top of the frame, I pushed and watched as the window popped open about an inch and in the next instant, Sancho was there looking at me, weapon in hand. "Here?"

"Here." I turned away, looking at the trailer court to my right and the bypass road and highway to my left, watching an 18-wheeler blast down I-25, headed south. Scanning the ground with my flashlight, I still couldn't see any prints but started thinking about carrying a child wrapped in a blanket with no shoes — how far you could go and who would it be that the child would let do such a thing without making any noise?

Turning back to the window I pushed it

up the rest of the way as Sancho reappeared from the hallway. "Something?"

"Who was at our offices last?"

He thought about it. "Probably Vic. After we got the call from search and rescue, she closed up shop, but then got the call on the missing kid."

"Came and got me and then straight here?"

"Far as I know."

"Do me a favor, head back and see if Donnie Lott's Jeep is still in our parking lot. I think he's been hiding out at the rodeo grounds — the heat was on in the announcer's room."

"Why there?"

"He came up here to get his son and for some reason I spooked him, but now I'm betting he's got Liam, and if they're in that Jeep then I'm not sure where they are, but it could be pretty far from here."

He dashed into the house, and I played the beam of the flashlight toward the road and the bypass, stepped over a short picket fence and down the barrow ditch to a pull-off. The ground was hard, and I couldn't see any tracks until I shone the beam farther back, where a set of tires with an aggressive tread seemed to have pulled over and sat.

Not proof positive, but it was a hunch.

368

I walked back to the road and, turning left toward the rear of my truck, thought about it. Why would Donnie go to such lengths to steal his own child? Even if his father-in-law hadn't been in the Casper hospital, he had every right to the child, so why not just come and take him? Was there something more going on in the family, or were there players I wasn't even aware of?

Keasik was still sitting in my truck as I walked by the window, Vic rushing over, breathless. "Anything?"

"Nothing . . . Liam must've known his abductor and gone with him willingly."

"So, you think this guy stole his own kid? But why?"

"I don't know, but if that Jeep is gone, I'll start knowing a lot more."

Static. "Unit one, this is unit three."

Vic slung the handheld to her face. "S'up?"

Static. "The Jeep is still here. Still parked. Still locked."

"Tell him thanks for blowing my theory."

She keyed the mic. "You blow." She looked up at me. "Shorthand." The tarnished gold sharpened like molten metal, and she glanced around. "Now what?"

"The old-fashioned way, I guess."

"Door to door?"

"For lack of anything else." I gestured toward the radio in her hand. "Tell Sancho to stay there for ten minutes, I'm sending over a visitor."

She nodded, and I went back to my truck. "Hey, it's looking more and more like I'm not going to make it home tonight, so your options are this truck or our offices. I sleep there all the time, and the shower downstairs has hot water that'll take the first three layers of your skin off, honest."

She stared at me, the chin held up a little in defiance before she lowered it and shrugged. "How will I get over there?"

"You remember the way?"

"I can use my phone. It's a small town."

"Take the truck, I'll hitch a ride with Vic, if I need one." Pulling the keys from my pocket, I handed them to her and flipped the driver's seat forward to allow Dog to escape into the yard, where he immediately began sniffing.

Scooting her own dog to the floor, she climbed over the center console, and settled herself in the driver's seat, adjusting it forward. "Jeez, daddy longlegs."

She fired it up, and I shut the door, stepping back and watching her go.

"You do realize you just gave a complete stranger your truck and access to the entire sheriff's department."

Dog sat on my foot and looked up at me as I reached down and ruffled an ear. "She seems trustworthy."

Vic rolled her eyes. "I'll take the other side of the road."

Watching her head across the street, I called out, "I'm going to have a quick chat with Jeannie Lott first."

"Fine."

My voice followed after her. "Why is it I get this side?"

"Because that way you get the trailer park."

"So, you've had absolutely no contact with your husband since he came up here?"

The woman composed herself, dabbing her eyes with one of the tissues that Sally Anders had provided. "Well, not really. I mean there were texts that he'd gotten here saying he'd gotten a motel room because it was late . . ."

"But nothing after that?"

"No." She stood and walked away from me and toward the front window, looking out at the flashing lights that intermittently lit up the neighborhood. "Look, I just want my son back."

"We're doing our best." I followed her.

371

"How about your father, anything from him?"

She continued looking out the window with her back to me. "No, we don't talk much."

"I'm assuming you didn't stop and see him in Casper on your way up?"

"No." She turned and looked at me. "Sheriff, I'm not sure you understand how alienated my family is from one another."

"I guess not, but I'm starting to get an idea. Do you mind if I ask what the source of all this animosity might be?"

She turned and walked to the sofa and leaned back, glancing around at the empty room. "I'd rather not."

"I'd rather you did."

"I don't think you realize just how difficult this is for me . . ." She studied my face for a moment. "Are you charging me with something, because otherwise I don't see it as being any of your business."

"Ms. Lott, I've got all my deputies and most of the northern Wyoming law enforcement community out there looking for your husband and child, so I think I'm due something of an explanation as to why they might be missing."

Suddenly gripping her hands into fists, she screamed in my face. "You need to do your job and find my family!"

I waited a moment before answering. "I'm trying, Ms. Lott, but you're not making it any easier for me."

She screamed again. "It's not my responsibility to make it easier for you — just find my husband and child!"

I stood there for a moment longer and then went into the kitchen, where I found the Anderses and Dog, who was bumming a piece of bread from Dave. "Walt, I don't know what to say . . ."

"Don't say anything — it's not your fault. If anybody it's me that should be blamed. I put you in a position that was untenable. I should've known that somebody was looking to abduct Liam and it's certainly not your fault."

Sally looked up at me with tears in her eyes. "Thank you."

Squeezing her shoulder, I smiled. "We'll find him."

I glanced at Jeannie Lott as I passed through the living room, but she pointedly avoided making eye contact with me, so I continued out the front door with Dog.

Who, what, where, and why?

I didn't have an answer to any of the W's.

"Walt!" I looked up to see Vic crossing the street. "Third door, and we might've caught a break." She gestured for me to meet and follow as she slowed. "The old guy across the street says he saw a vehicle cruising the neighborhood a couple of times and thought it was weird, so he was going to grab out his license catalog and look it up." She gestured for me to hurry. "License catalog, what the hell is that all about?"

Hustling as best I could, I caught up with her as Dog shot ahead. "Back in the day, the fraternal organizations — the Elks, Moose, and Lions clubs — used to sell these little yellow booklets that had the county plates referenced with everybody's name, address, and phone numbers — they used to sell them off the counters at the gas stations."

"You're kidding."

"Nope."

"A booklet for sale that had everybody in the county's plate numbers and personal information?"

"Crazy, huh?"

"Fucking-A."

We strode up the driveway to the porch door just as an elderly gentleman appeared thumbing through one such booklet. "Hello, youngsters."

I didn't know him, but that didn't mean he didn't know me, and I was momentarily charmed by the fact that there were entire cavalcades of people in my community with whom I never had any interaction in an official sense. "Mister?"

"Kling, Jack Kling." He reached down and petted the beast. "I think I've got him, pretty low number, so I had to keep going back to the front to cross-reference."

Vic folded her arms. "If you give us the number, Mr. Kling, we can have dispatch get us all that information in a few moments."

Adjusting his glasses, he peered into the now illegal booklet. "Oh, but what's the fun in that?"

"Mr. Kling, a boy's whereabouts . . ."

"Here it is. Low number all right, 24-387."

The number sounded familiar. "Who?"

He thumbed through a few more pages as Vic yanked the handheld from her belt. "Fuck me running through the forest." She clicked the toggle. "Base, I've got a plate number that I need run. It's Absaroka 387?"

Static. "Roger that. Hey, I'm assuming it's okay to let the Cheechoo woman camp out here and have a shower since she's driving the Boss's truck?"

"Whatever, we're here to serve and protect and promote personal hygiene."

Kling pinpointed a page with a fingertip. "Here it is. Now I've got the address I can find the name."

"Mr. Kling, if you give us the address, we can have —"

"Just one more second, young man." He lifted the finger and immediately lost his place. "Damn." Thumbing through a few pages again, he found it and then moved to cross-reference.

Vic raised the walkie-talkie to her mouth. "Base?"

Static. "Hold on, I've got a call coming through. How the heck does Ruby deal with all this crap at once?"

Kling smiled and nodded. "There he is. I thought that was it, but better to be safe than sorry, huh?"

Static. "Hey, you guys aren't going to believe this."

Vic keyed the mic. "What?"

Static. "Guess who's MIA at the Wyoming Medical Center down in Casper?"

The older gentleman looked up at us, pushing his glasses onto his forehead and smiling even more broadly. "Abarrane Extepare."

"Your reputation is spreading, even down in the Casper hospitals they're referring to an unofficial self-release as a *Longmire*." Saizar-bitoria met us at the top of the stairs. "How do you go from medically induced coma to stealing your '65 Travelall back from the impound lot in one of the largest cities in Wyoming and then driving a hundred and twelve miles to pull your grandson through a window?"

Vic reached down and scratched Dog's ear. "In a hospital gown, no less . . . Man, that's one hellaciously tough old bird."

I shook my head. "He must have been pretty desperate. And how did he find out where Liam was?" My staff looked back at me blankly, including Dog. "We've notified the HPs?"

Vic nodded.

"All right, where would he take him?"

She leaned on Ruby's desk. "The ranch."

Sancho shook his head. "The Outlaw Cave, the place has history for his whole family, and it's where he feels safe."

"Even after we carried him out of there?"

He tipped his ball cap back, a dollop of dark hair falling over his forehead. "That's my bet."

"Fortunately for us, we've got three officers and three units." I pointed at Sancho. "Call Double Tough and head down to the Middle Fork, but don't go into the canyon unless you see that Travelall. I turned to Vic. "You go to the ranch, and if he's not there you wait and see if he shows up."

"How come I get the ranch?"

I smiled. "Because you play cribbage."

"And where the hell are you going to go?"

"Up the mountain."

"The mountains, why?"

"He's got reinforcements up there."

"And you're going to go alone?"

"I've got Dog."

". . . And me." We all turned to see Keasik coming up the stairs from the basement, roughing her dark hair with one of our towels. She draped the towel over the shoulder of a fresh flannel shirt as Gansu joined her. "I've got nothing to do, so I might as well be good for something."

"Ms. Cheechoo, I'm afraid . . ."

"You sure needed some help the last time I saw you up there."

I shook my head. "I can't place a private citizen in danger."

She barked a laugh of dismissal. "He's a hundred years old, and he almost died of hypothermia."

"He's desperate."

"Look, I'll stay in the truck with the dogs, okay? I just think you need to have some-body up there with you just in case."

Realizing I wasn't making any headway and aware that the more time it took us to get moving the more chance it was that Abe and the boy would be even harder to find, I gave in. "All right, let's get moving."

Sancho headed down the front steps. "I'll call Double Tough from the radio in my unit and get Ruby to come in and pull an all-nighter."

Vic punched my shoulder as she passed. "If I end up spending all night getting cheated at cribbage with that crazy old bat with nothing to show for it, I'm going to be very pissed."

I yelled after them both. "Call in on the hour to see if anything has developed."

Turning, I watched as Keasik retrieved her North Face jacket and pulled it on. "So, I guess Miguel Hernandez is now officially on the back burner?"

"With all due respect, he's dead, and the boy, we all hope, is still alive."

The bright blue eyes looked a little ashamed. "Sorry, I guess this was the wrong time to bring that up, huh?"

"Actually, maybe not." I stood there, studying her.

After a moment, her chin stuck out the way it did whenever she was challenged. "What?"

"I'm trying to see what your place really is in all this, Ms. Cheechoo."

"What do you mean?"

I took a step closer, stuffing my hands in my pockets. "You seem to be taking all of this so personally, more so than what I would deem as normal."

"Normal." Her head dropped, and her voice became quiet. "What's normal anyway?"

I smiled in spite of myself and started toward the stairs, patting my leg so Dog would know I was serious about leaving. "If you're coming, let's go."

She scooped up her own dog and trotted down the steps after me. "My childhood, it wasn't a great one, so I hate to see children suffer."

"You think Liam is suffering?"

"I don't know, but I'd say it was a possibility — it's something I recognize."

I nodded and shut the heavy door, locking it and walking toward my truck. "You had a rough childhood?"

"Oh, just another abusive father who took his life's losses out on his children."

She stopped at the passenger door, and I opened it, allowing her to climb in. "We've got a long ride ahead of us, so maybe we can tell each other the story of our lives."

"I'm sure yours is much more interesting than mine." I shut the door and started around, letting Dog in and then climbing in myself and buckling up before hitting the starter. I sat there for what only felt like a moment staring through the windshield at the office, feeling something was wrong, something palpable.

After a while, I heard her voice from far away. "Are you all right?"

I turned and looked at her. "What?"

"Are you okay?"

"Um, yep. I've been having these spells since getting back from Mexico. Was I gone long?"

"A minute or two." I said nothing, so she added, "Have you been looked at? I mean it sounds like you went through a lot down there."

"I've got a friend over at the hospital who I check in with regularly."

She looked doubtful. "Is he any kind of specialist or anything?"

"On pretty much everything." Unlocking the emergency brake, I spun the wheel and hit the gas before stopping again to stare at the empty parking lot.

"What is it?"

"Do you see a black Jeep Wrangler out here anywhere?"

She glanced about. "No."

Stomping on the accelerator, we peeled out. "Neither do I."

15

Leaving the lights of town behind, we drove up the mountain, the conifers leaning over the road as we traced our way up the switchbacks toward Powder River Pass. We drove through the cloud cover to the top and you could see where the snow had receded, leaving a patchwork in the shaded areas, all of it illuminated by the full moon. It looked cold outside, like being on that moon, but it was warm and close in the cab of my truck with the heat on full and the four of us breathing. "In what way?"

"Well, he and my mother had had other mistakes, but my next nearest brother is almost twenty years older than me."

"More like an uncle."

"If he hadn't been a useless alcoholic, maybe." She followed the ice that had etched aspen branches on the inside of the windows with her fingertips. "He died about three years ago."

"I'm sorry."

"Why? He drank himself to death his whole life and finally got what he wanted." She reached down and petted Gansu. "Anyway, I had a dog — at least we thought it was a dog." She turned toward me. "A friend of ours had a pup, and I cried until they let me have it. I fed it scraps from the table — anything I could get my hands on and he got bigger. After about a year, it became obvious that he had wolf in him. He was the greatest dog I ever had."

"What happened to him?"

"My father shot him." She leaned back in the seat. "He was beating my mother, and I tried to step in and he hit me, and the dog went for his throat. They never liked each other." She looked out the window at the passing scenery. "Later that night, when the dog was asleep, he shot him."

"I'm sorry . . . again."

"Yeah, well this time you can be." She chuckled a bitter laugh. "Like I said, he drank himself to death, which had to be better than my grandfather who got run over by a train."

Static. "Walt, Scott Kirkman says they've got troopers on all the main roads, and no one has seen either of the vehicles."

I stared down at the Motorola and then,

plucking the mic from my dash, I keyed it, reassured that the real dispatcher was back in the saddle. "Thanks, Ruby."

Static. "Of course, that's only as of ten minutes ago."

I pressed the toggle. "Right, well thanks for coming in."

Static. "Find that boy."

"Yes, ma'am." I hung the mic back on the dash and took the turn toward Paradise Guest Ranch, moving along Hunter Creek and slowly climbing from the canyon, with the clouds stretching out over the plains, looking as if you could walk on them. "And that, is that."

"Meaning?"

"Scattered radio or cell phone contact until we make the ridge at the corrals, and once we're over, it's gone completely."

I watched as she pulled her phone from inside her jacket and checked. "Only one tick."

" 'One tick,' what does that mean?"

"Limited reception with only one bar of power." She pointed. "See, up here?"

She handed the device to me, and I hit a few buttons with my oversize paw, then handed it back to her. "I can't tell, but I don't know anything about those silly things."

She held it up but then stuffed it back into her pocket. "So, who is it we're supposed to be seeing up here in the middle of the night anyway?"

Switching into four-wheel drive because of the partially frozen mud, I turned a corner. "Well, Abe has run off with Liam; Donnie has run off with his Jeep . . ." I shrugged. "At least I think it's Donnie or the guys from search and rescue."

Slowing to study the tracks on the road, I looked to the right where Hunter Mesa began; a long ridge running like a wall from east to west. "And then there are the shepherds who are left — Jimenez, the camp tender, and Arriett. They both work for Abarrane."

"And are they somehow involved with the boy's abduction?"

"I don't think so, at least not in a direct way."

"But you do think the cases are related?"

"Possibly." We made the ridge and dropped off into the basin, where I could see that there were tracks that led north. "It would make my life a lot easier if they were."

She leaned against the door and studied me. "Does it usually work out that way?"

"Hardly ever."

She laughed and then cocked a head as

we drove by Paradise Guest Ranch, the golden ruddiness of the lights looking inviting. "What say we say the hell with it and get a cabin?"

"I think that's what they call a dereliction of duty."

She laughed. "You were in the military?"

"I was."

"You know, you don't give out with much." She kept watching me as I drove. "You don't really believe that old man is abusing his grandson, do you?"

"I don't, but I discount nothing at this point — strange things happen on the mountain." I glanced at her still hunkered next to the window. "I had a previous case that turned out to involve an abused boy and another who was murdered that didn't end well. But there was an element that became evident, one that I haven't completely come to terms with just yet." I continued driving. "I had a native friend, a man named Virgil White Buffalo, who helped me and Henry . . ."

"The one that broke my father's arm?"

"I thought it was your uncle."

"Um, no, my father."

I glanced at her. "Anyway, Henry seems to think that Virgil may be manifesting himself as this wolf."

Her expression didn't change. "And you believe that?"

"I'm not sure what I believe — that's the problem."

There was a long pause before she spoke again. "Look, I'm going to be honest with you." She turned and watched me as I drove. "I looked you up. There's a lot about you, but not very many interviews."

"I try and avoid them, if possible."

"There was even something about those Mallo Cup cards. What's that about?"

Pulling the one from my shirt pocket, I handed it to her. "The fellow I mentioned, Virgil White Buffalo, he used to leave the Play Money cards from Mallo Cups for me as some kind of shaman totem. Bread crumbs, I guess."

She studied the card in her hands. "Used to?"

Pulling up to a cattle guard and barbed-wire stringer, I stopped and turned to look at her. "Why are you asking me these questions?"

"I just thought it was curious, the Mallo Cup thing, I mean."

I nodded and got out, threw the hitch, and walked the loose strands of wire back across the cattle guard and left the stringer leaning against the nearest pole. Looking at

388

the stars, I breathed the scent of the big fir trees, wondering what it would be like to live up here year-round — cold, I'd imagine, but peaceful.

I could see her watching me as I climbed back in, started the truck, and pulled it forward through the double gate. Stopping once again but leaving it running this time, I shifted the three-quarter ton into Park and climbed out. Her voice trailed after me. "I think your dog needs to pee."

I glanced back at him through the open door. "How can you tell?"

"He was whining when you got out."

"Really?" I looked at Dog, who looked back at me with the inscrutability of the ages. "He almost never whines." She shrugged, and I opened the back door.

Never one to turn down an opportunity, though, Dog bounded a few steps over the deeper snow drifts. Then he turned to look at me as I walked behind my truck and restrung the wire back across and latched it. "Yep, I know."

I got the fence in place just in time to see Keasik Cheechoo climbing over the center console, jumping into the driver's seat, pulling the gear selector into place, and spinning the wheels, throwing snow on both me and Dog.

Putting a gloved hand up to protect my face, I watched as the taillights of my truck bounced along the trail and across the open area before going over a slight rise and disappearing.

Turning to look down at Dog, who sat in the snow and looked at me as if I were an idiot, I reached down and stroked his head. "Just as I'd planned."

Dog and I walked along the two tracks left by my truck. I shined the flashlight up the road and could see the spots where other vehicles had gone off cross-country. One set was very wide but not with the most aggressive tread, while the other was narrow, vintage, and with a more pronounced pattern.

"Seems like a party, huh?"

He regarded me, still unsure as to whether I'd lost my mind.

"I know, but there wasn't any other way."

Continuing the long trek, we broke into the first park where we'd found the dead sheep, and I figured it to be a little over a mile to Miguel Hernandez's wagon — about thirty minutes in these conditions.

Starting off again, I tightened my jacket and wished I still had my old sheepskin one that had been cut off of me over in South

Dakota. Lined jeans would've been nice too.

It was cool and clear, and I walked into my breath.

There was a noise off to my right but no tracks heading in that direction. I stopped for a moment and studied the timberline but couldn't see anything. Dog took a few steps but then stopped and turned to look at me.

"No."

He begrudgingly came back and fell in line behind me.

"I know, and I think it is too, but we've got a job ahead of us."

I watched as he periodically trailed to the right, but then seeing me looking at him would return to the tracks and follow.

The snow receded, tracing the diagonal tree line in a jagged representation of the mountains and giving the broad park a lopsided appearance. The drifts were gone where I climbed the rise, but the ground was still soft enough to leave tracks.

Making the ridge, I squinted at the narrow opening that led to the other park and thought I may have underestimated the distance by half.

Dog looked up at me. "I know, but there weren't any other gates closer." I started off again. "C'mon, we need the exercise — or at least I do."

There was more snow on the downslope, and I had to catch myself from slipping as we descended, finally sliding so much that I found myself sitting in the snow with Dog sticking his face in mine. "I'm fine, I'm fine." I lumbered up, heard the noise to my right again, and instinctively reached down to grab hold of Dog's collar as he made a slight lunge toward the darkness. "I told you, no."

Something was moving about a hundred yards away, slipping between the pines and then melting into the dark as if it had never been there. I waited but nothing showed, and I started off again.

There was a gradual rise leading to the narrow spot in the trees that opened into the next park where the wagon had been. Realizing I was about halfway there, I concentrated on making time rather than on being spooked by what might be in the woods.

I'd made it about halfway up the grade when I thought I could see something in the narrow aperture, right at the peak. Dog growled.

I was thinking wolf, but it wasn't.

"Hello, Jacques."

The man, backlit by the moonlight, said

nothing but readjusted the carbine in his hands.

Getting a little closer, I stopped about fifty yards from him.

"You need to go away."

"No, I don't think so."

"You need to go away now."

I started up again, but this time surreptitiously slipped my .45 from the holster and held it behind me.

"Stop."

I kept coming, Dog trailing out to my right again, just a bit.

He readjusted the rifle, aiming it toward Dog. "Stop or I shoot."

"You shoot my dog, and I will most assuredly shoot you."

He wavered a bit, settling the muzzle of the .30-30 back on me. "Stop, or I shoot you now."

I had effectively shortened the distance between us and had him at about forty yards, a point where I felt comfortable putting my Colt against the Winchester rifle. I stopped and turned just a bit so that I could bring my gun hand straight up for an off hand shot. "What do you think you're doing, Jacques?"

"You turn around and go back."

"Back where — Durant? You've got my truck."

"I don't have nuthin'. You turn around and go back down to that dude ranch — you'll be there in an hour or so."

"I don't think I will."

He was silent for a moment. "I don't want to shoot you."

I took a deep breath. "How many people have you shot, Jacques? Any? I've shot and killed so many people lately I can't even keep count anymore."

He shifted his weight and the palpable nervousness carried across the space between us. "I'll shoot you —"

"You're not going to shoot anybody, because you're not a killer." I sighed and turned to look into the trees at my right where I was sure something was there watching our little drama play out. "If you were, you would've noticed that I've already unholstered my sidearm with a round in the chamber and the hammer back and thumbed off the safety — ready for fire." I turned the Colt out a bit, allowing it to glint in the moonlight. "Have you even jacked the lever on that carbine? Are you sure there's a round in the chamber? Is the safety on? Have you checked any of that?"

"I'll shoot —"

"Of course you haven't, because it's not your job, you're a shepherd for goodness sake. I'm a sheriff, and I've had one of these things on my hip for coming up on a half-century. You're not going to shoot me, Jacques."

I looked at the sky and couldn't help but appreciate the beauty of the pattern of the stars, so clear, so remote. "The nearest star is the sun, of course, ninety-three million miles away. Did you know that it takes about eight and a half minutes for its rays to get to earth?"

He looked up.

"And out of the two thousand stars that we can see without help, about a dozen are already dead; we just don't know it yet."

I stopped talking, and his attention returned to me and the extended muzzle of my Colt .45, aimed directly at the spot between his eyes.

"Just like you won't know you're dead until it's too late, and the only thing that will happen will be a flicker of surprise as you hit the ground staring up at those cold, dead stars." I took a breath. "Drop it, now."

He did as I said, and the muffled thump of the thing falling to the snow was the only sound.

Lowering my own weapon, I walked the

rest of the way to him and stooped to pick up the carbine before thumbing the safety back on my Colt and holstering it. Lifting the rifle, I could see that the safety was indeed on.

"Aren't you going to hit me?"

I stood there, looking down at the small man. "Why in the world would I hit you?"

"They always do that in the movies, you know, because I held a gun on you."

"Jacques, if I belted every person that pulled a gun on me, I'd be the heavyweight champion of the world." Lifting the Winchester to my shoulder, I pushed my hat back. "If you don't mind my asking, and even if you do — what the hell is going on?"

"Please don't ask me."

"Then who can I ask?"

He gestured behind him. "Ask them. I'm not down there because I don't want to be party to it."

"To what?"

His head dropped. "Ask them."

"All right." I sighed, my breath creating its own cloud. "Get the hell out of here."

He looked at me. "No joke?"

I nodded. "I've got a suspicion that the fewer people involved in this the better." I stepped out of his way. "Head on down to Paradise — I'm betting they will spot you a glass of wine."

"I could use it — or something stronger." He started off but then stopped. "Hey, can I have that gun of mine back?"

I stared at him for a good long while. "You're kind of pushing your luck, aren't you?"

He glanced around. "There are wolves."

"Wolf . . . Punch the safety off." I tossed him the Winchester. "And don't shoot anybody."

He smiled the shy grin and trooped off down the hill in my prints, not quite making the distance of my stride, and slipping a few times. It was quiet for a minute or two until he began whistling to himself and whatever else might've been out there in the darkness.

There was a fire, and the sheep were bedded down around the area with only one mule tied to the wagon.

The vehicles were parked near it — a haphazard collection, my truck the closest. I could see my keys hanging from the ignition along with the mic and cord of my two-way dangling from the rearview mirror.

I could hear voices and see shadows reflecting off the wagon front where Saizar-bitoria and I had sat eating the stew and drinking wine with Arriett.

Dog stood a little ways off in a slight drift where the snow had once again taken advantage of the shade from the tree line to hang on for a few more days. He dipped his big head, sniffing the air again, detecting a million scents I would never even know existed.

Taking a few more steps at an angle, I could see into the space between the International Travelall and the black Wrangler to where two people were talking and laughing in a relaxed manner.

Patting my leg to get Dog's attention, I moved up between the vehicles and looked down at a dark spot in the snow, smaller spots trailing toward the fire. I slipped off a glove and felt the substance, lifting it to my nose. Blood.

I wiped my fingers off on my jeans, slipped my glove back on, took out my .45 and punched off the safety, holding it once again at my side. Moving up to the front of the Jeep, I paused at the fender, listening as Keasik, who sat on one of the tree stumps with Liam in her lap, the two of them wrapped up in a blanket, told him a story.

"There was a man, a brave warrior, who was known throughout the land as a great hunter, but one season a dark winter appeared and took hold of the land, a winter

398

unlike any before. The man and his wife and son were separated from the rest of the tribe and in the depths of this winter they grew hungrier and hungrier. Finally, the warrior told them that he must go out into the snow and get them food, but the warrior's wife and son cried for him to not go."

She propped Liam up farther on her knee and dropped her face so that the child could see her. "The warrior, realizing that they would die if he did not find them food went out into the storm, warning them to not open the flap of the teepee unless they heard his voice, which they promised to do. He searched the frozen land for any signs of game, but could not find any to kill. Finally becoming exhausted, he returned to the lodge where he heard his son crying in hunger and his wife assuring him that his father was a great hunter and would not return without food for his family."

I leaned against the fender of the International, and my movement must've caught her attention. She stared at me for a moment with those light-colored eyes and then continued. "The warrior turned back into the storm, but after a while he became weak and fell in the snow. Then he heard a voice calling out from the trees:

" '— Brother, why do you despair?'

" 'My family is starving, and I can find no food for them.'

" '— Brother, do you feel the warmth of my breath on your throat?' " She breathed on the neck of the boy and he squirmed and they both laughed.

" 'Yes,' he said as the darkness closed in, and he felt himself become unconscious.

" '— Know that with the power of my jaws I could kill you, but instead I will help you because you have a great responsibility to your family, but you must thank me.'

"When the man awoke again there was a great hunk of flesh on his chest, the hock of a buffalo, more than enough to feed his family. Wresting himself from the snow, he stood and called out to the trees, 'How can I thank you when I do not even know who or what you are?' The voice carried back from the trees on the wind:

" '— You will know me.'

"The warrior went back to the lodge and called out, and his wife opened the flap. They cooked the meat, and it was very good, but more than they could eat. Sitting there around the fire, they began drifting off to sleep when a voice in the warrior's own called from outside, asking to be let in.

"The warrior's wife said no, that there could be nothing surviving out in the storm that would bring them any good, but the warrior untied the straps and suddenly the largest wolf any of them had ever seen forced its head inside the teepee, first looking at the child, then the woman, and finally at the warrior. Realizing that he could not reach his weapons, the warrior decided to distract the wolf by throwing it some of the leftover meat, which the wolf devoured in a second, not giving the warrior time to get his bow and arrow. They sat there looking at each other, and then the wolf spoke in the voice he had learned from the man:

" '— I told you, you would know me.' "

Dog, sensing the story was about him or his kin, stepped in a little closer to the fire as Liam's eyes grew wide.

"The wolf lived with them and lingered fearlessly in their camp, and that is how we came to have dogs."

Dog wagged and circled the fire, standing a little away from them.

"Howdy."

They both looked up at me, Keasik enclosing Liam in her arms with the blanket. "That was fast."

"It didn't seem like it." I glanced around. "Where are the others?"

She cocked her head at me. "Where's Jacques?"

"On his way down to Paradise and a glass of wine."

"He's better suited to that." She glanced at Liam. "Are you tired, honey?"

He nodded, and she hugged him, and walked him toward the sheep wagon, carefully lifting him through the open door at the rear where her dog stood waiting. "You cover up with Gansu, and I'll be there in a minute."

He looked past her at me and then lifted something to his mouth and blew, the comical noise coming from the toy badge Saizarbitoria had given him.

I saluted, and he saluted me back, smiling as she closed the door and returned to the fire, pulling the blanket around herself and crossing her arms. "You don't seem surprised by all this?"

Holstering the .45, I shrugged a shoulder. "Oh, I'm sure there will be parts when I will be, but not by you."

"Starting with?"

"Your name. Henry said it's Cree for *'sky blue,'* eyes just like Jakes Extepare, and then when you slipped up and mentioned that your grandfather had been run over by a train . . ."

"You know that story?"

"Abarrane mentioned that he married a

native woman that night at the ranch, and that he'd been run over by a train."

"But that couldn't have been all?"

"Abe was the last person you called on your cell phone."

She stared at me. "I thought you didn't know how to operate those things?"

"I'm learning." I came around the Jeep and leaned against the grille guard. "You were the woman Miguel met at the house near the airport."

"So?"

"Whatever it was, was it worth killing him for?"

"I didn't kill him."

"Then who did?"

"Not me." Unconsciously, she glanced past me to the southwest and the trees where the shepherd had been hung. "How did you know?"

"You were the only person who knew that Liam had been placed with the Anders. You called Abarrane, and that's how he knew where to find him.

"You also slipped up and said Henry had broken your father's arm instead of the uncle that you mentioned earlier." I pointedly looked over my shoulder, slowly turning my head back to her. "Other than the family connection, what is it that has you and Abarrane working together?"

"A mutual enemy." She hugged herself tighter. "What was your childhood like?"

"I don't have time for this."

She raised her voice. "What was your childhood like?"

I stood there looking at her. "Uneventful."

"What the hell does that mean?"

"I didn't have an alcoholic father or a negligent mother, it was just — normal."

"Lucky you." She looked back at the fire. "By the way, I didn't say my mother was negligent."

"You hardly mentioned her at all."

"Victims are rarely leading roles in their or anybody else's lives." She reached in her jacket under the blanket and pulled out some sheets of paper, unfolding them. "I hope you don't mind, but I took the files on Miguel from the Immigration and Customs that were lying on the dispatcher's desk. Have you looked at them?"

I pushed off the Jeep, and Dog turned to glance at me. "No, I haven't had time."

"Good." She tossed them in the fire and watched them burn.

We both stood there like that for a moment, which I suppose was what she was trying to accomplish, but my conversational skills were running a little dry anyway. "By my count there would be three of them out there?"

She ignored me, her eyes staying with the fire.

"Are they armed?"

She continued to ignore me.

"I asked you, are they armed?"

The chin came up, and the eyes flared in the firelight. "Yes."

"Are you?"

"No."

"Good." I started to turn with Dog in tow but then diverted to my truck, where I pulled open the door and grabbed my keys from the ignition and my old blanket-sided canteen. Dog looked at me. "I know, but there are people out here with guns and they may not be able to tell the difference between you and a wolf."

He didn't move.

I unscrewed the top and took a swig of the cold water. "C'mon, kennel up."

He still didn't move.

"Truck."

He sat.

"Ham."

He jumped into the truck and turned around to face me as I closed the door. He sat, realizing he'd been had.

Coming around the front, I slipped the

canteen onto my shoulder, pulled the big Colt from my holster, and glanced at Keasik. "Don't go anywhere."

She nodded toward the wagon and then reached down, throwing another log into the fire. "I wouldn't leave Liam and Gansu or your dog, for that matter."

Starting off, I could see where a number of prints of different species had tracked through the snow in the direction of the hanging tree. It looked to be about a quarter mile to the tree line at the other side of the park, and the air was so motionless it was as if the mountain were holding its breath.

Her voice was soft, but in the dead silence it carried. "You could let it go, you know? Just turn around, get in your truck, and get the hell out of here."

I paused to look back at her, fully lit by the light from the campfire. "We both know I can't do that."

"It would be better, trust me."

I laughed a bitter bark of air and stared at the lone jenny tied to the wagon before starting off again. "One more thing?"

"Yeah?"

I growled my response. "You're missing a mule."

16

The drifts were high in spots, and I stumbled along in the frozen air, ice clinging to the stubble on my face as the temperature plummeted. I reached up to try to rub a little feeling into my chin and watched as the frost shards fell from the stubble on my face. Oddly, the scar that streaked the skin around my left eye felt warm, as if the hide was too tough to feel cold.

It's a common fallacy that cloudy nights are the coldest — it's the clear, glittering nights where a bone-shattering cold comes from the unending universe and descends upon the earth, shagging the trees with ice in a landscape that goes on interminably. The lodgepole pines and Engelmann spruces jostled as if jockeying for position at the timberline and waved their branches in anticipation of a race they would never run or, maybe, beckoning, calling me forward to whatever fate they held.

There was a gust every once in a while, just enough to let you know what windchill could do if it wished — coat you, bury you, or freeze you stiff where you stood. Taking the canteen from my shoulder, I took another sip of the cold water.

I saw the shot before I heard it and turned to look at it slap into the snow a yard or two to my right. I stopped and was fully aware that the only thing I could do would be to flatten out in the snow. "Just in case you don't know who I am, it's Walt Longmire, Absaroka County Sheriff."

There was no response.

"You've just shot at a police officer, which is a serious offense, so I would advise you to hold your fire."

Nothing.

"I'm coming ahead."

Still nothing.

Starting off again, I saw the slap in the snow a couple of yards ahead of me, seeing the evidence of the shot when the sound arrived. The next time, I saw the muzzle flash and raised my Colt, placing a round in the vicinity of the shooter before running to the left to make the shorter distance to the tree line before they recovered and took aim again.

There was another shot, but this one was

a good twenty yards to my right, which led me to believe that whoever was firing was either inexperienced or snap shooting with abandon. Either way, it was someone who wasn't used to being shot at and that gave me more of an advantage.

Just to keep him off-balance, I threw another round at the area, which was enough to get me to the first tree trunk, which was about half my width. Semicover not being what I was looking for, I kept charging until I got to a larger copse that was adjacent to the forest and then moved between the trees.

I allowed my eyes to settle in the gloom and walked softly in the direction of the shooter, the deep powder quieting my steps. Figuring he'd think I was going to try to flank him, I stayed near the front of the tree line, only dodging back when I needed the cover.

I stopped and smelled the air drifting from the shooter's direction. Cigarette smoke. Leaning a little to the side, I could've sworn I'd seen a smoldering ember. Then I saw it again, but now near the ground, as if it might've been discarded, but then it moved and grew brighter as if someone were inhaling a puff before lowering it to arm's length.

Careful to be soundless, I edged my way

to the left and started to circle — whoever it was didn't move, just continued smoking. I had gotten behind him and could see that the shooter was sitting at the base of one of the trees with a rifle in his lap, and a cigarette in his right hand.

Jimenez sat there, blood leaching down one side of his face. "Don't shoot, don't shoot again, *dios mio.*"

I holstered my Colt and knelt down beside him, tugged the scoped .243 from his lap, and stood it beside me, the bolt action open. I pulled back his do-rag to reveal a three-inch tear in his scalp where the round had skimmed alongside his skull. "Lucky shot."

He continued smoking. "No for me, damn it."

Pulling a bandanna from my coat pocket, I discarded the rag and then folded the flap of flesh back and tied the bandanna around his scalp. "Bleeding worse than it is, but it's a head wound, so that makes sense."

"My most hard part."

"Can you stand?"

"*Sí, sí . . .*" He started to get up but collapsed against the tree trunk. "Maybe not so much just yet."

I glanced around. "Where are the others?"

"Where you think?"

I turned and looked deeper into the high

forest. "I need to go, and I might not find you on the return trip, so I need you to get up and follow my tracks back to the sheep wagon where Keasik can take care of you."

He continued to smoke. "If there is a return trip."

I extended my hand again. "You better hope there is."

He looked at it for a moment and then stuffed the cigarette in the corner of his mouth, both hands grabbing mine as he slowly rose, using my hand and the tree for support. "My head, it hurts."

"Uh huh, I bet." Walking him to the edge of the tree line, I pointed toward my prints that cut across the park at a diagonal before straightening at the point where he'd first shot at me. "You see my tracks?"

"Sí, sí."

"Follow them. If you get in trouble and have to sit down and can't get back up, sing and I'll find you."

He looked up at me. "Sing what?"

" 'Twinkle, Twinkle Little Star,' for all I care, just make some noise so I can find you."

He nodded and then immediately regretted it as he started to slip sideways. I caught his shoulder. "Can I have my gun?" He swallowed and stretched his eyelids.

"Nope."

"Okay."

"Do you have more ammo for this M77?"

"*Sí, sí.*" He pulled a small box from his coat breast pocket and rattled it before handing it to me. "There's two more rounds in there."

Reloading the bolt action, I looped the sling over my shoulder. "Pretty sure of your shooting."

He stood there wavering a bit. "I didn't want to shoot you, Sheriff. The sooner I get off this mountain and get rid of this whole business the happier I will be."

I pointed. "That way."

Without another word, he started off and had taken only five or six steps when he started to sing. *"Twinkle, twinkle little star, how I wonder what you are. Up above the world so high, like a diamond in the sky . . ."*

Satisfied he was headed the right way, I turned, ran a thumb under the leather sling, and started off in the direction I knew by heart.

I looked through the Leupold scope and watched him standing by the fire. He cradled what looked to be the same Remington Model 11 shotgun in his arms.

Behind him, in the shadows, was a man

on a mule.

I held the bolt action at hip level and circled to the left so as to not come in straight at him. My first thought was to shout out and let the .243 do my work for me, but I wasn't sure what the animal might do.

Moving through the trees, I came at him obliquely.

"Hello, Abe."

He didn't even bother looking up. "Hello dere, Walter."

"Nice night for a fire."

He was wearing a pair of insulated coveralls, a heavy hunting jacket, and slip-on snow boots, probably the emergency clothes he kept in the Travelall. "Yeah, yeah dis is."

"Same shotgun?"

He adjusted the thing slightly in his hands. "Yeah, yeah . . . You get used to dese ol' tings and you just can't let go, you know?"

Now that I was in close, I thumbed the toggle safety, looped the strap of the Ruger onto my shoulder, and slipped out my Colt in one easy movement. "I do."

"You didn't hurt dem none, did you?"

I gestured with the Colt to make sure he saw it. "Talked Jacques out of it, but I had to deflect a .45 round off of Jimenez's hard head."

"Dat him I heard singin' so terrible?"

"Yep."

"Liam and my other relative, dat Keasik?"

"They're fine." I glanced over at a bloody faced Donnie Lott sitting on the mule with his hands tied behind his back, rope around his neck, his eyes wide and his mouth duct taped shut. "What are we doing here, Abe?"

For the first time his eyes rose to mine, and I could see how weak and depleted he looked. "Justice, we be doin' justice."

"That isn't what this looks like to me."

He took a deep breath and went back to studying the fire, his complexion gray and sallow. "Well, you don' know de whole story, now, do you?"

"I'm waiting to hear it."

For the first time, he turned toward me, but the shotgun remained leaning on his shoulder. "You done your duty — now go on home."

I stood there, unmoving.

"I don' wanna shoot you, Walter."

"And I don't want to have to shoot you, Abe." I took a step closer. "You're in no condition to be up here in the thin air, and I think you better slow down and think about what you're doing."

There was a long moment that passed like an ice age, and then in the near distance I could hear a low, mournful call that wavered through the thin air like a spirit itself.

Abarrane's head rose, and he smiled. "I hear you, you ol' bastard." We both listened, but there was nothing more. "He lonely, that ol' guy, but he ain't gonna find nobody like hisself." His eyes came back to mine. "He owe me a sheep, but I respect him."

I glanced at the man on the mule and then back at the old Basque. "Abe, let's try and stay with the subject."

"I am." He shuffled a bit, but then stood still. "You don' see dose animals takin' advantage of dere young, do you?"

"That's what this is all about?"

His dark eyes glinted in the campfire. "He kill dat man."

"Miguel Hernandez?"

"Yap."

"Why?"

"Because Miguel know what he done." Another deep breath and a tremor passed through him. "He confront dat bastard dere an dat son-of-bitch kill him."

"So, Donnie was the one who attacked Miguel at the Euskadi Bar?"

"Yap, and now I'ma kill him."

"It's your son-in-law, Abe."

"Dat man no blood of mine." He stared into the fire. "Dat boy, he try and tell his momma, he try and tell me, but nobody believe him, so he just stop talkin'." He shook his head and began sobbing. "Somebody do dat to a child, dere own child . . ." He glanced at Donnie, then looked back at me, tears lining his face. "I got to spell dat out for you? He abuse my daughter and his own son." He glared back at Donnie. "Hangin' too good for a man dat do dat."

"Abe, if he's done what you say then we'll take him in, and he'll be charged, tried in a court, and sentenced according to the law."

He shook his head, coughing. "Nope, nope, nope."

"Abe, do you want Liam to live his life knowing that his grandfather killed his father?" I took another step. "You're all he's got, Abe. Don't rob that boy of the only chance he has."

His jaw drew tight, and the word was barely audible as his hand slipped down to the trigger on the shotgun. "No."

"Don't do it."

The shine of the tears on his drawn face reflected as he stared at the popping and hissing fire, his breath fogging the distance of about twelve feet between us before being burned away into nothingness. "I think about my father, now dat was a man. He was rough, but he love us more dan anything in the world. I remember bein' ashamed of him when I find out he go to prison dat time for not even shooting Lucian . . ." His face turned to me. "Imagine dat, bein' ashamed of your own father?"

I became aware of some movement to Abarrane's right and could've sworn there was something out there in the darkness just as I had on the climb up. The mule was getting fidgety, his nostrils distended as he smelled whatever was out there and sashayed back a bit, forcing Donnie's head forward by the rope, the blood dripping from his face.

"Ashamed of family, imagine dat."

Straining my eyes past the heat wavering from the fire, I could see whatever it was had moved, and from the glint of the golden eyes out past the campfire, I knew exactly who and what it was.

The eyes didn't move but just hung there. They blinked.

777M.

He lifted his head and sniffed, probably picking up the blood on Donnie's face. He'd found something to eat in this exact spot before and probably thought he'd try the buffet again. "Abarrane . . ."

Paying me no attention, Abe stepped from the fire toward the man on the mule and raised the foreshortened barrel of the shotgun. "Sometimes I feel like dat some people's, some families is just cursed."

The wolf shifted to the left, and I could still see the glittering eyes and now the intimidating bulk of the thing. "Abe . . ."

He raised the shotgun straight up in the one hand. "You do what you got to do dere, Walt, but dat man, he gotta die."

"Abe . . ."

The wolf shot from behind him, perhaps confusing the blood dripping from Donnie's face with the mule.

Abe, surprised out of his wits, half-turned, stepped back, and fell over a loose log, the shotgun going off as he hit the ground beside the fire. The mule, already crowhopping to one side to avoid the wolf, bucked with an incredible screech before it bolted out from under Donnie. Galloping between Abe and me, he barely missed the fire but carried embers as he disappeared into the darkness with the wolf on his ironshod heels.

Abe sat there watching the helpless man kicking the air and swinging back and forth.

Running toward Donnie, I holstered my .45, the .243 and my canteen falling to the ground. I grabbed his feet and placed them on my shoulders and yelled up at him.

"Don't panic — stand on my shoulders!" He tried to continue kicking, but I held fast. "Put your weight on my shoulders, and it'll keep you from strangling!" I felt him steady a bit, but then he leaned forward. "And try and stay balanced!"

Looking in that direction, I could see Abarrane had stood and was backing up and stumbling away.

"Abe, help!"

He stopped and looked at me for an instant and then turned and ran, swallowed by the black of the forest.

"Abe!" There was no response.

Trying to help Donnie get his balance, I called out to him calmly. "Donnie, if you can hear me, just make a noise."

He whimpered.

"Good. Now look, we're going to have to get your hands free, and the only thing that'll do that is this knife I've got in my pocket, and I'm going to have to let go of one of your feet to get it out and hand it up to you, all right?"

He whimpered again.

"Now, once I get it out of my pocket, I'm going to reach up behind you and you're going to take it and cut that rope around your hands, then you can cut that rope around your neck, got it?"

419

He moaned.

Taking one of my hands away, I slipped my fingers into my pocket and pulled the stag-handled Case out. Carefully, I handed it up behind him, trying my best not to dislodge his boot from my shoulder.

I could feel him fumbling with his fingertips. "I'll try to get it higher." Pushing his boot closer to my head, I could feel him getting a better grip on the thing. "Do you have it? I'm not letting go until you're sure."

He whimpered again, but this time it was louder.

"Okay, I'm letting go, but whatever you do, don't drop it, because I don't have another one."

I could feel him adjusting his hands and assumed he had begun sawing at the hemp behind his back. Looking straight ahead, I tried to remember the last time I'd sharpened the damn thing and made a mental note to be a better knife owner in the future.

Donnie stopped moving.

"Hey, just keep working on that rope — whatever happens just keep cutting, you got me?"

He whimpered again and continued.

I felt something strike my back and heard something fall to the snow behind me.

"Please tell me you didn't just drop the knife?"

Silence.

I almost laughed. "All right, I'm going to have to stoop down and get it." He made no noise at all. "We have to have that knife and unless you've got a better idea, I'm going to have to let you hang for a few seconds while I get it." There was still no response. "I'll ease down and then grab the knife and come back up, so have your feet ready to rest on my shoulders — it'll only be a second, so hang on."

It was a poor choice of words, but I felt his legs tense and figured he was ready.

"Donnie, are you ready? Here we go."

I eased into a crouch and felt in the snow for the knife but couldn't find it. Desperately thrusting my hands into the snow, I came up only with a set of car keys on a Jeep fob. Hearing Donnie strangling above me, I stood quickly and placed his boots onto my shoulders again. "I couldn't find it, but I found your keys of all things."

There was no sound.

"Donnie, I need to try again." Looking up, I could see his face staring down at me, the pressure of the rope having turned it dark and distended. One eye was battered partially shut, and the other bugged out at me as he shook his head. "I need to get that knife."

He shook his head again.

"What?"

Looking down at me, I could see him struggling with the tape, trying to talk. After a few seconds he gave up and closed his eyelids, only to open them a second later with a passive resolve.

The next thing I knew, he'd kicked my shoulders away and was swinging his legs in all directions, clocking me in the ear with a hiking boot. I tried to grab his legs again, but he continued to struggle and refused to let me take the weight. After another outburst, I got ahold of his legs, but they were limp and lifeless.

Whirling about, I looked for where the rope might've been tied off, but could see nothing. Taking my flashlight from my belt I followed the hemp rope tied around the man's neck to a branch above where it looped over and continued.

Running behind him I finally found where the thing was secured to a lower limb on another tree, but with the tension on the rope and the tightness of the knot it seemed like it took forever to untie the thing. I watched as Donnie fell to the ground in a heap.

Lunging back toward him, I pried my fingers under the noose and freed it, but he remained motionless. I pulled off my hat and placed an ear to his chest. Nothing. Ripping away the tape and rolling his head to one side, I began attempts to resuscitate him, but he didn't respond. Finally, I sat back on my haunches and stared at the dead man.

After a moment I saw his hands still tied together, the one desperately clutched around something. Leaning forward, I pried his curled fingers apart to find my knife still there.

I found the mule at the edge of the park about a hundred yards away.

He was a little reluctant to return to the scene of the hanging, but even less enthused about staying out there in the darkness with 777M. Catching the leather lead, I walked him back and tied him to what looked to be a sturdy tree. I wrapped the body in the saddle blanket and loaded the dead man onto the mule's back. Kicking the remaining embers of the fire into a pile, I shuffled snow on top of it, effectively putting it out, and then coiled up the rope and hung it over my shoulder with the .243 and my canteen.

I made the clearing and could see the prints Jimenez had made inside mine, the only marks on the pristine snow. The mule got used to the idea of walking and took less pulling, finally matching stride with me as I tromped on.

Somewhere below zero I occupied myself with the sins of the fathers that are visited on the children and how strong a person it took to break those chains and stop a personal evil that is visited on the truly innocent.

When I crested the hill, I could see the fire from the sheep camp, as could the mule, which brayed to his friend, the jenny, tied up there, who answered his call with an ear-splitting response — so much for a stealthy approach.

Jimenez and the Jeep were gone, but two people still faced the fire.

Keasik Cheechoo sat huddled with a blanket wrapped tightly around her. Even from the distance, I could see her blue eyes focused on the dancing flames as she lifted a bota and swallowed some wine. Abarrane sat beside her still holding the shotgun.

Neither of them moved. I stepped back and carefully lifted the body onto the hood of the International in plain view. Hanging the Ruger on the grille guard of the old truck, I turned and unscrewed the top of the canteen, taking a swig. "Well, there's your handiwork — I hope you're proud."

His voice resonated in his chest as if inside a tomb. "You tink dis was somethin' I enjoy?"

"I would've hoped that it was something that was so distasteful that you wouldn't have done it."

"What if it was your grandchild, what if it was your daughter?"

I turned to her. "You stay out of this — you've done nothing but enable this entire mess, including the death of Miguel Hernandez."

"I did no such thing — he found out about it and confronted Donnie on his own. I begged him to not do it, but he was so adamant about the whole thing and that it had to be stopped."

"Did it ever occur to either of you to come to me with this?"

They sat there, silent.

"Well?"

Keasik glanced at Abe and then turned back to me. "The man was psychotic, he'd already killed Miguel. Do you think he would've stopped at killing Jeannie or Liam or any of us?"

"You could've come to me."

"And then what? Abarrane tried to save his daughter but she was paralyzed with fear not only for herself but for what Donnie had and would continue to do to their child, so Abe took him. What would you have done?"

Pulling the Colt from my holster, I reached around and took the handcuffs from my belt. "Stand up."

He didn't move.

"I said stand up."

Finally finding his voice, he shook his head. "No, I don' tink I will."

I loomed over the fire, feeling the heat. "Don't make me use force, Abe."

He rubbed his nose and smiled a sad grin. "I heard about dat force of yours from Jacques and I don' think I want helping."

"Put the shotgun down, Abe."

"No, I don' tink I do dat either." He stood unsteadily and directed the shotgun away from me, knowing I would fire in an instant otherwise. "I think about dat ol' man of mine, de one dat supposed to shoot Lucian?" He shook his head. "Crazy times dat was. I tink dem times is long forgotten, but now I see that crazy times is all around us waiting for de opportunity to step up and shake hands all over again."

There was a wavering sound that carried

426

in the high wind with a sorrow and loneliness that was profound. We all paused to listen, and Abarrane barked a laugh. *"Ezezagunen lurraldea otso lurraldea da."*

I listened for the wolf again, but there was only silence. "What does that mean, Abe?"

For the first time, his eyes met mine, and there was none of the singsong rhythm in his voice. "A land of strangers is a land of wolves."

I could see his hands tightening on the Remington. "Don't do it, Abe."

He stared at me, dark eyes glinting in the reflection of the fire, and I knew he'd made up his mind.

"It's like dat, you know — you kill a man and you kill yourself."

I raised the .45, leveling it at his chest.

"God is good, but he not crazy."

Suddenly, there was a whirring sound.

We all froze. There stood Liam on the steps of the wagon with a blanket wrapped around his shoulders, his bare legs exposed, and Keasik's dog Gansu beside him.

Abarrane stood unmoving, licking his lips, trying to find his voice. "Did Poppy wake you up with dat loud talk?"

The boy nodded.

"Well, you go on back in dere and stay warm."

"No, Liam, don't." The old man turned to look at me as I put away the cuffs and holstered the Colt. "Why don't you come out here and join us?" Walking around the campfire, I moved past Keasik and, wrapping him more securely in the blanket, lifted the boy into my arms and turned back toward the fire.

Gansu joined her mistress as I approached Abarrane with his grandchild tucked into my arms. The child smelled good, of warmth, sleep, and life, wiping away the smell of gunmetal and death with his small, fragile breaths. "Put the gun down and take your grandson, Abarrane."

The lines in his face smoothed and softened as tremors of emotion overtook him.

"Take your grandson, Abe."

A sob broke from his twisted mouth. The old man tossed the shotgun aside and reached out to take the boy, burying him against his chest with a retching cry that rivaled that of the wolf.

EPILOGUE

We sat on the tailgate of my truck and stared at another dead sheep.

"I'm thinking Larry is pushing his luck." I didn't respond. She gave me the same look she'd been giving me all afternoon, trying to read my unsettled mood. I watched as Butler and Kaplan worked the freshly killed carcass. "This one's only twenty-four hours old, so they'll be able to get a more definitive read on what killed it, right?"

"Yep."

She turned back to the grisly scene. "So, spoke with Larry lately?"

I didn't say anything.

"You think he's still out here?"

I studied the tree line leading to the high country. "In one form or another."

She sipped the coffee from the chrome lid of my old Stanley thermos and looked out at the fresh blanketing from two days ago. "Snow in May — welcome to the Bighorn

Mountains."

"The absence of all color."

"What?"

"White, the absence of all color — it's like nature has wiped the board clean and left nothing." I sat there, looking at the snow, feeling like I was falling into it and smiled a sad smile. "Rapidly becoming my favorite thing."

She stared at me. "What the fuck are you talking about?"

"Nothing, I'm talking about nothing, absolutely nothing." I took a deep breath and slowly exhaled, watching a thick haze lift into the air and dematerialize. "What day of the week is it?"

"It's Friday."

I stretched my side, trying to unkink the muscles in my ribcage without pulling my stitches. "Seems like a weekend."

"Uh huh." She handed me back the cup. "You sure you're all right?"

I refilled the cap and took a slug. "What time is it?"

"You having some kind of cognitive disassociation or something?"

"No." I lowered the cup. "I'm just wondering what time it is."

She glanced at her watch with all its buttons and dials. "It's four-twenty."

"The office will be closed by the time we get back down."

"Yeah, and it's still going to be Friday." Raising her voice, she called out at the two men. "Hey, when are you two possum patrolmen going to finish up here?"

Butler, the brand inspector, turned to look at her. "I'm sorry, are we interrupting your coffee break?"

"As a matter of fact, you are. Besides, there's a nice fire back at my house and a half-bottle of Chianti that's calling my name. So, let's get this wrapped up, shall we?"

Ferris Kaplan rose, distributing portions of the victim into Ziploc bags and removing his plastic gloves. "Can I come?"

Vic smirked at him. "I said a half-bottle, carp-cop."

Not taking the remark seriously, the bearded game warden stepped around Butler and crossed toward us. "Can't blame a guy for trying." He turned back as Butler stood and joined him. "Well?"

The older man tipped his signature black hat back and rubbed a calloused hand over his face before blinking and making the pronouncement. "Cat."

Kaplan nodded in professional confirmation. "Cat."

"Hallelujah." My undersheriff raised her face to the retreating sun and then turned back to them. "Wait, once they get the taste for human flesh is it hard to break them of the habit too?"

Ignoring her, I asked. "You're sure?"

They both looked at me, Butler frowning. "What, you wanted it to be your wolf?"

"No. Not really, but I guess I wanted to know if he's still here."

Butler shook his head as he glanced at me knowingly. "If he's not dead, he's moved on to greener pastures — too much activity around these parts, I'd say."

"Where would he go?"

He shrugged. "Back in the park, the basin or farther north into Montana would be my guess." He looked at Kaplan, who nodded in agreement. "Anyway, you don't get another public wolf scare with this one."

Vic looked up at me. "No such thing as a mountain lion scare?"

It was Kaplan's turn to shake his head. "Sometimes, but not much, which is kind of surprising in that they're much more capable killers, especially solitary ones. It's odd too, because unlike wolves they'll sometimes kill a dozen sheep in one attack just because they're moving. I mean, they're cats."

432

"Too much like us." They all turned to look at me. "Wolves, they're too much like us, which is why they scare people. Too much like us in their use of hierarchy, teamwork, cooperation, territory, ritual, and loyalty." I capped my thermos and moved toward the driver's side of my truck, opened the door, and greeted my own great beast in his part-time lair. Ruffling his ears in an attempt to get him over the grudge he'd been holding against me for about a month now, I jammed the thermos into the seat cushion in the back and turned to look at them. "Except sometimes humans aren't very loyal at all."

"So, he forgot and tied up the mule?"

"Yep." I navigated the switchbacks slowly, enjoying the ride down the mountain. "Donnie wasn't much of a cowboy, and given his state of mind I guess he forgot."

She reached back, letting Dog lick her open palm. "But he was the guy who beat up Miguel at the bar?"

"Yep, I got an inkling of that when Jeannie said she and her husband had taken line-dancing lessons and that he'd bought an outfit and hat."

"All this because Miguel found out about the abuse?"

433

"It would appear."

"So, Mickey Southern: Pervert Hunter was right?"

"In a way."

"What way?"

"Donnie Lott was Mickey Southern."

"You've got to be kidding."

"Sancho went back to the Denver PD, and because of the seriousness of the crime, they were able to get an injunction that forced the server folks to give up the info on the Southern site. I guess he's been doing this for years as some kind of recompense for his actions. There are no formal charges, but Jeannie admitted that there had been instances in the past that had been covered up."

"She protected the son-of-a-bitch?"

"It's not unusual."

"From the abuser of your own child, nevermind yourself?"

"Funny where those lines of loyalty delineate themselves, huh?"

She gave it some thought. "So, Miguel finds out Donnie is beating his wife and molesting his own kid and threatens to tell Abarrane, so Donnie gets the shepherd drunk and hangs him."

"There were also the arboglyphs that the shepherds were using to communicate between themselves, including the one with the man and boy — the one with the evil eye warning."

"What about the whole Columbian connection?"

"A diversion." We hit the straights past the runaway-truck cable system, and I gave the three-quarter ton a bit more steam. "By that time Donnie was on his last rope, so to speak. He'd accidentally run into me at the gas station and got spooked. He must've felt like the world was closing in on him, which it was."

"So, being an IT guy, he figured a way to crack into the Colorado Department of Labor and Employment files and insert the incorrect fingerprints?"

"He did, but the photos didn't match."

"How about the ICE guy, did he show?"

"Yep."

"And?"

"He got a nice tour of the museums in Absaroka and Sheridan counties before having a beer at the Mint Bar and getting back on a plane to DC."

"At least he knows where Wyoming is now." She shook her head. "What about the Choo-choo woman?"

"Keasik, Cree for 'sky blue,' like her eyes and like the eyes of her grandfather, Jakes.

She'd been in touch with Abarrane after following up on Miguel. I think she knew
about what was going on and used Hernandez as a point of contact. Then she and Abe
worked together to get Donnie."

"Teamwork."

"Once the investigation started, they saw
me as the real threat and her main job was
to keep an eye out and make sure I didn't
get too close."

"Territory."

"Blood being thicker than water."

"Loyalty." She shook her head. "So, all
the wolves go to jail?"

"Inchoate crimes."

"Excuse me?"

"A legal term relatively specific to the state
of Wyoming, inchoate crimes are attempted
crimes committed by accessories or by
conspirators. Both Abarrane and Keasik
were charged with attempted involuntary
manslaughter and arranged a plea hearing
and sentencing whereby they can plead nolo
contendere; they were promised that they
would be placed on probation, including
but not limited to whether or not they go to
jail."

"Verne Selby is okay with that?"

"The judge likes to see justice done."

"You talked to him."

"I did."

"You also talked to the prosecutor and explained that Donnie was an internet predator, a spousal abuser, a pedophile, and a child molester — of his own child no less — and the murderer of Miguel Hernandez."

"I did and also pointed out Donnie's decision to not extricate himself from the noose, which would warrant a more lenient treatment of both Abarrane and Keasik."

"You think he dropped his spare set of keys in an attempt to get you to let go of him?"

When I didn't respond, she shook her head. "Why not? I mean you beat your wife, molest your own son, and there isn't going to be much solace from anybody."

"No, there's not."

"So, time served and honest Abe is back at his ranch cutting hay to feed to the sheep the wolves are going to eat."

Rolling into town, I slowed and made the turn, pulling in and parking beside the jail. "More or less."

"And Keasik Cheechoo?"

"I don't know, and tell the truth, I don't care."

" 'Inchoate crimes,' it does have a ring to it." Once again, she stared at me. "Come over and help me drink wine?"

437

"I thought there's only a half-bottle?"

"I lied." She unbuckled her seat belt and knelt on her seat, placing her elbows onto the center console and breathing on the side of my face. "C'mon, I'll make spaghetti, and we'll have sex."

I shook my head. "I don't think I can do this anymore."

"Sex or spaghetti?"

I smiled. "Maybe I've finally had enough of what people can do to each other."

"I got there a long time ago."

I turned to look at her, those eyes very close. "So, why go on?"

"Because we're doing good, Walt. We're the only thing that holds the wolves at bay."

"That's unfair to wolves."

"Yes, it is. Here's where the hierarchy comes into play — we're the alphas, the ones that fight for decency and the common good."

"Think we're winning?"

"That's not important, the important part is the fighting. I can't believe I'm giving this pep talk to you. I don't know much, but I know you've got to stand for something in this life — you have to fight for something. Some people go their whole lives without standing up or against something that's wrong. I don't know about you . . . Actu-

438

ally, I do. We don't want to be those people, so that means we play by the rules, fight the fights, and take the shots."

It was silent there in the truck — the only noise was Dog's breathing. "I think I'll just go in and get a few things done and then head home, sit in my chair, and look out the window."

"Well, maybe that's the fight for today." She knelt there with her eyes on me for quite some time and then turned, sat, and opened her door. She slid out and stood with a hand resting on the handle. "Whatever you decide to do, I better be part of the equation."

I nodded. "Yep."

She quietly closed the door, and I watched as she climbed into her unit, fired it up, and swung it around beside me. She cranked down her window.

I stared at her with a questioning look.

"Just so you know, I lost the office pool." Rolling up her window, she jetted out of the parking lot at just under light speed, pausing only a moment to give me the finger.

I don't know how long I sat there, but it was dark and the next thing I was aware of was Dog sniffing my ear and placing his head on my shoulder. "You need to get out,

439

buddy?"

I could feel his weight shifting the truck as he moved to the suicide door behind me. I unbuckled my seat belt, opened my door, and stepped out to open his. I watched him as he leapt to the ground and trotted to the edge of the parking lot between us and the courthouse to relieve himself with the one-leg salute.

Standing there waiting, I studied the traffic lights and then turned and gazed at the red-stone front of the old library with its two columns and tall windows, one of 1,679 such buildings philanthropist Andrew Carnegie donated to communities across the nation from 1886 to 1919.

I felt as old as the building.

I glanced up at the dark clouds and scattered moonlight that was highlighting the Bighorn Mountains. Patting my leg, I made for the door and was surprised to find it ajar. I held it for Dog, who bounded ahead as I slowly followed him up the stairs.

Saizarbitoria was sitting on Ruby's stool leafing through a copy of *Wyoming Wildlife* magazine, tossing it onto the counter as I approached. "Welcome home."

"Thanks. What are you doing here so late?"

"Waiting for the results — neither wolf

nor dog?"

"Cat."

"A mountain lion. Do we have to worry about that too?"

"Probably not."

"Good, I don't think I've got the stamina for another scare." He stood, stretched, and yawned. "Ruby left a note for you in your office."

I stared at him. "A note?"

"Yeah, Boss."

With a deep sense of dread, I approached my office, and looked inside at the large envelope lying on my otherwise naked desktop. "Where's the computer?"

"She had me put it downstairs on the communal desk." He joined me at the door and peered over my shoulder. "I have no idea what it says."

Entering my office, I sat in my chair and studied the intimidating cursive handwriting, spelling out my full name. "I thought I was doing pretty well."

"The computer?" He crossed his arms and leaned on the doorjamb. "What, you want it back?"

"No."

He pulled something from his uniform shirt pocket. "I almost forgot. I was cleaning out the prisoner personal-possessions

441

locker and found the rucksack Keasik Cheechoo left behind and these fell out." He tossed the stack of cardboard coupons held together with a rubber band onto my desk — at least fifty Mallo Cup Play Money cards.

I gazed at them as if they might bite.

"I guess she figured they would spook you or something."

"Maybe."

"Well, at least one mystery solved." He turned to go.

Still staring at the cards, I called out. "Hey, Sancho . . ."

He reappeared. "Yeah, Boss?"

"Are you still having those dreams?"

The smallest trace of a smile played out on his lips. "What dreams?" I smiled back at him, and he saluted before disappearing. "See you tomorrow, Boss."

After a moment, I heard the heavy front door shut. My eyes returned to the manila envelope and the cursive *"WALTER."*

Picking up the oversized stiletto switch-blade I'd carried back from my most recent adventures in Mexico, I slid it across the flap and opened the envelope.

There was a photograph, a large, color 8 × 10 with, of all things, a Post-it attached. Carefully sliding it out, I was confronted

442

with the photo of Cady and Lola that I'd used as the screen saver for my now departed computer. Smiling, I read the Post-it:

Walter,
Sometimes it's best for us old dogs to not learn any more new tricks.
Love,
Ruby

PS: Get your own frame.

Standing, I patted my leg and Dog followed as I walked through the office turning out the lights, finally stopping at Ruby's desk.

I wasn't aware of it until I felt the tug at my coat and watched as my hand turned and opened — the Absaroka County sheriff's badge lying there in my palm after I'd evidently unpinned it from my jacket. I read the words and then recommitted the image to my mind — the open book for justice, the mountains for steadfastness, and the star for truth, but all significant of something so much more.

And this is how things end, not so much with a bang but with a whimper.

I gently placed the gleaming hardware on

443

the smooth, oak-grained surface of Ruby's desk.

Turning, I started to take a step but then stopped and stood there looking at the floor, my hand still resting on the surface of the desk.

You pin that star on and you think it's something you can just take off, but it isn't that way — it attaches itself to you. Unlike the glimmering pinpricks in the freezing winter sky, this star warms you and becomes a welcome weight that doesn't let go even if you want it to. If its closest kin, over ninety-three million miles away, were to simply switch off, the average temperature on earth would plummet to zero degrees.

In a year it would be a hundred below zero.

In a million years four hundred degrees below.

Better to not risk it.

I picked up the star and pinned it back on, immediately feeling warmer.

Dog followed me down the steps, where I flipped the last switch off, stepped outside, and locked the door behind me.

On the drive out of town under the blinking yellow lights, I mused on the Mallo Cup cards and all the different places that I'd found them, but I couldn't work out how she could've placed the one under the Travelall where the wolf, 777M, had been perched. Maybe she hadn't planted all of them after all.

Noticing that the gas gauge was nearing empty, I drove under the interstate highway and took a left through the empty opposing lane, to pull into the vacant lot of the closed Maverik station.

It was getting cold again, so I zipped up my horsehide jacket and flipped up the collar, tugged down my hat, and pulled on my gloves. Standing there filling the tank, I realized this was the exact spot where I'd confronted Donnie Lott, and I gazed at the motel across the street, and then to the I-25 northbound off-ramp.

Maybe I'd head south for a few days to entertain my granddaughter and annoy my daughter, the Greatest Legal Mind of Our Time. Maybe I'd grab Vic and head down to Hatch, New Mexico, where it was bound to be warmer — or maybe I'd just break into the store and steal a six-pack of Rainier beer and go home.

Instead I held a notion in my head for a moment: the image of a bright-red Jeep Wrangler coming off the highway, rolling to a California stop at the sign, and then driving toward me, pulling up at the other side

445

of the pump. A window rolling down, and me stooping to peer into the backseat, where a bundled toddler — my granddaughter — sleeps.

A toothsome redhead with startling gray eyes is at the wheel and glances up at me. "Hi, Daddy."

But that's not what was there.

My eyes refocused on the empty, stained surface of a concrete pad on the other side of the pump island, a skiff of snow cast across the hard surface, looking for something, anything, to attach itself to. I could see Dog watching me from inside the truck, and then on the center console, the envelope with the photograph of Cady and Lola.

Maybe Henry was right, maybe I was awaiting a vision that I wasn't ready for just yet. I wondered what you had to do to be worthy of such things and thought about a world where I would no longer have a place, a world where people always did the right thing.

Studying the envelope, I figured maybe a photograph of a vision was enough for now.

I looked back at the mountains and listened for the sound of the ever-present wind and the swaying of the trees as they mourned its passing — but more important, I listened for the cry of 777M if you will, or

446

Larry if you won't.

All I could hear was the whir of technology as the gas filled the tank.

And I sighed, wanting to hear that howl so badly.

ABOUT THE AUTHOR

Craig Johnson is the *New York Times* bestselling author of the Longmire mysteries, the basis for the hit Netflix original series *Longmire.* He is the recipient of the Western Writers of America Spur Award for fiction, the Mountains and Plains Booksellers Award for fiction, the Nouvel Observateur Prix du Roman Noir, and the Prix SNCF du Polar. His novella *Spirit of Steamboat* was the first One Book Wyoming selection. He lives in Ucross, Wyoming, population 25.

The employees of Thorndike Press hope you have enjoyed this Large Print book. All our Thorndike, Wheeler, and Kennebec Large Print titles are designed for easy reading, and all our books are made to last. Other Thorndike Press Large Print books are available at your library, through selected bookstores, or directly from us.

For information about titles, please call:
(800) 223-1244

or visit our website at:
gale.com/thorndike

To share your comments, please write:
Publisher
Thorndike Press
10 Water St., Suite 310
Waterville, ME 04901